Praise fo

"Compelling . . . Candice Fox
first of two thrillers about a serial killer. Exploring the concept
of whether killing for justice could ever be rationalized,
Hades is a chilling read."

"A _____ **DATE DUE** _____ ack plot,
strong characters, and feisty, no-nonsense writing."
—*Qantas* **magazine**

"A powerful book, an incredible read. The pace is extreme, the
violence and the fear are palpable. The plot is original and
twisted, black and bloody. Tension runs riot on the page.
Dexter would be proud!"
—**The Reading Room**

"Well written with a suck-you-in story and characters with
depth, *Hades* is an exciting read, a bit *Dexter*-ish. It moves at a
great pace and reveals the narrative twists and turns in a way that
keeps you playing detective as you read—and it has an outcome
I didn't see coming. It's a great debut novel."
—**The Co-op Online Bookstore: Staff Picks**

"A dark, compelling, and original thriller that will have you
spellbound from its atmospheric opening pages to its shocking
climax. *Hades* is the debut of a stunning new talent in crime
fiction. The narrative is engaging, compelling. The characters
are unique and well fleshed out. The story is strong, bold,
amazing. This is how a crime thriller should make you feel."
—**Reading, Writing and Riesling**

"Candice Fox grew up trying to scare her friends with true-crime
stories. If her intent was to try and create an at times chilling
and gruesome story as her debut, it is very much mission
accomplished. She certainly looms as an exciting new prospect
in the ranks of Australian authors."
—*Western Advocate*

HADES

CANDICE FOX

KENSINGTON BOOKS
www.kensingtonbooks.com

KENSINGTON BOOKS are published by

Kensington Publishing Corp.
119 West 40th Street
New York, NY 10018

Previously published in Australia and New Zealand by Random House Australia Pty Ltd.

All Kensington titles, imprints, and distributed lines are available at special quantity discounts for bulk purchases for sales promotions, premiums, fundraising, educational, or institutional use. Special book excerpts or customized printings can also be created to fit specific needs. For details, write or phone the office of the Kensington special sales manager: Kensington Publishing Corp., 119 West 40th Street, New York, NY 10018, attn: Special Sales Department; phone 1-800-221-2647.

This book is a work of fiction. Names, characters, businesses, organizations, places, events, and incidents either are the product of the author's imagination or are used fictitiously. Any resemblance to actual persons, living or dead, events, or locales is entirely coincidental.

ISBN-13: 978-1-61773-441-0
ISBN-10: 1-61773-441-1

First trade printing: February 2015

10 9 8 7 6 5 4 3 2 1

Printed in the United States of America

First electronic edition: February 2015

ISBN-13: 978-1-61773-442-7
ISBN-10: 1-61773-442-X

For my parents

As soon as the stranger set the bundle on the floor, Hades could tell it was the body of a child. It was curled on its side and wrapped in a worn blue sheet secured with duct tape around the neck, waist and knees. One tiny pearl-colored foot poked out from the hem, limp on his sticky linoleum. Hades leaned against the counter of his cramped, cluttered kitchen and stared at that little foot. The stranger shifted uneasily in the doorway, drew a cigarette from a packet and pulled out some matches. The man they called Hades lifted his eyes briefly to the stranger's thin angled face.

"Don't smoke in my house."

The stranger had been told how to get to Hades' place but not about its bewildering, frightening character. Beyond the iron gates of the Utulla dump, on the ragged edge of the western suburbs, lay a gravel road leading through mountains of trash to a hill that blocked out the sky, black and imposing, guarded by stars. A crown of trees and scrub on top of the hill obscured all view of the small wooden shack. The stranger had driven with painful care past piles of rubbish as high as apartment buildings crawling with every manner of night creature—owls, cats and rodents picking and sifting through old milk cartons and bags of rotting meat. Luminescent eyes peered from the cabins of burned-out car shells and from beneath sheets of twisted corrugated iron.

Farther along the gravel path, the stranger began to encounter a new breed of watchful beast. Creatures made from warped scraps of metal and pieces of discarded machinery lined the road—a broken washing machine beaten and buckled into the figure of a snarling lion, a series of bicycles woven together and curled and stretched into the body of a grazing flamingo. In the light of the moon, the animals with their kitchen-utensil feathers and Coke-bottle eyes seemed tense and ready. When the stranger entered the house he was a little relieved to be away from them and their attention. The relief evaporated when he laid eyes on the man they called the Lord of the Underworld.

Hades was standing in the corner of the kitchen when the stranger entered, as though he'd known he was coming. He had not moved from there, his furry arms folded over his barrel chest. Cold heavy-lidded eyes fixed on the bundle in the stranger's arms. There was a Walther PP handgun with a silencer on the untidy counter beside him by a half-empty glass of scotch. Hades' grey hair looked neat atop his thick skull. He was squat and bulky like an ox, power and rage barely contained in the painful closeness of the kitchen.

The air inside the little house seemed pressed tight by the trees, a dark dome licking and stroking the hot air through the windows. Hades' kitchen was adorned with things he had salvaged from the dump. Ornate bottles and jars of every conceivable color hung by fishing line from the ceiling; strange cutting and slicing implements were nailed like weapons to the walls. There were china fish and pieces of plastic fruit and a stuffed yellow ferret coiled, sleeping, in a basket by the foot of the door, jars of things there seemed no sense in keeping—colored marbles and lens-less spectacles and bottle caps in their thousands—and lines of dolls' heads along the windowsill, some with eyes and some without, gaping mouths smiling, howling, crying. Through the door to the tiny living room, a wall crammed with tattered paperbacks was visible, the books lying and standing in every position from the unpolished floorboards to the mold-spotted ceiling.

The stranger writhed in the silence. Wanted to look at everything but afraid of what he might see. Night birds moaned in the trees outside the mismatched stained-glass windows.

"Do you, uh . . ." The stranger worked the back of his neck with his fingernails. "Do you want me to go and get the other one?"

Hades said nothing for a long time. His eyes were locked on the body of the child in the worn blue sheet.

"Tell me how this happened."

The stranger felt new sweat tickle at his temples.

"Look," he sighed, "I was told there'd be no questions. I was told I could just come and drop them off and . . ."

"You were told wrong."

One of Hades' chubby fingers tapped his left bicep slowly, as though counting off time. The stranger fingered the cigarette he had failed to light, drawing it to his lips, remembered the warning. He slipped it into his pocket and stared at the bundle on the floor, at the shape of the girl's small head tucked against her chest.

"It was supposed to be the most perfect, perfect thing," the stranger said, shaking his head at the body. "It was all Benny's idea. He saw a newspaper story about this guy, Tenor I think his name was, this crazy scientist dude. He'd just copped a fat wad of cash for something he was working on with skin cancer or sunburn or some shit like that. Benny got obsessed with the guy, kept bringing us newspaper clippings. He showed us a picture of the guy and his little wife and his two kiddies and said the family was mega-rich already and he was just adding his new cosh to a big stinking pile."

The stranger drew a long breath that inflated his narrow chest. Hades watched, unmoving.

"We'd got word that the family was going to be alone at their holiday house in Long Jetty. So we drove up there, the six of us, to rattle their cage and take the babies—just for a bit, you know, not for long. It was going to be the easiest job, man. Bust in, bust out, keep them for a couple of days and then organize an exchange. We weren't gonna do nothing with them. I'd even borrowed some games they could play while they stayed with us."

Hades opened one of the drawers beside him and extracted a notepad and pen. From where he stood, he slapped them onto the small table by the side wall.

"These others," he said, "write down their names. And your own."

The stranger began to protest, but Hades was silent. The stranger sat on the plastic chair by the table, his fingers trembling, and began to write names on the paper. His handwriting was childlike and crooked, smeared.

"Everything just went wrong so fast," he murmured as he wrote, holding the paper steady with his long white fingers. "Benny got the idea that the dude was giving him the eye like he was gonna do something stupid. I wasn't paying attention. The woman was screaming and crying and carrying on and someone clocked her and the kids were struggling. Benny blew the parents away. He just . . . he pumped them and pumped them till his gun was flat. He was always so fucking trigger-happy. He was always so fucking ready for a fight."

The stranger seemed stirred by some emotion, letting air out of his chest slowly through his teeth. He stared at the names he had written on the paper. Hades watched.

"One minute everything was fine. The next thing I know we're on the road with the kids in the trunk and no one to sell them to. We

started talking about getting rid of them and someone said they knew you and . . ." The stranger shrugged and wiped his nose on his hand.

For the first time since the stranger had arrived, Hades left the corner of the kitchen. He seemed larger and more menacing somehow, his oversized, calloused hands godly as they cradled the tiny notepad, tearing off the page with the names. The stranger sat, defeated, in the plastic chair. He didn't raise his eyes as Hades folded the small square of paper, slipping it into his pocket. He didn't notice as the older man took up the pistol, cocked it and flicked the safety off.

"It was an accident," the stranger murmured, his bloodshot eyes brimming with tears as he stared, lips parted, at the body in the bundle. "Everything was going so well."

The man named Hades put two bullets into the stranger. The stranger's confused eyes fixed on Hades, his hands grabbing at the holes in his body. Hades put the gun back on the counter and lifted the scotch to his lips. The night birds had stopped their moaning and only the sound of the stranger dying filled the air.

Hades set the glass down with a sigh and began to trace the dump yards around the hill with his mind, searching for the best place for the body of the stranger and, somewhere separate, somewhere fitting, to bury the bodies of the little ones. There was a place he knew behind the sorting center where a tree had sprung up between the piles of garbage—the twisted and gnarled thing sometimes produced little pink flowers. He would bury the children there together and dig the stranger in somewhere, anywhere, with the dozens of rapists, killers and thieves who littered the grounds of the dump. Hades closed his eyes. Too many strangers were coming to his dump these nights with their bundles of lost lives. He would have to put the word out that no new clients were welcome. The ones he knew, his regular clients, brought him the bodies of evil ones. But these strangers. He shook his head. These strangers kept bringing inno-cents.

Hades set his empty glass on the counter by his gun. His eyes wan-dered across the cracked floor to the small pearl foot of the dead girl.

It was then that he noticed the toes were clenched.

1

I figured I'd struck it lucky when I first laid eyes on Eden Archer. She was sitting by the window with her back to me. I could just see a slice of her angular face when she surveyed the circle of men around her. It seemed to be some kind of counselling session, probably about the man I was replacing, Eden's late partner. Some of the men in the circle were grey-faced and sullen, like they were only just keeping their emotions in check. The psychologist himself looked as if someone had just stolen his last nickel.

Eden, on the other hand, was quietly contemplative. She had a switchblade in her right hand, visible only to me, and she was sliding it open and shut with her thumb. I ran my eyes over her long black braid and licked my teeth. I knew her type, had encountered plenty in the academy. No friends, no interest in having a mess around in the male dorms on quiet weekends when the officers were away. She could run in those three-inch heels, no doubt about that. The forty-dollar manicure was her third this month but she would break a rat's neck if she found it in her pantry. I liked the look of her. I liked the way she breathed, slow and calm, while the officers around her tried not to fall to pieces.

I stood there at the mirrored glass, half-listening to Captain James blab on about the loss of Doyle to the Sydney Metro Homicide Squad and what it had done to morale. The counselling session broke up and Eden slipped her knife into her belt. The white cotton top clung to her carefully sculpted figure. Her eyes were big and dark, downcast to the carpet as she walked through the door towards me.

"Eden." The captain motioned at me. "Frank Bennett, your new partner."

I grinned and shook her hand. It was warm and hard in mine.

"Condolences," I said. "I heard Doyle was a great guy." I'd also heard Eden had come back with his blood mist all over her face, bits of his brain on her shirt.

"You've got big shoes to fill." She nodded. Her voice was as flat as a tack.

She half-smiled in a tired kind of way, as if my turning up to be her partner was just another annoyance in what had been a long and shitty morning. Her eyes met mine for the briefest of seconds before she walked away.

Captain James showed me to my spot in the bull pen. The desk had been stripped of Doyle's personal belongings. It was chipped and bare, save for a black plastic telephone and a laptop port. A number of people looked up from their desks as I entered. I figured they'd introduce themselves in time. A group of men and women by the coffee station gave me the once-over and then turned inward to compare their assessments. They held mugs with slogans like "Beware of the Twilight Fan" and "World's Biggest Asshole" printed on the side.

My mother had been a wildlife warrior, the kind who would stop and fish around in the pouches of kangaroo corpses for joeys and scrape half-squashed birds off the road to give them pleasant deaths or fix them. One morning she brought me home a box of baby owls to care for, three in all, abandoned by their mother. The men and women in the office made me think of those owls, the way they clustered into a corner of the shoebox when I'd opened it, the way their eyes howled black and empty with terror.

I was keen to get talking to people here. There were some exciting cases happening and this assignment was very much a step up for me. My last department at North Sydney had been mainly Asian gangland crime. It was all very straightforward and repetitive—territorial drive-bys and executions and restaurant holdups, fathers beaten and young girls terrorized into silence. I knew from the media hype and word around my old office that Sydney Metro were looking for an eleven-year-old girl who'd gone missing and was probably dead somewhere. And I'd heard another rumor that someone here had worked on the Ivan Milat backpacker murders in the 1990s. I wanted to unpack my stuff quickly and go looking for some war tales.

Eden sat on the edge of my desk as I opened my plastic tub and began sorting my stuff into drawers. She cleared her throat once and looked around uncomfortably, avoiding my glance.

"Married?" she asked.

"Twice."

"Kids?"

"Ha!"

She glanced at me, turning the silver watch on her wrist round and round. I sat down in Doyle's chair. It had been warmed by the morning sun pouring in through the windows high above us. I knew this and yet my skin crawled with the idea that he might have been sitting here, moments earlier, talking on the phone or checking his emails.

"Why'd you take this job?"

I could smell her as I bent down and lifted my backpack from the floor. She smelled expensive. Flash leather boots hugging her calves, boutique perfume on her throat. I told myself she was probably late twenties and that women that age looked for guys a bit older—and the ten years or so I had on her didn't necessarily make me a creep. I told myself she wouldn't notice the grey coming in from my temples.

"I lost a partner too. Been alone for six months now."

"Sorry." Again that flatness in her voice. "On the job?"

"No. Suicide."

A man approached us, circled the desk and then sat down beside Eden, one leg up on the desktop, facing me. There was a large ugly scar the length of his right temple running into his hairline like white lightning. It pulled up the corner of his eye. Eden looked at him with that embarrassed half-smile.

"Frankie, right?" he grinned, flashing white canines.

"Frank."

"Eric." He gripped my hand and pumped it. "This one gets too much for you to handle, you just let me know, uh?" He elbowed Eden hard in the ribs. Obnoxious. She smirked.

"I'm sure I'll be fine."

I began to pack my things away faster. Eric reached into the tub beside him and pulled out a folder.

"This your service record?"

I reached for the manila folder he was holding. He tugged it away.

"Yeah, thanks, I'll have it back." I felt my tongue stick to the roof of my mouth. Eden sat watching. Eric stood back and flicked through the papers.

"Oh, look at this. North Sydney Homicide. Asian gangs. You speak Korean? Mandarin? Says here under disciplinary history you got a serious DUI on the way to work." He laughed. "On the *way* to work, Frankie. You got a problem with that? You like to drink?"

I snatched the folder from him. His wide hand thundered on my shoulder.

"I'm just giving you a hard time."

I ignored him and he wandered back to the group of owls. He jerked his thumb towards me and said something and the owls stared. Eden was watching my face. I scratched my neck as the heat crept down my chest.

"Fucking jerk." I shook my head.

"Yeah." She smiled, a full-size, bright white flash. "He's good at that."

2

I found out Eric was Eden's brother minutes before we got called away from the station to a crime scene. I don't know why the resemblance hadn't struck me before. They shared the same bold dark features, the same contained power and malice. Bored and powerful—misfit siblings. Eric looked wilder than Eden. I couldn't decide who was older. She sat in the driver's seat beside me, both hands on the wheel, chewing on her bottom lip as though she had heavy things on her mind. She seemed like someone holding on to a terrible trauma, something that stained her days and picked at her insides at night. Secrets and lies. Eric struck me as the life of the party, uncontrollable and unpredictable in turns.

The traffic was at a standstill on Parramatta Road almost directly out from headquarters on Little Street, heading in towards the distant blue outline of the city. We crept across an intersection and stopped again outside a Greek restaurant where a young man was scraping spray-painted snowflakes from the windows, months late. A giant red and yellow sign hanging over a DVD rental place asked if I wanted longer lasting sex, in bold typeface lit up by an already blazing sun. The Greek boy's father came out and hustled him to work faster, gesturing at the Thai restaurants wedged on either side with their immaculately polished windows.

"So, a drinker and a serial marrier." Eden smiled suddenly, as though only just remembering. "No wonder your partner necked herself."

"Give me a break."

"Don't let Eric get to you. He's just having a dig."

I struggled not to burst into profanities. I knew that being bothered by what he had done would only make things worse. So I'd been DUI-ed. Who hadn't? So it had been on the way to work. I'd had a rough year.

"Working with your brother. That's a little incestuous, isn't it?"

She smiled. I'd expected a laugh. She shifted lanes, flicked her blinker with her little finger like she'd owned the car for years.

"We're never partnered," she offered. "Conflict of interest, you know."

We pulled up at a small marina on Watsons Bay, east of the harbor and between the Navy base and the parkland. The street was lined with rendered pastel-colored apartment blocks, with the obligatory banana chairs on the balconies and striped beach towels hanging artfully on chrome racks. The local butcher's shop advertised garlic and rosemary sausages on a chalkboard, eighteen bucks a kilo. Everyone, it seemed, knew the dress code: boat shoes and cargo pants, men and women alike. The change in scenery was jarring. What seemed like minutes earlier we had been driving past the above-shop brothels of North Strathfield, through the shadowed shopping districts of Edgecliff. Now, for some reason, sausages were ten dollars dearer and wet exotic plants brushed the windows of the car as we parked. I sighed and got out, feeling unwelcome.

Eden stood by the car, polishing her Ray-Bans on the edge of her shirt and glaring coolly at the dozens of apartments at the edge of the road. Boaties locked off from their yachts and gawkers from the surrounding parklands were perched on the hill, holding their hands up against the white glare of the morning and ignoring the insistent tugging of a variety of compact dogs on leads. Poop bags jangled on key-chains. They spotted a couple of homicide detectives straight away, nudging each other and pointing. *Yes, things just got interesting. Grab a latte and settle in for the long haul.* Some journalists snapped shots of Eden talking to a security guard. They seemed to miss me.

At the epicenter of the gathering of cop cars and paramedics was a lone young man wrapped in a grey blanket, sitting on the edge of an open ambulance. The overkill meant something god-awful had happened to him. I stood to the side, studying the man's downturned face and desperate eyes, and let Eden go in. People made way for her. I was surprised no one wanted to accidentally brush against her, try to soak up some of that power and beauty. They seemed to know her, seemed to possess some prior knowledge of her dangerous nature.

"Go ahead." She flicked her chin at the man in the blanket.

"I told that cop in the hat I didn't wanna make a statement," the man trembled, nodding towards a chief standing smoking by the gates. "You got what you need. I wanna go now. I wanna get outta here."

I was beginning to notice bumps and scrapes on the man, blood matted in his hair. His ankles were rubbed raw and his left foot was splinted. He jogged his right foot up and down, sniffling and letting his eyes dance over his surroundings.

"One more time." Eden slid her notebook out of her pocket. "Then we can think about letting you go."

There were track marks on the man's arms, purple and wet as he ran a hand through his damp hair. He seemed to want to pick at an old sore that wouldn't heal on his left cheekbone. He glanced at me. I leaned against the ambulance, my arms folded across my chest.

"I was up on the road." The junkie shuddered, nodding towards the boat ramp leading down to the marina. "I was trying to get a ride back to Bondi where I'm staying with mates. But none of these posh fuckheads would stop. It was maybe . . . three in the morning. I saw a guy backing a van up through the gates, pulling it alongside a boat. The gates were open so I thought I'd, like, see if I could slip in, you know? I was gonna set off by myself down the marina but I decided to keep watching the guy with the van."

"You were going to roll him?" I asked.

"Maybe. I was thinking about it. I was trying to make out what he had. I reckoned whatever he was shifting at that hour might be good for me. Whatever he had was locked down tight in one of those nice shiny steel toolboxes you see tradesmen carrying on their SUVs—about a meter long. He must've been a big bloke because he was carrying it lengthways across his chest with an arm on either end. He set it on the boat and went round the van. I waited to see him come out the other side but he didn't. I waited for ages and he just didn't come. I was just going to shift around the back of the trees to see where he was when I hear this massive *crack* and then there was just nothing."

The junkie reached up and touched the back of his skull, feeling stitches. Eden stood with her boot on the folded ramp at the back of the ambulance, watching the man's eyes.

"I woke up on the deck of the boat with a big chain around my ankles." The junkie twitched, scratching at his stubbled beard. "I didn't think we'd left the marina, the boat was so still. It was getting light so I must have been out of it for ages. There was blood everywhere. I rolled over and saw him shoving the toolbox towards the edge of the deck. I followed the chain attached to my ankles and saw that it led to the box."

"Christ." One of the cops behind me laughed. I looked over my shoulder at him. I'd forgotten about the crowd around us, all street cops with their arms folded, cigarettes between their teeth. The water beyond the pier sparkled between them. I squinted.

"I went over." The junkie trembled, his right leg jogging faster, up and down like a piston. "I hit the water."

The junkie in the blanket burst into tears. The cops around me twisted and looked at each other and shook their heads and scoffed and laughed. Eden was perfectly still, her sharp face resting in the palm of her hand, her elbow on the knee of her jeans. Breathing, long and slow. The junkie swiped at his eyes with a skeletal hand. Long fingernails. Before he could resume his story, one of the cops piped up:

"So how the fuck are you sitting here, Houdini?"

The junkie tossed an evil look at the men and women around him.

"Broke my foot when I was a little kid," he murmured. "Clean across the middle—dancing."

"*Dancing?*"

"Yeah, dancing," the junkie sneered. "I was fucking dancing in one of those primary school talent shows. I jumped off the stage and landed on it wrong and snapped it right in half behind the toes. It's been off ever since. When I was going down I was pulling and tugging and struggling with the chain. As I got deeper I just reached down and broke it again."

Everyone looked at the splint running up the side of the junkie's ankle. A low moan of appreciation went up from the bodies around me.

"You must be the slipperiest fucker alive."

"Hallelujah. You been touched by a goddamn angel, son."

"You got a lot of will to live for someone who spends all day jacking themselves with deadly chemicals," another cop said.

The junkie wiped dried blood from his nose onto the back of his hand.

"Thanks, mate." He scowled. "Thanks for that."

"No problem."

"Okay, okay," I cut in. "Back to the story. Did he see you when you came up?"

The junkie bristled. Eden was watching me, expressionless.

"When I got up he was long gone," he said, staring at the concrete in front of him. "I got picked up by a couple of guys in a small boat and brought back here maybe an hour later. Was too far out to swim and I couldn't use my foot. I thought I was going to get my arse eaten by something. I thought I was really gone, you know?"

He sobbed once, hiding his face in his fist. There was silence all around us.

"So what are we looking for?" I sighed, taking out my own notebook. "A man, a boat, a silver box."

"I can't help you with the descriptions," the junkie said. "I tried already. He was wearing a jacket zipped up to his nose and a fucking hat on top. The boat was white. I don't know nothing else about it. Big. White. Boat-shaped. You want to press me about it, go ahead. That cop in the hat already tried."

"What about the silver box?" I asked, putting my foot up on the ramp so I could balance the notepad on my knee. "It have a name on it? Anything written on the side?"

"No," the junkie shook his head. "It was plain, like all the others."

"All the others?" Eden asked, her voice ringing out so much finer and smoother than those around her, like a birdsong. "What do you mean, *all the others*?"

The junkie wrapped his arms around himself and stared at the ground, his lip trembling like he wanted to cry again.

"When I was going down I had time to look around me," he gasped, squeezing his eyes shut. "The morning light was cutting through the water. There were others down there on the bottom of the ocean. Heaps of them."

Blood had soaked into the sheet around her head, there were bloody prints on the cotton. Hades unwound the duct tape holding the sheet and rolled her out onto the floor. Tape around her wrists and face, sticking in her hair. She howled as he ripped it off her mouth, long and loud and full of fear.

"There's another one," he said to himself, hearing his voice tremble as it never had before while his fingers fumbled with the tape at her eyes. "He said there was another one."

Hades left the girl on the floor and ran out of the house, his fingers slick with the blood that had coated her face. He smeared it on the keys as he tugged them from the ignition of the beaten-up red Ford, on the trunk as he shoved them into the lock. The little girl tottered drunkenly out of the house behind him, her long dark hair lit gold by the light of the kitchen. She watched soundlessly as he opened the trunk and dragged the other bundle of sheets from the darkness, her eyes lifeless orbs in a mask of red.

"Oh please," Hades heard himself murmuring. "Come on. Please."

The head of this body was soaked through with blackness. He pulled the damp sheets away and cradled the broken skull in his fingers. A face carved from onyx. Gaping mouth and sunken eyes. The man pushed his fingers into the slimy neck of the child. There was nothing. Warmth and stillness.

"Come on, boy. Come on."

Hades didn't beg. Not to men, anyway. He'd begged plenty of race-horses in his time. Begged greyhounds zipping across static screens. He was begging a boy now. Begging him to live. He bent his stubbled mouth to the boy's wet lips. The girl watched, her hands gripping the front of her dress. Hades pinched the boy's tiny nose and chin in his huge fingers, watched the little chest inflate and deflate like a wet balloon. As he pumped the small birdcage chest with his palms he looked up at the girl, watched her shaking in the light from the kitchen without really seeing her. The seconds lagged on. Peacocks made from twisted pieces of an old car stood and watched the happenings before the house. A bronze wolf howled in silence. In the kitchen, the stranger's blood made a thick dark pool on the linoleum.

The body in his fingers bucked and coughed. Hades shook the boy roughly and thumped his back.

"That's it," he growled. "Come back now. Come on back."

The boy vomited, gurgled, fell limp again. Hades knelt over him in the gravel and dust, his heart raging as it had not done in some time. He reached down and wiped the strands of matted black hair from the massive wound in the side of the boy's head. Clotted flesh and frayed skin, the beginnings of bone underneath. Hades looked up at the sky and hated the stranger. Hated him over and over as the boy slept.

The girl followed Hades as he carried the boy into the kitchen. The child was so much smaller in the light, white skin between ink black and ruby splashes and streaks. He lay the ruined doll out on the table. Hades looked down at the boy, inspecting him like a butcher with a slab of meat, noticing the bulbous joints where cartilage strained and contracted, the limp feet and curled hands. He turned and looked at the sagging body of the stranger in the chair, and then his eyes fell to the girl who stood close by, her hands by her sides, her eyes locked on his face. Breathing, thinking, sorting through frantic voices in his head. For a moment the man and the child simply watched each other and wondered what was to come next. Hades seemed to decide what it was and reached out, encircling her thin arm in his massive fingers.

"Come with me," he murmured, pulling her forward. She let herself be led. In the cramped hall between the bedroom and the living room Hades rose up onto his toes and reached over the top of the ornate plastering that lined the wall, punching a hidden button. The wall sunk and slid away, folding into itself seamlessly. He pushed the girl into the tiny room. She glanced about her at the shelves that lined the three walls, the stacks of cash and dismantled weapons, the locked boxes and safes, the dozens of passports and forged birth certificates lying in neat piles.

And then she turned back to him. He reached up and pressed the button again.

"No!" she gasped, holding her hands out as the hidden door slid shut. "No! No!"

She screamed. Hades felt his face burn as the door closed and her fists began pounding on the other side.

"It's only temporary," he grimaced. "I'm sorry. It's only temporary."

He was speaking more to himself than to her. He could barely hear himself over her cries.

3

Eden coordinated everything from the shade of a blue plastic tarp strung up between two paddy wagons, leaning with her long legs crossed against the edge of a makeshift desk. She held a map of the marina in her hand and with her fingernail she drew a line around the boundary where she wanted the place cordoned off, her eyes lowered with the unenthusiastic appreciation of someone reading a tabloid magazine. The junkie was stripped, wiped down and photographed, and the ambulance where he'd been sitting driven off to the lab. The junkie himself she had driven away for a proper forensic examination. He put up a fuss but she ignored him. Her directions had a calm finality to them as though to defy them would be an act of idiocy.

Within an hour the barricade at the entrance to the marina was packed with spectators. Nothing will make strangers talk to each other more than a good scandal. The place was abuzz with gawkers leaning, murmuring, pointing, folding their arms and predicting. Helicopters whumped overhead, winding a circuit up and down the coastline. Four patrol boats were being prepared to deploy divers in selected spots around the bay.

I stood by the desk and sipped a coffee someone had brought in on a cardboard tray. I felt like mentioning to Eden that there was little chance the junkie had been in his right mind when he saw the other boxes, chained as he was to a weighted toolbox and sailing towards the bottom of the ocean in the dim morning light. What he'd thought he'd seen were probably rocks, submarine pipes, crab cages or illegally dumped waste. I didn't say anything though. Eden hadn't consulted me on the coordination process and so I was happy to let her make a fool of herself if it all went pear-shaped. She folded her arms and stared out at the hive of activity around her like I wasn't standing there. I cracked a couple of jokes and she ignored me. I could see the cool arrogance of her brother in her then.

One of the technicians, a young Filipino guy with acne scars on his cheeks, brought a laptop over and dumped it beside Eden. I recognized him as one of the frightened owls from back at headquarters. He ignored me as he opened the computer and clacked away, adjusting a wireless modem and linking up to a satellite service.

"What have you got?" I asked, moving around behind him. His shoulders seemed to lift up around his ears as I spoke, as though he were bracing for a blow. Eden squeezed in beside me and the technician shivered.

"I've got a link to the main patrol boat's computer," the owl murmured uncertainly. "They're going to feed us the diver's vision. The coast guard has spoken to the two guys who picked up the witness and got their GPS position. Calculating current, drift and the estimated time he was in the water, we've got a pretty good idea of where he was dumped. We're going to put a team of divers down and see if they can locate the boxes. We've tried to pick them up on sonar but it's not precise enough at that depth."

The owl pulled up a GPS map of the coastline beyond Watsons Bay. The sea was illustrated in a pristine, depthless blue. There were animated arrows and markers on the screen, ten or twelve vessels depicted with Xs and triangles. I watched the tech click away at the black laptop keys. In minutes he was showing us heavily delayed muted vision from a camera that was strapped, it seemed, to a diver's helmet. The screen showed a blurry shot of the patrol boat deck with the commander of the team giving a briefing as other divers suited up around the one with the camera.

Eden and I stood behind the owl and watched as the briefing was conducted. The divers zipped up their suits and moved into position. The sun was warm on my shoulders and I shrugged off my jacket. When I turned up my shirtsleeves, Eden glanced at my tattoos. I folded my arms and closed my eyes, feeling drunk on the warmth of the morning. It was the kind of day for lunching in outdoor cafés on the harbor, for strolling home and snoozing in the afternoon with Eden stretched out beside me. Her long white limbs sweat-slicked and stark against the sheets. Who wanted to work on a morning like this? The weekend was coming. The surf would be up.

The divers submerged and the camera delayed for a moment or two with the jolt of the water around the diver's head. More people had crowded in around us. For ten minutes there was nothing but blue and black shadows dancing on the screen. The audience murmured in anticipation. I glanced over and saw Eden's limbs had tightened, the stringy muscle of her forearms flexing in the shadow of the tarp.

Twenty minutes—and nothing more than the flailing of the nameless diver's limbs and the occasional glimpse of the others as they sunk together. The rise of the seabed materialized on the screen, and there was a notable shift in the mood of everyone around us. There, on the screen, was the rocky edge of what looked like a wide sea cavern. And in the cavern were about twenty weed- and sludge-covered toolboxes.

It was two hours before Hades opened the door to the hidden storage room again. The little girl was crouched in the corner farthest from the door, her arms tucked against her chest and her eyes wide. Hades hefted the limp body of the boy up onto his shoulder and spread a thick blanket out on the concrete floor. He let a pillow fall from his fingers and laid the body down. The girl watched, taking in the bandages around the boy's skull and his sunken eyes with barely contained terror. The boy was wearing an unfamiliar man-sized T-shirt. Hades groaned as he crouched above the boy, spreading a thinner blanket over his sleeping body and tucking it under his chin. When it was done he stood and met the girl's eyes.

"Come with me," he beckoned, reaching out his hand.

She didn't move.

"If I was going to hurt you, I'd have done it by now."

The girl shifted on her bloodstained feet, thinking. She rose up slowly, taking tentative steps towards the man.

Hades took her hand and led her into the kitchen. He directed the girl to sit on the edge of the table where the boy had been lying minutes before. The stranger's body was gone, the pool of blood mopped up and bleached away. There were bundles of bloody rags on the table beside the girl, cotton bandages and the clipped ends of medical wire, an open first-aid kit and a pair of scissors. The girl recognized her brother's soiled clothes dumped in a black garbage bag on the floor.

Hades filled a bowl with warm water. He set it beside the girl. Her eyes followed everything—his hands, his face, his tired steps back to the sink where a bottle of Johnnie Walker now stood. He poured two glasses. The girl shook violently as he approached her, her tiny nostrils flaring.

"This'll make you feel better," Hades said, taking her hand and pressing one of the glasses into it. Her fingers were sticky with blood. She looked at the whisky, then at his face. Hades swallowed his drink and set the glass down with a sigh. The girl hesitated.

"It's okay. I promise."

The girl gulped the scotch as she had seen the man do. She winced and coughed.

"Good work," Hades said.

He half-filled her glass again. When he picked up a cloth and rinsed it her brother's blood turned the water in the bowl a pale pink. Hades tried to take the girl's chin in his hand but she flinched away. He seized her face in his wide fingers and she whimpered.

"Settle down."

The scotch worked quickly in her veins. As he began cleaning the mask of blood away she was stiff and resistant. She soon softened up. Hades dipped her face and inspected the deep gash in her forehead. It was about four centimeters long, running across her hairline. He put down the cloth and looked at her. She had a chiselled appearance that would make her seem sharp and calculated when she was older. Dangerous and beautiful. Both children were greyhound thin. Hades wondered which dead parent they took after. The girl sighed with exhaustion as Hades cleaned her hands.

"What's your name, girl?"

"Morgan."

He spread her fingers and examined the scrapes on her palms. Her face was inches from his, her big eyes downcast to the ruined flesh. He tried to guess how old she was. Probably five, he supposed.

"What did they hit you with, Morgan?"

"A stick," she whispered, tears sliding down the edge of her jaw.

Hades wrapped her hands in bandages. He took out the needle and the wire and her eyes followed his fingers, drunk and sad.

"Did they mean to kill you both?"

"I think so. They said so. They made us kneel on the gravel. They yelled at each other."

Hades nodded, threading the fine wire through the soft white flesh surrounding the gash in her head. The girl didn't flinch. She stared at his chest, licking her wet coral-colored lips.

"What's going to happen to Marcus?" she asked.

"He'll either wake up or he won't."

"Are we going to stay here?"

"For now," Hades said, pulling the second stitch tight. "Don't worry about it. I'll figure something out."

Outside the house, beyond the mountains of trash, a truck blasted its horn on the highway. The sound spoke of the world outside the kitchen, an unimportant and distant place. A place of lost things. The girl's tears were silent. Hades rested his palms on her forehead as he worked to pull the wound closed. When he was done he patched the wound with a clean cotton bandage and stood back like an artist assessing his work.

The girl whose name was Morgan sat still, studying the floor as though she had forgotten he was standing there, as though consider-

ing some terrible decision. Hades frowned and felt a knot grow in his stomach. There was a strange coldness to her eyes now. It gave him the feeling that something he couldn't name, something that had been there only moments before, was now dead and gone.

He had never seen a child look that way.

4

We opened the first box on the concrete marina between two police buses, protected from the media by more blue plastic tarps. Everyone was pretty sure what we were going to find, but rather than driving people away it sucked them in, a macabre freak show. Eden and I crowded around the box with the area chief and a forensic specialist while the nobodies of the investigation whispered and shushed each other. The sun beat in on the side of the tarps, illuminating the shadows of dozens of bodies.

The forensic guy knelt down and wedged a chisel under the rusted lock of the toolbox, prying it open gently. Eden stood over him with her arms folded. She took off her sunglasses and her dark eyes examined the careful process, her head tilted slightly as though she could already smell the terrible stench that would erupt when the sludge seals were broken.

I saw the face first. The girl hadn't been cut up to fit into the box, as we found later that many others had. She was curled in a fetal position with her hands and feet tucked under her body, her torso a perfect fit for the confines of her coffin. Her face was pressed into the dark corner, her nose a little lifted and her milky eyes wide open. She was fresh. Around a week dead by my guess. Tiny life-forms panicked and streaked over the surface of the water in the box, taking shelter in the folds of her body. The girl's long blond hair was tangled around her throat, swirling like seaweed in the disturbed water. There were wounds on her, deep grooves in her lower back, but the inside of the box was dark and I couldn't see them properly at my angle. Her thin bony back was milk white, blotched here and there by the draining of blood and fluids. It was as though she had curled up in there to hide and someone had sunk her to the bottom of the ocean.

I looked at Eden. There was no emotion in her face. She stared down at the girl as though she were reading the fine print on a contract, attentive but distant. The area chief covered his mouth and nose with his hand against the smell.

"What is she?" I asked the forensic guy. "Sixteen?"

"Eleven. Twelve."

I chewed my lip. When no one spoke, I shrugged and said what everyone was probably thinking.

"She's pretty fresh. Probably that missing girl."

"Shut it up," Eden ordered, turning and pulling away a corner of the tarp where men and women scrambled back to let her through.

Most people hate the smell of mice. Jason had never understood that. There was something earthy and wet and warm about the smell of rodents, something natural that defied the sterility of the modern home. It brought him back to his childhood, to the caverns and tunnels and alleyways made by the beams beneath the house. He would crawl in there and dig treasures into the dirt, peer through the floorboards, listen to conversations. There were mice and rats under the house, nestled into crevices and squeezed into dugouts, small cities of rolled and coiled newspaper and dried grass. Jason liked to watch their little families, the licking and stroking and picking they imposed on each other, the silent ease with which they decided to sleep or play or fight. Things were not like that in his family. There was only noise and pain, locked doors and crying in the night. The mice didn't care if he picked his nails, if he couldn't recite his multiplication tables, whether his shirt was ironed or his face clean. The mice couldn't hurt him. The mice couldn't call him names. He envied their uncomplicated lives.

Jason was fascinated by the things that humans shared with the animals and the things they tried to leave behind. Bonds really puzzled him. Curled in his bare immaculate room, reading silently beneath the blankets by the light of a small flashlight, he had read that brolgas—those lanky, dancing, stony-colored birds that strolled the lake near his home—found a partner to breed with and stayed with that mate for life, no matter what. Imagine that. Jason had set out the next weekend on his lone wanderings to find a brolga and see this incredible natural magic in action. On the way he encountered some of his schoolmates—cruel, freckled, sun-bleached kids who threw pencils at him in class and made fun of the way his mother cut his hair. They were huddled in a group skipping rocks by the edge of the lake. When they set upon him, sneering and laughing and pointing and interrogating him about his purpose, he explained what he knew about the brolga and that he planned to catch one alive. All day under the wicked sun he labored to catch one of the swift, graceful, wide-winged birds. He used every conceivable trick he could think of—creeping, swimming, snaring, baiting, trying to strike them down with rocks. The schoolkids had hounded him like a rabble of street dogs, yabbering and rolling and barking laughter every time he failed. When Jason finally got hold of a bird and its mate had rushed out of the water, squawking and honking and flapping its wings in fury, the children had fallen silent, awed, and Jason had laughed, victorious. He'd teased the angry bird by wringing his partner's neck, slowly, gently, scattering the feathers in the wind. The male bird filled the air with its noise. Jason turned to his schoolmates and grinned, showing them the limp bird.

"See?" he said. "They love each other. Animals can love each other too."

Sometimes the animals he hunted and trapped and played with in the wild weren't enough. Jason liked to have animals in his life. His ever-expanding collection of beetles, lizards, snakes, his encouragement of stray cats and dogs, got him beaten and locked up and starved plenty of times but the impulse never completely died. The animals didn't want anything from Jason other than food, affection, warmth. He loved their stupidity, their simplistic natures. Make a dog your own, secure its loyalty, and you can beat that dog within an inch of death and it will return to you, love you, guard you. Jason knew that. He admired loyalty. It reminded him of the brolgas. Jason was fascinated by the intersection between wild and dependent things, becoming a slave of one creature to another. The unnaturalness of it. Much of life was like that. He wanted to scratch, to bite, to fight, to crawl away into tight holes and forget the world outside. Instead he was a loyal dog, a beaten yet obedient creature, an enemy to his own instincts. A mouse living in a tank instead of a hole.

The small dark apartment in Chatswood wasn't right for anything larger than a tank of mice but the adult Jason didn't mind. He sat by the tank in the mornings and watched them going about their business—digging or sleeping, running madly on the little plastic wheel.

When he put his finger into the tank one of them rushed forward and gripped on, hoisting its warm velvet-soft body up onto his hand. Trusting. He sat in the light from the venetian blinds, cracked open just enough to allow some view of the outside world, and ran the mouse over his hands, smiling at its frantic dash from one palm to another, over and over, never recognizing where it had been, no care for where it was going. People were inexplicably like mice. Panicky, wide-eyed, utterly at the will of a callous, fleshy-palmed god.

Jason put the mouse on the table and watched it sniff and scurry around the objects lying there, the scalpels of various sizes lined up in foam trays, the glass bottles and packets of paper towels, the rolled bandages and coils of medical wire. The mouse stopped and munched on the edge of a stack of papers littered with names, ages, birthdates, blood types, addresses. Beginning at the corner of the page, it tore tiny strips off with its pink paws.

Taking a scalpel from the tray, Jason pinched the mouse's ear between his thumb and forefinger gently, feeling its impossible thinness and softness, his most careful touch surrendering the creature's entire head to his will. A whisper of flesh. He looked at the scalpel, considered, then gave the ear a wag. He let the mouse go, stroking its curved spine with the flat of the blade. Ticcing, twitching, jittering life beneath the fur. Jason lifted the scalpel, let it dangle, point down, before releasing it. The point of the scalpel dug into the table a few centimeters from the mouse's right front paw. The animal was unfazed. Jason pried the instrument from the wood, lifted it again, higher this time, and aimed better. The scalpel chunked into the wood, just missing the mouse's nose.

The television, barely audible, caught his attention. On the screen police officers were swarming on a pier like ants, crawling over it, meeting each other, gnashing pincers and pawing, all in black. In one sequence a young man was being ushered unwillingly into a van. Jason had encountered him in the early hours of that morning, a man he had been certain he would never see again. More panning shots of the crowded marina and then one of a steel toolbox. Jason felt fury and pride tingle in him briefly before the familiar calm smothered the emotions. He sucked air between his teeth.

When the story ended he looked back at the creature on the table, carefully cleaning its whiskers by his hand. Careless, brainless thing. Jason lifted the scalpel at a full arm's height, squinted, let it settle in his fingers for a long moment before letting it go.

5

We found a quiet corner of the café on the marina to use as a base for the afternoon. It was near enough to the crime scene that specialists and witnesses could come and report to us, but distant enough from the fray that we could organize ourselves without the distraction of the chaos down on the water. Eden finally passed me some responsibility—rounding up security tapes from the marina, calling in marina staff for interviews, sending a progress report back to the station. She sat across from me munching spicy potato wedges between phone calls, glancing out now and then at the sinking sun glinting on the water. A troop of bicyclists clad in spandex of every color of the rainbow took a nearby table, clacking in on plastic shoes, ordering gluten-free chips and smoothies, laughing with long teeth. Yellow and lime-green fish circled the pier pillars beneath us, visible through the glass that lined the balcony. I watched them as I spoke, envying their calm, meaningless paths.

In time we'd made all the calls and taken all the notes we could. I ordered a scotch and Coke, and Eden asked for a bourbon on ice.

"So there's not much we can do until the forensic team gets back with the report on the bodies. We should catch up tonight," I suggested as the café staff began packing up the cutlery on tables around us. "We're going to be working pretty closely from here on. It might be nice to know something about each other."

Eden smirked. I felt a lump in my stomach.

"I like a bit of professional distance. It'll make it easier to *not* take a bullet for you one day."

"Oh, come on, a couple of drinks."

"The whole homicide team goes out together now and then." She lifted her eyes to mine briefly. "They'll be at The Hound tonight from six. If you want to bond, we can bond in company."

"The Hound? Urgh. Woman, where are your standards?"

She paused, staring at her drink. "Eric will be there." It sounded like a warning.

"Why would I care if Eric's there?" I asked, the lump in my stomach growing. "He's my partner's brother. We should be mates."

"Yeah, I guess." She smiled and shrugged. "It's worth a shot. Don't be surprised if he doesn't want to bump chests with you. It takes a long time to become close to Eric."

I raised my eyebrows in answer. The revelation didn't surprise me.

* * *

I'd been to The Hound before but never liked it as a hangout. Too many cops. A drunken night out at The Hound tended to turn into a dick-measuring contest between street cops, encouraged by grizzled detectives and captains and presided over by nonchalant paramedics and firemen. At The Hound officers fresh from training at Goulburn, surprised and disheartened by the lack of understanding and appreciation they received from old hands in their new occupation, could mingle with their heroes in the business—cops who'd been on the beat a good six months longer than they had. This kind of mingling encouraged war stories and the comparison of arrest tallies, the showing of scars and narration of chase tales. Abilities were questioned and motives examined. Fitness feats and beep-test scores were lamented over. As the glasses emptied, fights erupted and poured out onto Parramatta Road, where the missed swings and pained howls were watched by families of every conceivable ethnic origin who lived in apartments above the neighboring Haberfield shops. No arrests were made, of course, and the black eyes and split lips that ensued were chuckled over in the office the next morning. Promotions, easy beats and pay bonuses were awarded to young guns who could land a fist after ten schooners. I didn't like that kind of competition. I preferred to drink alone, the older I got.

Like a schoolyard, the bar was divided into status groups organized by occupation. The morgue attendants and body handlers crowded quietly in one corner, making sick jokes and drinking themselves unconscious. The forensic specialists, who generally left early, engaged in their strange technical language over vodkas and light beers at the outdoor tables. The street cops huddled in booths along the walls, sunburnt and testy.

The homicide squad kept to themselves, separate from the

rest. The owls, strangely deliberate-looking in their tailored jeans and cotton shirts, sat wedged together on leather couches by the jukebox. The conversation was sparse and the music loud, so although they looked uncomfortable they were able to pull off a general feeling of community just by drinking and smiling at each other. Eric had perched himself on the arm of one of the couches and was making loud wisecracks about each owl in turn, which everyone seemed to think was hilarious. I sat beside Eden at the bar, watching him work the room like a debutante. Of course he knew everyone in the pub. They all greeted him like they hadn't seen him in years. Some of the women whispered in his ears and held his fingers lovingly as they talked.

"You guys locals?"

"We're from Utulla, out the back of Camden." So, about half an hour down the Hume Highway from me. Eden took a long breath and let it out slow, like keeping her secrets from me was going to be a long and arduous process. I wondered what she was hiding. I ordered her another drink and she seemed grateful.

"Where you from?" she asked.

"Bankstown born and bred."

"Go the doggies."

"Damn straight."

"Got family out there?"

"Nope." I smiled, not bothering to disguise my relief. "Got any in Utulla?"

"My father." She nodded.

It sounded strange to me, the way she said "father" instead of "dad," like she deliberately wanted me to understand that she had been the fruit of this man's loins. She bent to adjust her boot and I noticed a long scar running the length of her hairline, faint and barely detectable.

"Okay," I said. "So what's your deepest, darkest secret?"

She coughed over her drink and smiled.

"Come on, Frank. The whole my-partner-is-my-soulmate thing has been seriously overcooked by *Law & Order*, don't you think? We don't have to be intimate to be effective."

"I *want* to be intimate with you." I grinned.

"Uh huh. You'll get over that."

"I'll tell you mine."

"I don't want to know yours."

"We'll start simple." I spread my hands out on the bar as though clearing room for a party trick. "I once climbed out a girl's bathroom window after a one-night stand while she was cooking me breakfast."

Eden nodded her appreciation. More drinks arrived.

"Okay." She smiled sheepishly, after some long and deep consideration of the challenge. "I did a week of dog squad training out at Rockdale in the early days. There was a dog there that really hated my guts and they kept giving it to me for assessments. One time, when no one was looking, I kicked it. Kicked it hard, right in the backside."

I made a big deal, hooting and hollering, waving my hands in the air. She punched my arm.

"You're a *bad* woman," I said.

"You got no idea, pal."

"I rigged a police charity raffle once. Won myself a holiday to New Zealand. It was Kids with Cancer."

"Oh!" she cringed. "You're a monster."

I felt exhilaration creep over me. I didn't know if it was the bourbon or if there was a possibility that Eden was actually warming to me. I'd never imagined her as she was now, sniggering over her drink and shaking her head of long dark hair.

"Okay. I let another girl in my Year Five class take the rap for stealing from the teacher's handbag. Her mother made her move schools."

I slapped my hand on the bar and ordered another drink. Eden opened her wallet and laid a twenty on the counter, turning and looking over her shoulder at the crowd. I went on blabbering, not realizing that her smile had disappeared.

"I slept with my Year Twelve English teacher." I grinned. "She was probationary. Naive and new age. I convinced her to stay behind and help me with my grammar. I was such a hound dog."

I caught the look on her face. A splinter jabbed in my heart.

"Oh, come on!" I clapped her shoulder. "I was seventeen! Gimme a brea–"

"I'm gonna do a round of the room, Frank," Eden murmured and slinked away. I followed her eyes across the room and caught Eric watching us, surrounded by people who were talking and grinning nervously.

I'd just grabbed ahold of myself and was about to let loose at the urinal when I felt a hot rush of breath on the back of my neck. Eric's voice whispered in my ear:

"Can I give you a hand, honey?"

I jolted and shoved back into him and he thumped me on the shoulder. The sound of his laughter filled up the room. There was piss on my shoes.

"You're so uptight, Frankie."

"There's a certain code of conduct when someone's taking a piss," I snarled, immediately regretting the overreaction. Eric chuckled and took a urinal two down from mine, victorious.

"You've got up Eden's nose already," he noted, looking down at himself. "She's abandoned you." I said nothing. One of the owls came through the door, saw us standing there and retreated.

"Well, you know, she mustn't have liked the track I was going down. Not my fault she's got something to hide."

"We've all got something to hide, Frankie." Eric grinned, zipping up and turning towards me. "You don't want the rest of the crew finding out about your assault charge, do you?"

I almost zipped my cock up in my fly. I couldn't help myself. My hands lashed out, gripping the front of his shirt. I shoved him into the wall. Though I put the full force of my body behind it, I felt that he was letting me hurl him around, letting me know there was power in his body that he was choosing not to unleash on me. His large, strong hands folded around mine. He squeezed and I heard my knuckles crack.

"You punched your ex-wife in the head."

"It was a misunderstanding," I growled. "A *confidential* misunderstanding. You've got no right going through my files."

"This job is about knowing each other, Frank. It's about knowing each other's secrets and ignoring them. We're all good guys here. No one's better than anyone else. We're all dirty. We've all got something shadowing us."

"The others know your secrets, then, and they ignore them—is that right?" I shoved him into the wall again and it felt good. "Then why are they so fucking scared of you? Why don't you tell me what *you're* hiding, Eric?"

I didn't even see him move. His big wide hand shot up and smacked the side of my head. He didn't punch me, he slapped me, and it was intentional, because though he hadn't made a fist the impact hurt like nothing I'd ever felt, like his hand was made of iron. Humiliating, the way the sound of it rippled out and away from me, the way my ear was instantly on fire. At the same time he kicked my legs out from underneath me. I sprawled on the bathroom floor, landing hard on my elbows.

"You're running with wolves now, Frankie. You've got to be faster than that." He laughed as he turned to leave. His wolf howl echoed around the large tiled room.

I didn't leave, even though it seemed that Eden had disappeared. I wasn't giving Eric that satisfaction. I went out into the bar and sat at the counter where I'd been sitting with Eden, my head throbbing. I ordered a drink and the barman glanced at me worriedly for a moment before turning and pulling a bottle off the shelf. Eric's eyes were on my back, hot and heavy, his presence in a group of people by the door like a siren from across the room.

My first wife and I had married young and we'd taken up cocaine pretty early as a way of avoiding the depressing sink into monotonous suburban life. I'd been a street cop then and the coke had been easy to come by—just about every man and his dog was carrying it, and asking for it never raised an eyebrow. We thought that because we had a habit and a hotted-up car we were different from the Mary Janes and Uncle Bills in the rows of cheap prefab houses in Sydney's West. My wife and I'd only known each other on the party scene in the city and got married because I knocked her up in the third week. We thought we were *bad*. We thought we were different and in love and all that crap. Suburban life crushed that. Things went from a hundred Ks an hour to a laborious jog in three seconds flat. Suddenly we were watching

Who Wants to Be a Millionaire? every Saturday night and arguing over dishwashing liquid brands.

Louise hid the coke from me during the pregnancy but I knew the whole time what she was up to. I didn't care. I had two lives by then. My time at home with Louise was a waiting game between shifts on the street. I didn't love her, not really, and as the baby grew inside her we started to fight. I just wanted to be on the job all the time, roughing up perps and throwing my weight around. Driving fast. Bursting into houses. Getting free drinks and pretending I could have any chick I wanted. I wanted to stay out all night drinking with the other street cops and relishing the secret language of the force. Louise wanted someone to care for her. I wasn't that guy. I was much too into myself then.

She had a stillborn, a girl, at 2AM on a Tuesday in November. I wasn't there. Not being there when that happened was the thing that finally ruined us.

We fought for months, daring each other to be the one to throw in the towel. She used to hurl things at me, lunge at me, claw at my face. The neighbors heard the screaming and got involved once or twice. I hit her one night, mainly to get her off me, and it was the last time I ever saw her. I was charged and pleaded guilty and was barely allowed to keep my job.

I was thinking about the baby as I sat at the bar staring into my drink. I glanced at the mirror behind the counter and spotted Eden sitting by the window, watching the traffic, an old Lebanese woman selling roses between the outdoor settings. I was about to leave when I accidentally slid my hand into the small red wallet sitting on the counter beside me.

The wallet was square and flat, the size and shape of a man's, only it was made from what looked to be dark red eel skin. I'd seen wallets like that in Chinatown and Oxford Street, surrounded by rabbit-foot key rings, flashing phone covers and coke pipes. I knew instinctively that it was Eden's. I sat stock still and stared at it, aware of the heat spreading out through my limbs, the thumping of my heart in my temples. Watching her in the mirrors, I slid the wallet across and opened it. Her homicide squad ID was at the front behind a clear plastic window.

There are two ways you get to know the heart and soul of a woman. You sleep with her or you rifle through her things. Both actions carry the acute risk of winding up with a stiletto heel in the side of your neck. I didn't care. Eric had pissed me off. I wanted something to arm myself with, something that might draw me into his and Eden's elite circle.

Gun club membership. University library card. Business card for a kickboxing club. Discount card for Genie's Nails.

There was a small piece of paper tucked behind Eden's ID, separate from the others. I noticed it because of its age. It was yellow and frayed, like it had been handled for years. I slipped the paper out carefully, listening to it crackle as I pressed it open.

Six names. Four had been crossed off. Two were left untouched at the bottom of the list, written in blue ink by a shaky hand.

Jake DeLaney.

Benjamin Annous.

I read over the names a couple of times. Then I pulled a photograph out of the same pocket. The picture was of an old man, the ex-thug type, with heavy shoulders and a boxy head. Like an ageing Rottweiler. He was leaning back in a wooden chair and holding his hand up, cringing playfully in front of the camera, holding a short glass.

I knew this man from somewhere. I knew the way he held his gnarled hand up, shied from the cameras, quiet and yet threatening. He struck me as someone who might have appeared in a newspaper, leaving a courthouse or two. Infamous. He had that infamous look to him.

One of the owls nudged my shoulder as she ordered a drink from the bar. I slipped the photograph and the piece of paper back into the wallet and left it on the counter. Eric met my eyes for a moment, smiling, as I pushed through the exit.

Hades let the girl out of the room at night when the trucks had stopped rolling over the horizon of trash and the sorting center workers had left through the gates. He went down on the first morning and discreetly took some clothes that he thought might fit the children, stuffing them into a garbage bag and hauling it up the hill. He also found a fluffy black toy dog that he thought the girl might like.

She was waiting for him when he opened the secret door, standing there with her eyes raised to his face, the boy still unconscious by her feet. She looked sick and pale. He sat silently by her side as she ate the spaghetti bolognaise he had cooked for her. Color came slowly back into her cheeks. The little girl ignored the stuffed animal, letting it slip to the floor beside her chair.

When Hades took her bowl away her eyes rose to the ceiling, examining the colored bottles and chains and cracked teacups hanging there, the broken mobiles and pieces of bone and polished machinery parts. She reached out and touched the huge black wing of a dead bird he had nailed to the wall by the table, following the long dorsal feathers with her fingertips. He watched her, wondering if he'd spot that strange look he had seen the night of the murders, the darkness in her eyes that he had only ever witnessed in the eyes of the damned. He didn't see it and he told himself that he must have imagined it. When he beckoned her into the living room she followed obediently and sat curled on the very edge of the sofa, as far away from him as she could get. He switched over to The Simpsons, *thinking it was something she might have watched in her other life. She didn't laugh. Not once.*

The boy moved through layers of consciousness, but was never really awake. Hades set a routine of checking on him twice in the middle of the night, which sometimes woke the girl suddenly and got her screaming and crying.

On the third day the boy was still out. Hades thought about driving him to a hospital and dumping him at the doors, but what would he do with the girl? She had seen his face. She had seen his house. Hades worried incessantly about the boy, sometimes peeling his eyelids back and staring helplessly into his vacant eyes. He didn't want the boy to die. More than that, he didn't want the girl to know it before he did. He changed the bandages on the boy's head and cleaned the vicious wound.

He let the girl out that afternoon. It was a Friday and there were few workers about. He had dropped hints to the sorting center staff about an old flame who was giving him trouble about his children and who'd threatened to dump them on his doorstep. He led the girl down to his workshop at the bottom of the hill. She sat on the edge of a bench and watched him work on his latest creation.

Finally he seemed to have found something that brought life into her eyes. She watched with rapt attention as he ground and welded and beat the salvaged materials into the shape of a fox. Her lips formed shapes of wonder. When he waved her over from the bench she dashed to his side, reached out and touched the still-warm metal, stroking the snout of the giant beast tentatively as though it were living—and dangerous. She watched for hours, saying nothing.

As they walked back to the house she reached up and took his huge fingers in her hand. Hades looked down at her and it seemed to bring her out of a daze. She realized what she was doing and snatched her hand away. The setting sun made her cheeks look flushed pink and her eyes a glittering gold. She seemed like a living doll to him. He worried that his clumsy hands might break her.

The man and the girl stopped inside the doorway to the little shack. The boy was in the kitchen, crouching, one hand steadying himself against the floor. He was looking at the ceiling. Hades realized with shock that he had left the door to the secret room open. The girl let out a howl and flew at the boy, encircling him with her arms. He was confused and shaken, couldn't stand properly. Hades had never seen the boy's eyes open of their own accord. They were even sadder and more soulless than those of the girl.

"Marcus?" the girl sobbed, taking his face in both her hands and shaking it. "Marcus? Marcus? Marcus?"

"Easy now," Hades cautioned, moving her hands away gently. "Just be careful with him."

Marcus looked up at Hades with the cool detachment of a mental patient. Hades worried that he might be permanently brain damaged. The do-it-yourself stitch job had pulled the corner of his right eye up slightly. Crooked and broken. Hades sat the boy down and took his chin in his wide hand, lifting his face into the light.

"Do you know your name, boy?" the man asked.

"Yep," the boy answered, licking his cracked lips. "Do you know yours?"

6

I'd taken a girl home. I do that now and then. She was someone I'd found while dropping into my local for a double scotch to put me to sleep before wandering up to my apartment. There's an odd moment that passes between perfect strangers sometimes when, without words, their eyes meet and both have a look on their faces that says how lonely they are, despite the vague successes of their lives, despite their manufactured identities. All I'd had to say was, "Let's get the fuck out of here." In the morning I wasn't lonely anymore and I don't think she was either.

We were snapped awake by my mobile phone. I knew who it was and ignored it. It was five and still dark. The girl groaned at the noise, her sharp toenails carving lines of protest down my shins. The phone stopped ringing and seconds later there was a pounding knock at the front door. I grabbed the blanket and pulled it up over our heads, pushing the girl over and gripping her around the middle so she wouldn't go, addicted to the heat of her body in the bed.

"Just lie still and be quiet and she'll go away."

"Frank! Get up!"

"Who is it?" The girl asked.

"No one."

Eden knocked on my window. I pulled the blanket down tighter.

"Go away, devil!"

"They've got nine bodies for us. We need to go."

"They'll keep. It's the middle of the fucking night. What's wrong with you?"

"Bodies?" the girl sat up sharply, shoving the blanket aside. I sighed. "What are you, like, a cop or something?"

"You didn't wonder about the handcuffs?"

"I'd liked to have known you were a cop. I don't like cops." She frowned over her shoulder at me.

"Only crooks say that."

She started gathering her things and I crawled, shivering, from the sheets. That beautiful smell of warm bodies and slept-in sheets and gentle exhalations evaporated. I tore open the front door and Eden's eyes dropped to my naked crotch, then rose to the eagle tattoo on my chest, then finally met my own. She looked aggrieved.

"Frank."

"This is what you get, you come to my place at this hour."

"Put some fucking clothes on and get in the car." She shook her head and walked away. I laughed as she descended the stairs, swivelling my hips so that everything jumbled around.

"Get a good look," I called. "You won't do it again!"

I was still laughing as Eden passed my elderly neighbor on the level below. She was stopped by the stairs, washing basket in her arms, looking up at me. I covered myself and walked inside.

The nine bodies were laid out on two rows of morgue tables in the Parramatta District Hospital mortuary, each with a clipboard detailing the autopsy. Some had been reassembled. Others were curled up as they had been to fit the shape of the boxes, the pathologists and forensic specialists reluctant to straighten their limbs in the preliminary stage of investigations. I wandered between the gurneys, looking at each of the corpses. There were four females and five males. The youngest of the females was the girl who'd been in the first box we opened. The youngest male looked about fifteen.

I stopped by the boy's body. His face was tucked against his knees but I could see in the shadow of his limbs that his eyes were closed. His hair was falling out around his skull as his body decomposed. The smell coming off him was unnatural in its intensity, the powerful reek of rotting flesh having been added to with toxic chemicals. I stared at his curled fists. Eden came up beside me and I shifted my eyes away. I felt strangely ashamed.

"We began with the bodies that were the least decomposed," said the pathologist, a lanky Asian man. "There are twenty bodies. We estimate that around half will have to be identified by dental records. These are the only ones with faces."

My stomach turned. Eden was staring coldly at the body of a man on the table next to us.

"There's a unifying cause of death, which makes things easier for you," the pathologist said pleasantly, pointing his pen at my nose. "All these bodies were bled out. Each of them had a surgical wound that was not closed."

"A surgical wound?" Eden frowned. "Give me an example."

The pathologist pointed to the boy beside me.

"He's missing a heart." He turned and pointed to another. "That one's had her lungs removed. The young girl by the doorway, she's lost both of her kidneys."

"Christ." I shuddered. "Some sicko's nicking body parts?"

"This isn't a sicko, not in the traditional sense. The person you're looking for is a cold, calculated businessman." The pathologist lifted a sheet from a body at the end of the row. I stared at the bloodless cavity in a young woman's torso where some part of her had been removed. The pathologist pointed into her with the end of his pen, like an explorer following the edge of a map.

"These wounds are clean and meticulously positioned and the organs have been removed with the utmost care in the manner prescribed for direct transplant. Each of the victims has sedatives in their system. He's been doing this for some time. He's trained— and he's experienced."

Eden was chewing her thumbnail. She looked at the ceiling and let the air out of her lungs as though she was glad to have them.

"An organ thief," she whispered miserably. "This is a new one."

7

Martina Ducote had woken up plenty of times experiencing the strangely thrilling sensation of not knowing where she was. The moment before she opened her eyes was usually filled with the leftover giddiness of a night on the town and the dread of wondering who she was lying next to. This time was different. The moment before she opened her eyes was filled with pain and, as her body twisted to gauge its surroundings, she felt cold steel and rust, not the softness of an unfamiliar mattress.

She opened her eyes.

The drugs she had been slipped in the wine bar on Oxford Street had ruined her depth perception, so when she reached out to touch the bars around her she bashed them awkwardly with her knuckles. She was still wearing the little black party dress but her wrists were adorned with bruises like strange bracelets and her lip was split from what felt like a punch to the mouth. Her earrings were missing and so was her watch.

She rolled onto her knees and rested against the door of the cage, trying to will away the sickness.

It didn't work. Martina retched and vomited on the cage floor beside her water bowl.

"Help," she rasped, the sound barely loud enough for her own ears. "Help."

The common need among all forms of police is food. You've got to keep your calorie intake up if you're going to maintain the kind of reserved edginess required for an occupation constantly fraught with danger. For the homicide detectives it compensates for energy spent on anxiety about the case, puzzlement as events develop, the horrors of the crime scenes. Stress for the small stuff. Eden sat down in the conference room, placed her iced coffee within arm's reach and tore open the wrapping around a bacon and egg roll she'd bought for breakfast. She took the switchblade from her belt and cut the roll in half, then licked the blade on either side. I peeled the top off my breakfast pie, perusing the autopsy photographs before me. Unlike Eden, I would regret my high-fat breakfast, even though I knew it was necessary. She didn't look like anything other than protein shakes and rice crackers ever passed her lips. I wondered if she worked out. Her hands were veined and strong. A fighter's hands.

In silence we read through the ten autopsy reports. Eden put her boots up on the table, reading at twice the speed I did. Journalists she knew called her a couple of times. She ignored them.

There had been others milling around the front of the station, flicking cigarette butts in the garden as they waited for us.

I felt better after a bit of breakfast. Eden was watching me as I finished up the last report, licking gravy off my fingertips. I made a call to the forensic office to make sure the toolbox serial numbers were being traced. The marina CCTV was useless. Like the junkie said, the guy was covered up pretty well and the boat had been rented the day before with a fake license. We were having the images examined to get a height and weight on him, and the boat rental office attendant was being quizzed for a sketch.

"So what we've got to ask ourselves is whether we believe this guy's chopping pieces out of his victims as part of a psychotic ritual or as part of an organized transplant operation."

"He's so meticulous," Eden murmured. "So careful. None of the victims has any signs of sustained abuse. He's not violent. He's not escalating. It doesn't fit with the profile of a psychotic. My bet is he's transplanting."

"To who?" I shook my head. "He'd have to have willing recipients."

"The donor waiting lists are packed in this country. There must be plenty of people out there who'd buy a kidney off the list for a good price if it were offered. For themselves. For their children."

I looked down at the flakes of pastry left over from my pie. It seemed to me that we were discussing a nightmare, something absurd, unreal.

"Naw, come on," I scoffed. "You can't tell me a civilian would go for this. You can't tell me your average Joe would buy a kidney from a murder victim."

"I'm not talking about your average Joe. I'm talking about wealthy, desperate people. Who's to say they understand where their organ is coming from? Even if they do, you can convince yourself of anything if you think about it in the right way. Who deserves life and who doesn't is an age-old question with no real answer."

Something seemed to flicker in her then, some thought that wanted to push its way up from inside and make itself known. She shook her head as though to clear it away.

"I mean, you, Frank, have bought drugs off the street with no idea who suffered and died for their production. We cause pain and suffering and death in countries across the world simply because we are addicted to a certain way of living. We never see or meet or hear about these people. We ignore the inconvenient. It's in our nature."

A cold chill rushed through me. I liked the reference to my record. It was cute. Nasty, but cute. She was letting me know Eric had filled her in. On everything. She continued reading like she hadn't said anything.

"So he approaches people on the list," I thought aloud. "People who have money. How does he select the victims? How does he know they'll be a match?"

"We'll have to consult some specialist physicians." Eden clicked the top of a stainless-steel pen and made a note. "See who has access to the donor list, how long it is, what sort of transplants have occurred here and what kind of training he'd need. I'm only guessing, but he'd have to find a victim with a tissue and blood-type match. He'd have to have access to the medical records of his victims to ensure they don't have any health problems of their own. He'd also have to know the potential recipients had money. He'd have to be privy to their financial situation."

"This guy's got a hell of a lot of private information at his fingertips. That tells me he's either operated as a physician or a transplant surgeon or he's got someone inside the system feeding him confidential patient information."

Eden nodded and sipped her iced coffee. The condensation from the plastic bottle was wet on her fingertips.

"The organ recipients aren't going to be forthcoming with the details," I continued. "They'd be putting their heads on a chopping block. What would you call a charge like that? Conspiracy to murder? It's receiving stolen goods at the least."

Eden smirked. I felt the smile drop off my face as Eric entered the room. He was wearing gold-tinted aviators to cover his hungover eyes. The collar of his black shirt was open, hinting at an ornate tattoo on his collarbone. His shoulder holster was crooked. He looked like a men's magazine model someone had dressed up as a cop for a joke.

"Morning, comrades," he grinned, nodding at me. "Frankie."

I felt the desire for violence flex in me. A long breath eased through my teeth. I wanted Eden to trust me, as her partner and as a man. She was weird but I liked her. Eric was the predictable catch that came with having a dangerously beautiful and darkly mysterious woman fall right into your lap. I could handle him. He was a prick, a prick with knowledge of my past, but I'd dealt with plenty of pricks in my time.

"Something we can help you with?" I asked. "We're kind of inundated here."

"Hold your fire, cowboy. I come bearing gifts."

Eric slapped a plastic evidence bag on the table.

"What would you do without me?" He grinned sweetly at Eden. She rolled her eyes.

I pulled the evidence bag across to me, jiggling the object inside into one corner. It was a gold bracelet, covered in grime and rust. I felt it through the plastic with my fingers.

"It was in the box with the young girl in it."

It was an identity bracelet with a small pink jewel embedded beside a name. Eden leaned over to see the name on the gold plate.

"Monica," she said.

Our team had known the little girl in the box was the girl missing from Maroubra for hours. You could see it in the shape of her face and limbs and how these compared with photographs of the missing girl, though the look of a person changes dramatically after death and a little decomposition. But we couldn't give a definitive answer to the parents, not until dental records and DNA had come back. No matter how certain you are that a body is a missing person, you never inform the family until you've got scientific evidence. Doesn't matter if they have the same tattoos, birthmarks, goddamn amputated limbs. You never tell the family until you have the DNA. I remember my first homicide chief drilling that into me as I stood in his office for the first time in my brand-new suit and blindingly polished shoes. I got to wondering if his passion for the subject came from learning it the hard way.

The news that the bracelet was described on the missing persons report came back at the same time as the DNA. Even then it wouldn't have been enough to give the parents an answer. When we left the station to go meet them at around 11AM they'd been waiting a solid twenty hours or so to find out if their daughter was still alive. I sat back in the car as we headed for Maroubra and stared at the airport between tunnels of orange lights, the city skyline black against a gathering squall of rain. Cake's "Short Skirt/Long Jacket" came on the radio. Eden sang softly to herself. It surprised me.

"What happened to Doyle?" I asked.

Eden gave me a piercing glance. When she stared ahead there was a border collie grinning at us from the back of an SUV. She looked the dog up and down as though confused by its presence.

"Doyle copped a bullet in the face," she exhaled. "Simple as that. We were chasing a dealer who we thought was unarmed. We called for backup but they didn't get there in time. He waited for us around a corner. Doyle was faster than me. He went first. Got it right between the eyes."

"You see the shooter?"

"I put in a sketch. Got nothing back."

"Bullet?"

"Hollow point. Can't trace it."

"I heard you had his blood all over you."

"Where'd you hear that?"

"Dunno." I shrugged. "Police report?"

I'd lifted the file that morning, sifted through pictures of Eden standing by the ambulance covered in the blood and brains of her former partner. Her hair hanging in her face. Her palm to her temple and teeth bared. She hadn't looked upset. She'd looked angry. Disappointed. Almost as though she'd wanted it to happen another way, a more dignified way.

Eden's lip curled in distaste. I shrugged.

"What? Eric's the only one allowed to go digging in old police reports for personal interest?"

"I'd prefer it if you directed your personal interest elsewhere. I was right behind him," she said. "I saw him get shot."

I let some time go by.

We entered the eastern suburbs, hills laden with a tight mixture of weatherboard hovels, brick terraces and apartment buildings and glass-front mansions rolling towards the sea. Surfers milled on street corners, bare-chested and tanned. There were tribal tattoos and filigree scripts on skin everywhere and a stark absence of anything but white faces. I knew this city, had gotten myself drunk and fallen asleep on the beaches here many times as a troublemaking boy. It was a dangerous place for the Lebanese and Koreans, although they were safe at the larger beaches like Bondi. There was an unwritten code here about the faces that belonged on the scrub-fringed footpaths, those that belonged in the water, on the sand, in the pubs. In fact, everywhere but behind the counter of the local newsagent. At Maroubra even those strangers who met the criteria of ethnicity could take their boards and head up to the very southern tip of sand, never to the main beach where they would get in the way of the more experienced surfers. They were welcome at the Seals Club until ten and the main hotel until eleven. Maroubra had its local families who were born and raised here. Everyone else was a guest, and guests behaved themselves or were promptly and unkindly put out.

I leaned against the window as the car rolled and dipped over hills, around the cliff edges. The rain began to patter on the windscreen and the surfers on the street corners didn't move. I could make out more in the water, bobbing on the waves like lumps of driftwood.

"Must've been hard," I said. "You and Doyle were partnered for three years."

Eden sneered and there was no humor in it.

"It's supposed to be hard to see anyone shot in the face, Frank."

Hades didn't know how the children came up with their new names. One morning they just started calling each other by them and naturally he followed. From the moment that Eric awakened, Hades felt distanced from the girl. He hadn't been close to her in those initial days but she and Eric engaged in a relationship that was utterly exclusive and strangely intimate. They spoke in a language of gestures and looks. Now and then Hades heard them whispering in the night when they were supposed to be sleeping in the secret room, and he could never make out what they said.

The decision to keep the children never really happened. In the beginning he'd put off the heavy, painful question of what was best for them—and for him—until he knew whether the boy would survive, and then he put it off again until he was sure the boy was going to keep on surviving. Before he knew it three weeks had passed and he was taking the children into account when he ordered his shopping. Whenever thoughts crept into his day about how he would raise them and where he would keep them and just how fucking ridiculous the entire idea of running his nighttime business alongside being their father was, Hades simply banished the thoughts and did something else. It was easy to do. The children were always there. Hanging about under his feet or cuddling into his chair with him or trying to tell him stories in their wandering, illogical, wide-eyed ways. A month flew by and a routine fell into place.

The children revealed themselves to be different almost from the very beginning. Eden was a quiet and mysterious child. She kept secrets that he could find no sense in keeping—like where she had been for hours at a time, even if she was only down at the sorting center helping to fold clothes or over at the gate watching the morning crew arrive. She sang quietly to herself. She did anything Eric asked of her, dropping whatever she was doing to follow him out into the mountains of trash. But she had agency of her own, despite her obedience to her brother. When Hades went to his shed she would be there trailing behind him, strangely frightened that she was unwelcome in his workshop. She would watch him for hours as he sketched and built and experimented with his sculptures.

One morning he found her alone there, copying one of his design sketches. He had snuck up behind her and watched with fascination as her surprisingly skilled hand took in the shape of the iron dragon, never faltering, never needing to be erased. When she had followed his design as far as it went, she began to add things, change things, stripping away the bulkiness and clumsiness of Hades' original plan, adding details he hadn't considered. When she had discovered him watching she burst into tears, figuring somehow that she was in trouble.

Rarely she let him put his arms around her. When he held her that day she confessed miserably that she had always wanted to help him build the trash animals. When he asked her why she hadn't told him before, she couldn't answer.

If the murder of her parents had made Eden a reserved and damaged child, it had awakened something wild in Eric. He was exactly the opposite of the girl. Eric wandered in the garbage from sun-up to sundown, playing imaginary games, talking aloud to himself, engaging in one-man wars with the workers. He made elaborate plans to harass the staff—spying and keeping surveillance records, organiz-

ing booby traps, playing them off against each other until fistfights erupted that he'd watch with glee. He collected treasures from the garbage and buried them in secret locations, tinker boxes of machinery parts, jewelry, notebooks and maps. He was outgoing and curious. He questioned everything. He would return to the house as the sun was setting, ragged-haired and feral-eyed, starving and short with his words. But when Hades played the radio in the kitchen in the morning Eric would play air guitar and sing aloud, displaying an impressive memory for lyrics.

At night Hades read to the children in the tiny living room, sunk into the couch with one on either side, a scotch resting in his lap. He couldn't think of another way to educate them. He read to them from Dickens and Wordsworth, James and Haggard. When Eric showed interest, he read them Patrick Suskind's Perfume *and the dark tales of Poe. He indulged Eden with Shakespeare, which Eric hated.*

Whenever Hades was confronted by a decision about the raising of the children—how to answer their questions about the world, explain away their fears, how to direct them towards making the right decisions in their simple black-and-white lives—he found himself working more through experiment and chance rather than personal experience. All he remembered of his own mother and father was the glow of the house fire that consumed them, being so young when they disappeared from his still-expanding world with their tenderness and unconditional love in tow. After them had been the street, for how long he didn't know, where he'd lived like an animal without a use for things like fairness and respect. The only way Hades had got off the street was through demonstrating his natural talent for brutality. A man had died to earn him his place in the care of some of Sydney's most evil men. No, there was nothing in Hades' past that he could use as a model for a healthy childhood. He'd learned about respect by beating it into people, and fairness was something he'd rarely witnessed—it was like the blur of a beautiful creature retreating from him into the dark. He was sure a couple of people had loved him over the years, but never in a parental way and never with the vulnerability of a child. He wasn't even sure he could spot love in someone else, let alone demonstrate it himself. Uncertainty itched at the man's insides. There seemed to be no rules and Hades didn't like that.

The first time the children killed they were eight and ten.

Eden and Eric had settled into a life at the dump that seemed to Hades to be uncomplicated and comfortable, the kind of life that children who had been broken needed to repair their hearts. He gave them free rein to explore and play and dream and run wild during the day. At night he schooled them, following Eden's interests into classic literature and European history and Eric's passion for science and war. Hades didn't risk sending them to school. Though he had commissioned the forged birth certificates and medical papers and other things he would need to prove their legitimacy, some part of him feared that one day someone would recognize them from the newspaper reports and television clips and missing posters that had followed the slaying of their parents. Some part of him feared that one day they would be gone from his life as abruptly as they had come. Though villains of every nature still arrived at his door seeking his help, the little ones gave him a reason to believe that not all of his life was dedicated to evil.

Hades had watched the news religiously in the beginning to try to understand how such a colossal fuckup could have occurred, though he could only do this when the children were in bed and he was sure they were asleep.

From what he could gather, their father had been a lanky, quiet guy who made some discovery about isolating a gene that encouraged skin cancer and the scientific community had gone nuts about it. The mother was some kind of well-recognized creative type, a jill-of-all-artistic-trades who every now and then wrote snappy feminist columns for the newspapers. She was a dark, glamorous woman who was pictured with paintbrushes holding up her shimmery black hair or clay dust drying on her long, slender fingers, a woman who was always laughing and talking and touching people's shoulders when she talked.

There was plenty of news footage of the huge house on the lake, the shattered windows and the white-clad forensics officers tiptoeing through the chaos taking photographs. There were pictures of a set of gates with flowers and teddies and angry scrawled messages of vengeance towards the killers. The news reports likened the Tenor children to the three Beaumont kids who'd disappeared from a beach near Adelaide in the '60s, and within days the assumption seemed to be that they were dead. Newspaper opinion pieces called for the kidnappers to burn in hell and other rather uncomfortable punishments. Much of the initial rage and hurt at the missing children made Hades stir in his bed with guilt. But not a single relative was mentioned in the media during the hunt for the Tenor family killers and interest in the case died, however slowly. He consoled himself by standing in the doorway to the children's bedroom and watching them sleep, oblivious to the angry ripple they had caused in the world.

Now and then the children romped and wrestled in the little room he had built at the back of the house that served as their bedroom, but it was minor stuff, nothing like the night he discovered their secret. Hades had ignored the sound of them jumping from bed to bed as he sat reading a newspaper at the kitchen table. When Eden started screaming Hades looked up from the printed words. Taking off his reading glasses, he stood and moved silently down the hall.

"Don't, Eric, don't! I don't like it! Don't, don't, don't!"

Hades opened the door. Eden was midair, flying from one bed to the other away from Eric. She landed on the pillow and saw him standing there. Her smile disappeared. There was instant silence in the room. Eric's hands slid under his backside and his eyes scrutinized Hades' face with the cold calculation of a predator.

"What's going on in here?"

"Nothing." Eric grinned. "Nothing. We're sorry. We were just having a bit of fun. We're sorry, aren't we, Eden?"

"Yes." She nodded.

Eric took a long breath and let it out quickly. Hades let his eyes travel cautiously to Eden. Her cheeks were red. Hades looked back at Eric.

"What are you hiding?"

"What? Nothing." Eric shook his head. "I'm not hiding anything."

"What have you got there?" Hades frowned, pointing at Eric's hands. The boy shifted awkwardly and brought his hands out from under his backside, waving them around innocently. Eden's eyes were wild.

Hades felt a twinge in his heart. There was anger there and yet there was hurt. The children knew what evil he hid under the layers of trash out there in the dump. Eric had been curious enough to work out the science of it, the way the acidic leachate, built up from years of rotting garbage—fed and synthesized and collected as it was by Hades' unique system of layers and channels—dissolved the bodies buried beneath it. The children knew that this had been meant for them. They knew that Hades was flawed. So there was no reason they should hide things from him. Hadn't he shown them they could trust him?

"I don't want you to hide things from me, Eric," Hades sighed. "I don't want either of you to hide things from me. I'm asking you to show me what you've got. If you've got something you shouldn't have, then I'll punish you. But if you keep lying to me you'll lose my trust. Show me what you've got, boy."

Eric considered this silently. He looked at Eden for confirmation. Hades bit his tongue. He didn't feel that there was anything to consider. It seemed for a moment as though Eric was weighing the loss of Hades' trust against the punishment, judging the worth of each.

Eventually the boy pulled an object from under him and set it in Hades' palm. Hades studied the object in his fingers. It seemed to be an animal tail.

"What is this?"

"It's a cat's tail. I was trying to touch Eden with it. That's why she was screaming."

"Where did you get it?"

"I'm sorry, Hades." Eric tried to compose his face into what he thought was remorse but all he achieved was a quizzical frown. "We're both sorry."

That word again. Sorry. It was a learned thing. They thought they could say it and make things better, but they had no conception of what it meant. Eric scratched his brow, shadowing his stony eyes.

"Where did you get this?"

"I found it."

"No, you didn't."

Eric knotted his fingers together, looking at Eden for support. She remained silent. There was an icy tension in the room.

"Eden and I found a duckling," Eric said resignedly. "It'd been attacked by one of the cats. It was dying. The duckling's parents were there, and they were making a noise like . . . like they were screaming. Eden was upset. There are just so many cats out there because of *all the meat in the garbage. They're all feral, and they're all un-wanted. I just . . ." He cleared his throat. "Eden was so upset, you know, so I just . . ."*

Hades waited. There was no more.

"Why did you take this?" he asked, weighing the tail in his hand.

Eric chewed his fingernails.

"It didn't suffer," Eden piped up.

"Shut up, Eden," Hades snapped. She jolted. Eric's eyes searched the carpet, as though the answers were hidden there.

"Is this the only time you've done this?" Hades asked the boy. Eric was still. Hades went to the bed and shoved him aside, reaching under the bed to where he knew Eric kept one of his treasure boxes. He pulled it out and tore off the lid. The children watched as he heaped the ball of cats' tails out onto the floor, watching them uncurl like furry worms of every conceivable color—black and burned orange and chestnut and white. There were eighteen in all.

Eden started to cry.

8

According to the missing persons report filed by her parents, eleven-year-old Courtney Turner had disappeared on the short walk home from a sleepover at her friend's house. Courtney had left the Oberon Street house at seven o'clock in the morning, crossed the Randwick cemetery on Malabar Road and gone missing somewhere between Elphinstone Road and her house on Jacaranda Place. Nobody saw a thing. I knew that area. It was quiet and leafy and narrow back there behind the cemetery—rolling hills and shadowy lanes and plenty of housing commission flats. Endeavour House was near there, full of navy and army boys.

At eight o'clock the morning she went missing, Courtney's parents had phoned her friend's house. At half past, they'd gone for a drive. At ten o'clock they'd arrived at the Maroubra police station and sat in the waiting room among the families of drug addicts and drunk teenagers for an hour. They were turned away.

It was too early to file a report, they were told. At midnight they'd sat down with an apologetic Constable Alan Marickson to make a full report. Courtney was long gone by this time and everybody knew it. Gone, baby, gone.

It had been two weeks since Courtney disappeared when Eden and I turned up on the doorstep of the Turner house. Until now, the case had been handled by the missing persons department. From my discussions with them that morning it seemed they'd tried to hand the case over to homicide after a week and had been knocked back due to lack of evidence. And the big bosses were reluctant to cause a stir in the press by hinting that a child killer might be lurking around its pretty beachside suburbs. Lately, it seemed like missing persons had been whining a lot about a steep caseload and no one had taken them seriously. The discovery of the Watsons Bay bodies seemed to justify their concern about an upsurge in their work.

Courtney's mother clearly recognized Eden from the news reports about the bodies in the boxes. Her knees went and I caught her before she hit the deck. I heard her husband calling from the kitchen.

Soon the screaming stopped and the numbness set in. The four of us sat around the glass-top table in the Turners' stylish dining room, burning in the silence. Courtney's mother, puffy-eyed, sat beside Eden, staring at her reflection in the microwave. The father chewed his knuckles.

I'd been in this situation a number of times and this was usually how it went. They howled and denied and threw things around. They sobbed and moaned and blamed each other. After a while the awkward presence of the cops was noted and everyone was invited to sit down. Then the parents closed up.

Eden was making notes quietly in her notepad. It looked like she was plotting a novel. I glanced around the kitchen, counting the purple tiles on the splashback above the sink.

Courtney's mother was a small, thin blond woman. Her husband, by contrast, was huge and red-haired, like a caricature Viking. Agony was thick in the air. There were framed photographs of the girl everywhere. On the kitchen counter sat a stack of posters with her face. I couldn't draw a correlation between the smiling preteen beauty in the "missing" posters and the sunken-eyed corpse I'd seen in the morgue only hours before.

I lost track of the conversation thinking about Courtney. Eden was cracking her knuckles. She made a few pages of notes from the barely whispered words of the mother.

"Who's Monica?" Eden asked softly. Eliza Turner bit her lips. She took a breath and sighed. The gold bracelet found in the box with Courtney's body was in the center of the table, still in its evidence bag.

"We have another daughter, two years older than Court," Eliza whispered, glancing at her husband. "Derek and I have been fighting ever since . . . ever since that night. We sent Monica to stay with Derek's mother. In Richmond. So she. You know. So she . . ."

"So she would be protected," Eden said.

"Monica and Court sometimes swap bracelets. They have a matching pair. I don't know why they do it," Eliza sniffed. "They've always done it."

I noted the mother's use of the present tense. It made me want to chew my fingernails. I looked around and took a closer look at the photographs I'd been avoiding and noticed that, yes, there were two daughters. They looked so alike that on first impression it seemed an extensive collection of school portraits and dance troupe action shots and grinning Christmas pictures of one girl.

Courtney and Monica—two peas in a pod. There were only a couple of them together and they seemed like twins.

"None of our other victims were found with jewelry," Eden said carefully. "We're missing wedding rings and earrings and piercings. Can you think why Courtney might still have had this with her when we found her?"

Eliza and Derek looked at each other. He shrugged.

"The girls were very protective of these bracelets. Court was almost paranoid. Maybe she . . . hid it from him. I don't know."

"Seems to suggest she knew what was going on. That she felt threatened," I said.

"Jesus." Derek rubbed his eyes.

"So, Derek, you're the girls' stepfather?" Eden asked.

"Yes."

"Where's their biological father?"

"He died. In 1998," Eliza chipped in. "Heart attack. Monica was four when Derek and I married. Courtney was two."

Eden continued writing.

"Ever had any problems with the two girls, Derek?" I asked.

"Why is that relevant?"

"I'm not suggesting anything. If I was trying to ruffle your feathers, you'd know about it. Everyone has problems with their step-kids. I'm just trying to get a picture." ——

"They were both pretty good about it," Derek sighed. "They were young enough that it didn't really matter. Courtney gave me some a few years ago about not being her father but . . . I guess that's pretty normal."

"Did you notice anyone suspicious hanging around your neighborhood or your house in the days before Courtney's disappearance?" I asked. "Did you have any strange phone calls?"

"No."

"My colleagues tell me you guys moved into the area just a few months ago," Eden said, looking at her notes. "The girls started at a new school. Anyone at the school you're having trouble with?"

"No, no one." Eliza sniffed. "Everyone's been lovely. All the neighbors . . ."

"We answered this sort of stuff with the missing persons people," Derek murmured.

"I know. We have to ask again, in case anything new comes to mind."

"Courtney's blood type was O negative," Eden said carefully. "Which is reasonably rare. If you had to make a list of people who knew that, who do you think you'd start with?"

"Jesus. I don't know."

"Try," Eden said. "As best you can. Take your time."

Eden passed her notepad to Eliza. Eliza took one look at it and rose from her seat, walking drunkenly into the kitchen.

"I'll make tea," she said. "We should have tea."

"That's rough," I said. We were in the car. The rain had cleared and the afternoon sun was blazing red between the billboards advertising new apartment buildings over fenced-off sandy wastelands. I'd offered to drive but Eden said she liked it. I could understand what she was talking about. Concentrating on the road. Avoiding hazards. Analyzing and predicting the actions of others. Anything but the thought of your child suffering. Anything but the thought of the years ahead without her.

"For the money or for the love. What do you reckon?" Eden asked eventually.

I thought about the question. How much was our killer making by offering a new life to patients staring down the barrel of oblivion? Was he doing it because he wanted to profit from the suffering of others? Or because there was a certain thrill in deciding who gets the chance to live and who slowly wastes away in the hospital waiting for the stroke or car accident that would bring a new kidney, a new heart, a new set of lungs?

"He gets a kick out of this," I concluded. "He has to. There are twenty bodies that we know of so far. You don't do something that many times for the money. You don't do something that many times because it's a chore."

"I wonder if they knew, the recipients," Eden mused. "I wonder what he told them. He could easily have spun some lie to make the whole deal more appealing. If you were dying and I told you I had a kidney that I was shipping in from some death-row inmate overseas, would you take it? I mean, it has to go somewhere."

"I don't know."

"You've been on the waiting list for six months. Ten months. Two years. You've been bedridden for two years."

"I'd have to think about it," I sighed. We passed a billboard advertising end-of-fiscal-year clearances in bold red letters. *Prices slashed!*

Neither of us spoke.

Jason stood in the field by the boarded-up house and looked at the mountains. A storm was creeping towards him from deep in the dusty West, and though he couldn't see it, its earth-stirring smell had reached him an hour before. He had gone out into the long grass to wait for it.

Storms always reminded Jason of his father, whose return from the office each day had been very much like the stomach-thumping power of Mother Nature. The bright heat of midday always made the little house on Greendale Road seem like a dark cave because his mother, a slave to the drowsiness the heat produced, would pull down the blinds and shut the doors and windows, turn out the lights and let the quiet soothe her into a doze. The temperature dropped, the silence came, and he and his slobbering, bumbling little brother Sam played in silence in those afternoon hours as the pressure slowly mounted. His mother woke each afternoon at four and busied herself with preparations for his father's arrival, spinning and spinning around the house in faster and ever-tightening circles, crackling with energy, brushing and scrubbing and polishing things. When his car rumbled into the driveway she would stand with the two boys at the end of the hall and listen to his footsteps getting louder. The adult Jason remembered these times with terror and glee as he stood looking at the black mountains, the white light snapping between their jagged tops and the dark ocean blue of the clouds above.

He stood in the field and remembered the perfect storm, one of the last storms before he and his father left the house on Greendale Road. It had come from another of Jason's experiments. Jason was just about finished with his games with the birds and their strange, wordless marriages in the wild. But he was still thinking about the bonds between creatures. He'd been inspired to find out more about the bond between mother and child when he discovered the deflated body of an infant brown dove at the bottom of a tree by the lake, its gnarled claws and hollowed eyes crawling with ants, its thin leather skin receding from the tiny skull. Jason looked up and spied the nest, and almost in the same instant heard the chirping and pipping of the other babies in their bowl of sticks and mud and feathers. He was amazed. What was different about *this* baby that it had been forced to suffer such a cruel fate? How did the mother, who he was sure could feel and share love, switch off her love for this offspring so completely? He walked home, carrying the tiny dried carcass in his hands, placed it carefully on a tissue atop his tiny wooden desk and began to read.

The night of the greatest storm had begun like any other. The darkness of the afternoon descending over the house, his mother's bare feet crossed at the end of the tightly made bed, the quiet tumble of wooden blocks on the polished floorboards as Sam played. Jason watched Sam for a long time—the clumsy grip of his pudgy fingers, the translucent string hanging from his dimpled chin. Jason knew there was something different about Sam. Something weak. His mother had told him that Sam had to be treated gentler than Jason's other little cousins because Sam wasn't as strong, that he hadn't grown as well, that something had gone wrong in Mummy's tummy when Sam was in there waiting to be born. Sam was different from the other babies. Jason watched Sam and wondered. Why didn't his mother push Sam out? Did she want to? Was something stopping her? Was pushing Sam out the *natural* thing to do?

As usual Jason's mother woke at four o'clock and began her polishing and scrubbing and spinning around, pushing open the windows, wiping the countertops, fussing with the couch cushions and muttering to herself. She fixed Jason's collar and combed his hair and wiped his cheeks like she always did, sighing with annoyance at the dirt on his palms and the leaves in his shirt. Then she looked around for Sam. Father had come home and she wasn't ready, and the two of them got to talking quickly and loudly and then to shouting. Jason watched, curious. His mother started crying and his father erupted, and soon enough the two of them were screaming and running around to all the rooms in the house, their voices loud as thunder. As they ran out into the yard calling Sam's name, Jason followed, his head cocked, trembling with excitement as his experiment unfolded.

They'd never find Sam.

9

It was my turn to pick Eden up the next morning. I hadn't slept. My night had been filled with steel toolboxes, with scalpels and needles. The junkie had yelled at me all night. *I just reached down and broke it. I just reached down and broke it.* The kind of desperation that would cause a man to break his own bones. I knew that as I slept. More than once I woke sweating and listened to a storm rolling overhead. It had been a while since a case had touched me like this.

I pulled up in front of Eden's apartment block. It was a nondescript redbrick place that might have been one of those ultra-trendy reclaimed and fitted-out factories. I could see through round windows on the wide street that all the top floors had lofts, and all the beams inside looked exposed. The old loading dock on the ground floor had been turned into a tiny café with only stools to sit on and everything written in chalk. Eden peered out at me briefly from a set of balcony doors on the third floor. I raised a hand in hello but she didn't answer. It was while I was searching the emptiness behind her that I noticed the painting on her wall. I lifted my eyes to the circular window above her and spied a couple more paintings and something covered in a paint-stained sheet. A grin spread over my face.

Finally, one of her secrets.

She opened the apartment door and jolted as she saw me standing there. She had a short black military-style jacket on over a black blouse, tailored jeans that hugged everything. She swept her long hair off her shoulders briskly.

"You didn't have to come up, Frank."

"Show me your studio." I smiled.

Eden froze, giving me one of those brief obligatory looks in the eye.

"I don't . . ."

"Come on, Eden. I can see it from the street. Share this secret with me and I promise you one in return."

"Frank." She lifted her shoulders as she breathed, let them drop. "Don't."

"I'm not backing down." I folded my arms. "I'll stand here all morning."

Something flitted across her face. Rage. Shame. I'd caught her naked fantasies laid bare and I wasn't letting it go. She covered her emotion with one of her crooked smiles and a roll of her eyes. I didn't care. If this was what it was going to take to know something, anything, about her, then I was willing to force her a little.

Despite the run-down exterior, the apartment was large and modern. Polished hardwood floors met vast white walls where she had hung a great number of paintings, giving each the appropriate light and space to allow it a world of its own. Some of the factory's original structures—strips of iron and bolts up the walls—had been left and painted over. A black leather lounge set hugged a huge plasma television set against one corner. Bloodred curtains hung against the balcony doors.

"Wow."

She sighed and tried to figure out what to do with her hands as she stood impatiently by the door. I hesitated before heading for the twisting iron stairwell to the loft floor. There was too much to see. The paintings on the walls were like little universes, cut off and independent from each other. All of them in dark thick oils and pigments, hollow faces obscured by dream. A burning farmhouse. A man standing on a seaward-facing cliff. A small girl playing with a black stuffed toy dog in a room with bloody walls.

"How could you not tell me about this?" I scoffed.

"You're not into art, are you? Art is a very personal thing."

I tentatively touched the base of a polished wooden statue, two naked warriors caught in battle. One was strangling the other, trying to drive a blade into his ribs. I climbed the stairs to the studio. Gold Spanish horses rearing, their necks twisting, teeth bared. One wall was black and covered in brush marks and smears where Eden scuffed her brushes clean as she worked. The effect was a colorful vortex swirling in on itself. I examined the paintings silently, feeling I wouldn't have enough time to appreciate them all. A stocky, thickly built man welding a piece of iron, live sparks hitting his shoulders and neck, spraying into the air. A thin black-haired teenage boy staring at a mirror, reaching out. Some of the paintings were of seemingly ordinary things but they each had a menacing quality to them, like a snapshot of a moment about to go horribly wrong. I wandered over to the sculpture I had seen from the window. It dwarfed me by at least half a meter on its steel frame. Eden stood by the stairs, folding and unfolding her arms. She strode forward, grabbing the speckled sheet and tearing it down from around the piece of work.

Again, two men. Smooth, impossibly black marble. One was pinned on his back, his legs and arms curled in defense, muscular feet and ankles anatomically perfect, grinding at the body of the other man. The warrior with the upper hand had the man on the ground by his throat, the other arm raised, a long sword hovering ominously in the air above the victim's face. I looked at the victim's chiselled cheekbones and howling lips. I bent and peered into his mouth, noting teeth shaped expertly from the marble.

"Where did you get this?"

"Italy. It comes in a series of large blocks." Eden's face seemed to flush a little with pride as she illustrated with her hands. "It weighed about half a ton originally. I had to get an engineer to tell me if the floor would hold it."

The warrior's lips were drawn back over his teeth in a snarl. Both men were naked. My fingers, with a will of their own, ran down the sculpted abdomen, wanting to know the ripple of the marble.

"What's it called?"

Eden paused, studying the sculpture. I waited.

"*Vengeance*," she admitted.

Without knowing why, I felt a little afraid in her presence at that moment. I got this strange feeling that every painting in the house, every sculpture, every bar of color and stroke of darkness were connected. They all meant something and Eden was nervous that I was wandering around in one giant temple dedicated to that thing. She was worried that I would *get it*. I didn't get it, not then. But I wanted to. There was fear and yet there was a longing. I wanted to understand her and I knew I'd have a fight on my hands.

"You're incredibly talented."

"Can we go now?"

"Yes, we can go now." I turned and headed down the stairs ahead of her. Color flashed in her cheeks. Tangible relief.

"I won't forget the secret I owe you," I told her as she closed and locked the front door.

"Yeah? Well, it better be a fucking big one," she said.

Dr. Claude Rassi's office was on the sixteenth floor of a building on Darlinghurst Road, a few blocks down from St. Vincent's Hospital. It was a short stroll up the road to the convict barracks, then on to Hyde Park, laden with bug-eyed ibises and the homeless, coffee vans and lawyers on lunch breaks. I liked the idea of coming to work here every day. It seemed like a hive of activity, crisscrossed by angry motorists and cops on horseback.

From the look of his office interior, it was clear that Dr. Rassi hadn't done much slicing and dicing in the past few years, aside from what he prepared for his dinner. There were four identical filing cabinets taking up one wall of the office and two other walls dominated by shelves of medical texts and journals. There were two stacks of papers on his large glass desk, one going in and one going out. Both were at least twenty centimeters high.

A floor-to-ceiling window gave the feeling of being able to walk right through the office and off the side of the building. I stood at the glass and looked down at the people on the street, enjoying the weightlessness.

"I haven't got long, I'm sorry," Rassi began, taking the huge wingback chair behind the desk. "I'm actually leaving the country this afternoon to consult at a seminar in India."

"We shouldn't take up much of your time," Eden said. "We just want a brief rundown of the whole system."

A stunning young woman clopped in on stilettos, all glossy hair and straining muscle, and set a mug of black coffee in front of the doctor. Eden ordered a white tea and I waved my refusal. The woman smirked at me with wet red lips and left. I felt like I'd just been slapped.

"My understanding from our phone conversation is that you've got a vigilante surgeon doing organ transplants?" Rassi said, raising his eyebrows. Put like that, even I found it hard to believe. I nodded anyway. He shook his head.

"From what I saw on the news so far, it's a fairly large-scale operation."

"We've recovered twenty bodies."

"The first thing I have to tell you is that you're probably going to find more," Rassi sighed, rubbing his eyes. "Something this . . . *primitive* would take a few goes to get perfect. Even with extensive training, adapting the transplant process into a one-man, garden-shed job is a significant medical feat. It's not something I would try, even with my background."

He waved at a series of framed certificates hanging on the wall. I looked them over and tried to make a suitably impressed face, something like a slow nod with my bottom lip poked out.

"So how can I begin to help you?" Rassi shrugged. "Organ donation rates are always a heartbreaker. There are around seventeen hundred people on the list at any one time and last year less than half the demand for organs was met. Things are getting better but they're never satisfactory. A lot of factors influence such an unmet need. People have misconceptions about organ donation. People think it's against their religion, that they're somehow cheating what their god intended. But that's just a load of codswallop. Few scriptures mention it simply because it just wasn't conceivable."

"What else stops people from donating?" Eden asked, her pen hovering over her notebook.

Rassi smirked bitterly, as though recalling a personal insult.

"There are plenty of myths and legends. A common story, which always happens to friends of friends, is the doctor failing to resuscitate car crash victims because their driver's license shows they're a donor. Harvesting without familial consent is another one. In optimum cases you can use a donor body to save up to ten lives and people are scared by the idea of a doctor sacrificing them to up his survival rates. The general impression that *someone else will do it* or *I'll never need one* dominates people's perception. There's also a sort of ickiness that people don't like about the concept of one person's organ living and thriving in the body of another. It's seen as unnatural. Particularly when you get into animal-to-human transplanting."

Eden nodded as she wrote. I was beginning to feel the ickiness that the doctor spoke about looking around at the artistic diagrams on the walls, the ancient oil paintings of primitive organ surgery. In one, a tall man stood astride the body of a young man held down by several nurses, a long saw in his fist. In another, a corpse lay beside the body of a living patient, grey in the face, while black-cloaked figures discussed their plan of attack.

"How long would a patient expect to be on the organ recipient waiting list?" I asked.

"Anywhere between six months and four years. Most of our organs are recovered from cerebral vascular accidents—blocked blood vessels in the brain, strokes and the like."

"What's the actual process of organ transplant?" Eden asked. "You mentioned that it would be difficult, near-impossible, as a one-man job."

The doctor drew a breath and puffed out his cheeks.

"It's possible but it would be difficult, yes. Heart transplants, for example, are a five-hour procedure with a team of six. A person doing this alone in a chop shop, as they're commonly called, could get by with a heart and lung machine, a monitoring system, a defibrillator and a hell of a lot of drugs. It would be risky. Things would be made easier for the survivable transplants by the fact that only one of the patients has to survive. Like I said, I think the man you're looking for probably tried and failed a number of times before he got the technique right."

"So it's possible we've got recipients as well as donors in our body pile," I told Eden. She looked downtrodden.

"What kind of drugs are we searching for here?"

"Anticoagulants, antiseptics, sedatives, anesthetics. Adrenaline. The real money shots would be the anti-rejection drugs. Various immunosuppressants. They're not easy to get, even on the black market. A patient's critical stage is just after the transplant operation, when the body fights the foreign organ because of the unfamiliar DNA. The anti-rejection drugs stop this process. Organ transplant recipients need to be on a program of anti-rejection medication for the rest of their lives."

"We'll need a list of the most common anti-rejection drugs and their manufacturers."

"I'll have my secretary print you one out."

"Can you speculate about the sort of prices a recipient would be looking at?"

Again, Rassi shrugged.

"He could charge whatever he liked. Transplant tourism is rampant in China, encouraged by their lax medical consent laws and Mao's barefoot doctor program. There are places in provincial China where you can get a kidney for ten grand Australian, but you run the risk of unskilled surgeons, money scams and disease. A well-organized, confident and discreet surgeon, operating out of your home country, with a record of success—forged or legitimate—could charge upwards of eighty grand."

"Jesus," I said.

"How do you put a price on life, Detective?" Rassi eyed me curiously. "If you had the money, would you play your hand on the waiting list?"

I didn't answer.

We spoke for an hour or so, going back over the process of transplantation, the necessary materials and skills. It seemed to me, as I sat quietly calculating in my leather armchair, that the killer had outlaid a million or more on his setup costs alone. The profits of the business were mild in comparison, but unlimited. Rassi provided documented cases of transplant tourism operating in China, the Philippines and Pakistan. There was no reason, he concluded, that our killer could not be going global with his business. There was no reason why he wasn't conducting a transplant operation every couple of weeks.

When we were ready to leave he pushed a bunch of papers towards us. I looked at a list of names followed by basic personal information.

"This is the organ transplant waiting list." He nodded at the paper. "I could have waited for a warrant but, like I said, I'm leaving this afternoon and I'm the only one with the authority to release it. I've taken the liberty of highlighting the names of forty-nine patients who have taken themselves off the list before receiving an organ transplant in the last year."

"Thanks." I raised my eyebrows.

"Before you get excited, Detective, you won't find that this is a comprehensive list of your suspect's buyers," Rassi told me. "When the need for a transplant is recognized the patient is added to the list automatically. It's not unusual for patients to remove themselves from it. Some do so for religious reasons, as I mentioned earlier. Others feel that they're too old, or too far gone, to be worthy of a transplant. Some seek alternative medicines to cure their disease. It's a personal choice."

"Okay," Eden said as we drove off, folding the list out on her knee. "So we'll start at the top?"

10

The cage was a cube with one-meter-square walls of iron bars, the kind that might be designed, Martina supposed, to house a large, vicious dog. The cage was placed a meter or so out from the wall of a large room with boarded-up windows. There were faded shapes of pictures that had once hung on the walls. She listened hard but heard no sounds. Not a voice, not a car. Nothing but the howling of unabated wind.

For the first two hours Martina had screamed for help. Now and then she burst into tears. The sounds she made, the moans and cries, were unfamiliar and frightening to her. For the next few hours she lay against the side of the cage and tried to think.

She went over and over the night out with George and Stephen, the laughing and the teasing, the Baileys shooters and the pulsating in her ears and chest as the music hummed through her. Oxford Street. Random police searches by the side of the road, homeless men aggravated, abusing the cops and struggling out of their gloved hands. Groups of young men brushing against her shoulders as she passed, poking their tongues between their fingers, simulating oral sex. George and Stephen rushing up the stairs of The Pleasure Chest, sword-fighting with meter-long dildos, grabbing her wrists and forcing her hands onto anal plugs, anal beads, penis rings. The shop owner scowling at them. Stephen reading a porno by the front windows, suggesting a threesome, pulling her hair. The cold night air as they spilled out into the street again. She had left the boys to meet Sascha at The Stonewall, where there were drag shows on the hour every hour and they let patrons dance on the stage. The strange thrill of being a straight girl here, the looks the girls gave her, her embarrassment. The last thing she remembered was the illuminated stairs leading onto the street from Arc Nightclub, the sound of her heels as she ascended them.

Martina chewed her lips. She had not drunk any of the water in the bowl in the corner of the cage, though she desperately wanted to. She closed her eyes so that they would not wander as they had earlier across the room to the open doorway, through the doorway and into the next room where she could see the edge of what she was almost certain was a table.

A steel table.

The kind one might find in an operating theatre.

The sound of footsteps broke her out of a sickly half-slumber. Martina rose up on her vomit-stained high heels, crouching absurdly against the door of the cage.

"Help!" she wailed. "Help me, please!"

A man stepped into view. Framed by the doorway, he seemed enormous, his broad shoulders taking in the width of the entrance, his head of cropped brown hair almost touching the top. He was wearing a white collared shirt that had been immaculately ironed.

"Stop yelling," he said.

Martina swallowed a sob. He stood watching, as though waiting for her to say something, to promise she wouldn't call for help. Deciding that no answer would come, the man walked towards her and crouched before the cage door. She watched through tear-blurred eyes as he took a pair of latex gloves from his pocket and pulled them onto his large smooth hands.

"There's not a soul for miles around," he murmured, his grey eyes downcast to his fingers. "No one's going to hear you."

"What do you want?" Martina cried. When he didn't answer she felt a wave of rage rise up inside her. "What is this, you fucking creep?"

The man reached into the cage and swiped at her. Martina cowered, but there seemed nowhere to hide from his long arm. She howled as he wrenched her wrist through the cage, her shoulder slamming into the bars as he pulled the limb as far out as it would go. He sat and wrapped his arm around hers. She was helpless to tug at his shoulders and neck.

"Please! Please!"

"I'm not going to hurt you, girl," he said. The alcohol was cold in the crook of her elbow. Martina gagged as the needle bit her skin, her legs trembling under her weight.

"You've got the wrong person," she sobbed. "My . . . my name is Martina Ducote. I'm a fucking bartender. I'm no one. I've . . . I've got nothing. I don't . . ."

"It doesn't matter who you are or what you used to do," the man smiled, capping the syringe full of her blood. "If your records are right, you're blood type AB negative, you don't smoke and you've never had a heart problem. That's all I need to know."

He released her arm and stood, fitting the syringe into his pocket. Martina screamed as he turned his back to leave.

"What are you going to do to me? What are you going to do?"

Hades liked long-term staff. He got plenty of interest from youths at the dump—the work required little experience and it paid well, the perfect job for university students in summer or for high school drop-outs wanting to build muscle in the sun. Now and then the local council tried to tempt him with benefits to hire mentally disabled people to work in the sorting center or to run the car-crusher, but Hades never took on any of them. He liked a worker he could get to know, someone he could draw in close enough so that they were aware, however vaguely, that they shouldn't fuck with him. He made sure he knew where they lived, had spoken to their girlfriends or wives over the phone, had their medical records and was familiar with their cars. Hades liked a worker who could be influenced by the other workers around him, who would become one of the fold, steady under the pressure never to go against Hades, no matter what you saw or heard or the strange feelings you got alone in the darkest corners of the dump. Hades paid Christmas bonuses, birthday bonuses, Easter bonuses. He noticed everything—a change of cigarette brand, a new haircut, a limp, a rise or fall in motivation. He took care of dental bills, over-looked criminal records. He was a boss who was only ever present as a round silhouette by the door of his little shack on the hill, surveying everything for a moment or two, trusting that things were being done right. It was an ancient game. Hades had been playing it, in one form or another, all his life.

Greg Abbott and Richard English were new and this made Hades nervous. The two men came as a package deal from a contractor and seemed to want to keep to themselves—something that further unsettled Hades. They were younger than the other staff, louder and smoked a lot.

Eric, who often stalked the workers like a restless monkey, seemed to take an instant dislike to them. In the second week Hades had been forced to reprimand English for shutting Eric out of the staff parking shed and clipping him over the ear. Nobody told his boy where he could and couldn't go. Nobody touched his son. Eric had no reason for wanting to hang around the parking shed, had never taken an interest in the place before. English had some kind of meat-head muscle car and was probably worried about it being scratched. Hades suspected Eric's behavior was an attempt to piss English off. Eric seemed to have a special talent for understanding what people didn't want him to do.

When Greg Abbott knocked on his door two months in, Hades was falling asleep watching the news, his bare feet on the cluttered coffee table. It was after working hours. He let the book he had been reading to Eden before she went to bed slide off his belly and onto the couch.

Hades put the hall lamp on and opened the door, throwing light on his guest and leaving his own face in shadow. Abbott was standing on the bottom step with a plastic shopping bag in his hand. He said nothing when Hades looked down at him.

"It's seven," Hades said. Abbott, freckled and sun-bronzed about his muscled torso, nodded and chewed his lip in apprehension.

"Have a chat?" the man asked.

"It's seven," Hades repeated.

"It's important. It's about Richard."

Hades let Abbott stand there squinting in the light a little longer, right to the edge of an uncomfortable silence. Then he turned and trudged back down the hall.

Abbott closed the door. He took the chair nearest to it at the kitchen table, watching carefully as Hades went to the television and muted it. The old man sat in his customary chair and shifted the newspapers aside, clearing a space on the table. Abbott rifled in the shopping bag.

Two weeks earlier, English had fallen ill suddenly, an asthma attack or something. It had happened in the shed while he was in his car. English had gunned the engine and slammed into the car in front of him, pushing it into the staff lockers, buckling them in two. The young man's windscreen shattered. Hades hadn't checked what had happened exactly. He didn't care and had been too irritated about the ruined lockers to bother. They were new. He never bought anything new. Hades had assumed he'd hear about English from Abbott at some point, probably seeking a loan to cover the damages to the car—or, if he was cheeky enough, workers' compensation. He hadn't expected it to come at night.

"What is this?" Hades asked, flicking his chin at the bag. "Late-night shopping?"

Abbott took a shimmering handful and spread it on the table. Hades looked at the thin fragments of glass. He could see the bends and warps of molding in some of the pieces. A sharp bulge and a tiny nib on a flat surface, like the nipple of a glass doll, a little blackened by heat.

"You know what this is?" Abbott asked.

"A broken lightbulb."

"Two broken lightbulbs," Abbott corrected. Hades felt the corner of his mouth tighten. Abbott was sitting there, across from him, motionless, expressionless, waiting for a reaction. Hades refused to give it. He *folded his arms and began planning in his mind the violence he would enact if this stupid game continued. Abbott was a university type, he could see this now. They were always questioning and being open-minded and "thinking critically," looking for ways to do things better. Letting people come to their own conclusions. Hades hated university types.*

"One of these lightbulbs, I reckon, was your average-sized house-hold bulb." Abbott sifted through the glass carefully with a finger, isolating what was obviously the rim of the larger bulb. "The other was a smaller one—tiny, in fact, the kind you might find in an oven. It was small enough to fit inside the larger one. When I found these fragments, the rims of the larger and the smaller bulbs were sealed off with masking tape."

"Fascinating."

Hades kept his eyes locked on Abbott's, not once taking in the glass.

"I found these glass fragments in Richard English's car," Abbott continued, dividing the pile of glass in half with gentle fingers. "There was more masking tape there too, which would have been used to attach the larger bulb with the small one inside to the panel behind the brake pedal. The first thing you do when you get in a car is put on the brake, right? English gets in, shuts the door, stamps on the brake and, crunch, there go the bulbs."

Hades said nothing. Abbott sat back and waited. On the highway beyond the horizon, an ambulance was wailing. It reminded Hades of the sad howling of dingoes. Hades felt his temple ticcing and wondered if Abbott could see it on his leathery skin.

"You know what Yperite is?"

Silence. Hades waited.

"Its common name is mustard gas," Abbott said, leaning back in his chair. "You take synthesized ethylene, which you can extract from

barbecue gas bottles, and you mix it with refined chlorine, which you find in pool-cleaning chemicals. Nasty stuff, mustard gas. You breathe it in deep enough it'll make Swiss cheese of your lungs. Kill you in minutes, if it's strong enough."

"You're saying someone mustard-gassed your friend English," Hades sighed, letting his head loll to the side.

"Got it in one." Abbott nodded. "Not only did they rig this ingenious method of delivery, they also snapped the inside handles off the doors of Richard's car and jammed the windows shut. When he put his foot on the brake he got a lungful of one of the most deadly vapors ever made. If not for his quick thinking in turning the car on and ramming it forward, which broke the windshield, he'd be dead. Right now, they don't know if he's ever going to talk again. Burned a hole in his esophagus the size of a fifty-cent piece."

"You got all this from glass fragments in a trash-filled car, some fucked-up doors and a busted window?" Hades shook his head slowly. "You oughta write penny mysteries."

"Come on," Abbott scoffed, "you know what your boy did, Hades."

Hades had been smiling and looking at the floor, appreciating his own dry humor. Now his eyes widened and flicked to the man across the table. Abbott shifted a little in his chair, his Adam's apple bobbing.

"My boy?"

"Eric has been hounding us like a fucking dog for weeks. He plays with chemicals he finds around the dump all the time. Hades, you know he—"

"It's Mister Archer to you, you little punk." Hades panted, just once, feeling the air come hot and heavy against his tongue, thick with rage. "You're saying my boy did this?"

"I—"

Abbott's words faltered under Hades' stare. The man stared at the table in front of him. In the bedroom, Hades could hear the children *whispering, moving in their beds. He let the sound carry his mind away as he sat like a lion watching Abbott.*

A generous silence lingered.

"You and English will receive your severance pay in the mail," Hades said quietly. *The sound of his voice made Abbott start. "I don't recommend you come back here for your things."*

Abbott stood and Hades watched him rise. The glass sparkled on the tabletop in two distinct piles like shavings of ice. The younger man let the plastic bag settle on the chair he'd been sitting on and turned awkwardly towards the door. When he reached the threshold he turned back, seemed to consider something. Hades waited, tense.

"You're going to have trouble with them," the man said, his hand on the door. "They're not right."

Hades stood. Abbott disappeared. When he was gone, Hades released a breath and let his body succumb to the trembling that the rage insisted upon. He walked stiffly to the secret room, extracted two bundles of cash and stuffed them into envelopes, muttering to himself all the while. That would shut them up. Not that they had anything to say. No one was going to believe a story like that. And all the evidence was still on his kitchen table. Hades forced himself to unlock his jaw.

When he returned to the kitchen, Hades stood at the sink and looked at the darkened doorway, thinking. He went to the oven, crouching and tugging open the door. The bulb was missing.

11

Afternoon, the quiet and constant call of brown doves in fig trees that lined Alloe Street in North Sydney. Eden and I sat in the car watching the town house for ten minutes. It seemed strangely turned in on itself, the face of the building hidden by overhanging bougainvillea vines and a large red awning, and the windows disappearing behind ornate iron bars.

We had visited two other houses that day. One belonged to a man who had removed himself from the transplant list because he thought he was too old to endure the surgery. His widow had answered the door, sheepish and confused about what we wanted, smelling of Vicks. The second, a woman in her thirties with pancreatic cancer, had made the arduous journey down her apartment stairs to greet us on the street. She was seeking alternative therapies and was wearing a sprig of some leafy plant in a tiny glass jar around her neck. Her eyes were bright beneath the colorful headscarf and her skin was white and soft like milk. When we left I felt surprisingly charmed and optimistic. Her smile had been infectious and knowing, like she had something on me. Like she'd known I was coming and had set a hilarious booby trap.

"What are you doing tonight?" Eden asked without looking at me. The question caught me off guard. It sounded like she was asking me out on a date. I knew she wasn't but that strange kind of ludicrous hope flickered.

"Dunno. What are you doing tonight?"

"It's State of Origin Two."

"I noticed," I said, nodding at the blue streamers on the car in front of us.

"Yeah, well, the guys at the station have this stupid roster for the football season where we have to watch a game at someone's house every two weeks. Captain James started it to develop some camaraderie and no one's got the balls to drop it."

"And you've got it this week?"

"Uh huh."

"Sucks to be you. Are you inviting me?"

"Well, I suppose it would look weird if you weren't there."

"You sure know how to make a guy feel special. I'll have to check my diary. I was going to clean my shower."

Without warning she got out of the car and walked towards the house. I jogged after her, laughing.

Knocking on the door of the Sampson place didn't raise anyone. I walked around the back of the house but found it locked tight, the venetian blinds closed. Eden stood on the doorstep, looking down at a pile of Woolworths catalogues that had wilted in the rain.

The two cars registered to Ronnie and Julie Sampson were parked in the street. The red sedan had a ticket stuck to its windshield and bird shit all over the hood. Ronnie had been on the transplant list for a year and a half and wasn't much nearer to the top than when he'd been diagnosed. The local football club had raised a few thousand dollars in coin tins to help out his wife and kid during his hospital stay, but aside from that the great suburban empire of the Sampsons had been slowly crumbling, the doors of their furniture shop closed and their kid missing days at school. Ronnie had removed himself from the list two weeks earlier and no one had heard from the family. I kicked some leaves around on the porch and thought for a while.

"Skipped out?" I asked Eden, trying to imagine what was so fascinating about Woolworths catalogues. I looked at her eyes. She wasn't seeing. She was thinking.

"They're dead," she concluded in a tone that made it sound like she was telling me the time. "We should get a bus down here."

I stood looking at her for a moment, trying to take this in. When I didn't move she pulled out her phone and dialed the forensic team herself.

"Wait up a minute here," I scoffed. "What makes you so sure?"

I had the gut-clenching feeling that I had missed something obvious. I looked about me and sniffed the air. It was silent and cold in the street and that smell, that warm, wet smell I and my colleagues in homicide spent so long tuning our noses to, wasn't here.

"Can't you feel it?" she asked.

"Feel what?"

"The *emptiness*."

"You're weird," I said. She shrugged and waved her hand dismissively at the door. I guessed she wasn't in the right shoes for it.

Eden pulled a pair of rubber gloves out of her pocket as I kicked my way in. She gave the barest wrinkle of her nose as the smell engulfed us. She flipped on the lights and walked right into the hall, through the living room and into the kitchen like she knew the place. I staggered forward, bewildered, and came to a stop behind her. Eden stood looking up at the hanging corpse of Ronnie Sampson, with blue-green face and swollen features. From where I stood, I could see the limp legs of a child and a spray of blood on the wall in the next room. The tight rooms had contained the smell. The air was thick with the feral animal scent of spilt piss. There was a gun on the table. A half-empty bowl of cereal, the milk lumpy and congealed.

Eden walked around the man's body and lifted the back of his soiled cotton shirt. The corpse swung gently on the end of a nylon towing strap wrapped around a ceiling fan. Eden ran her fingers over the curved scar where Mr. Sampson's poisoned kidney had been removed and replaced with a new one, a clumsily stitched gash that hugged the curve of his right love handle.

"You see a note?" she asked me. I looked around. There were bills tacked to the fridge that were never going to be paid. On the table by the cereal was an orange piece of cardboard with "Student of the Week" printed on it and a spattering of gold stars.

There was no note. I walked into the bedroom and looked at the bodies of the mother and child. Mrs. Sampson had hugged her arms around the girl like she knew it was coming.

"No note?"

"Nah."

Eden walked to the windows, a long row of louvres looking out into a weed-filled garden. Her silhouette barely moved as she breathed. She opened her palms and looked down at them as though considering them for the first time.

I watched, trying to forget everything, trying to blink the bodies of the mother and child from the backs of my eyelids and take in the image of my partner instead. There are some things you know you will never be able to unknow, to unsee. In this job you don't talk about them. You don't think about them. You collect them, carefully and deliberately, until your retirement from the force, at which time you have every right—no, you are *expected*—to completely lose your shit, to become one of those vile, unforgiving old men who no one can stand. I wondered idly if that was the sort of stuff that fuelled my weird reluctance to fill my life with people. The way I pushed women and their dreams of babies away. I didn't want to see their faces there. In my dreams. It was easier if it was just me and the strangers.

Sirens on the hill. Through the front windows I could see press vans arriving, having heard the call on their scanners.

Eden met me at the door to the child's bedroom, her eyes taking in the bodies, the fireworks of blood splatters on the bedspread, the walls, the toys. I shuddered, shaking myself from head to toe, and she pursed her lips and nodded like she agreed.

"So this party," I said, following her out to meet the vans. "Am I supposed to bring something?"

I ended up bringing two bags of Doritos and some salsa, having paced the snack aisle for a good fifteen minutes, analyzing the implications of various choices. I avoided anything with the words "light," "grain," "decadent" or "sensuous." Having narrowed it down to "classic," "crunch" and "salty," I grabbed the first thing that fell under my fingers.

Eden opened the door to her apartment and gave me one of those smiles that made her look like she was being pinched somewhere I couldn't see. There was music playing and a couple of the owls were perched on the back of the sofa, too noncommittal to sit down.

"You look beautiful," I told Eden. She gave me an awkward frown. It was true though. She'd let her hair out and it was falling dead straight over her shoulders and brow. Helplessly angry eyes. The only enthusiasm she'd expressed for the theme of the night was a Bulldogs pin on the neck of her tight black shirt. I felt instantly dumb in my Blues jersey. Neither of the owls were wearing team colors.

"Got a cooler going?" I asked, lifting up my six-pack. She led me to the massive stainless-steel refrigerator at the back of her kitchen. It was hardly a cooler but it seemed to do the job.

"Forensics confirmed the Sampson case as a murder-suicide," she said, taking my beers. "No note, but Ronnie Sampson has a number of public phone calls on his mobile leading up to the day he removed himself from the transplant list. And we've got a specialist saying the transplant wounds are consistent with the style of the bodies we found at Watsons Bay."

"The *style*?" I asked.

"Yeah, all surgeons have a style apparently. Some cut here, some cut there. Some are neat, some aren't. I don't know. Don't ask me, I'm not a quack."

"So someone approached Sampson and he agreed to take the deal, and then the news reports spooked him. Thought he'd check out and take the family with him before we came a'knocking."

"Looks like it."

"What a prick."

"We're holding a press conference tomorrow morning, so don't get pissed."

"How are you going to take advantage of me on the couch after everyone's gone if I'm not pissed?" I asked.

"No one's taking advantage of you," she sighed. "Will you just help me with these?"

I was filling thick black china bowls with snacks on the kitchen counter when Eric walked in from the balcony, carrying a glass of red wine. He was wearing a textured, collared shirt of black and deep blue weave. Eric smiled at me and grabbed a chip from one of my bowls.

"I like the jersey," he crunched. "You look like you're about to crack a stubby and smack your wife."

"I like the shirt." I nodded at his chest. "You look like you're about to get a pedicure and a brow wax."

"Enough," Eden snapped. "One of you answer the door. I've got my hands full here."

Eric gave me a sidelong glance and headed for the door. I noticed Eden had taken some of her paintings down. The ones she had left were figureless. Dark landscapes and unlit houses snuggled in rainforest nests. She'd replaced the violent sculpture of the fighting men with a floral vase. I noticed other little things had been tucked away—notebooks and stacks of papers, trinkets and photographs.

Darkness was falling beyond the balcony rail. A deep purple hue had taken over the horizon. I drank the first two beers quickly. Eden avoided the chatter around the television set by playing the overworked host, but it looked like she was just finding things to do. Some of the female detectives gathered in the kitchen and began whispering conspiratorially. She didn't join them.

There was an air of fakeness to the gestures and voices of the guests. Nervous looks and harsh laughter. People glanced discreetly at their watches. Eric sauntered around like a prison warden, smugly enjoying the company of his inmates.

"Let me do something," I told Eden, who had worked up a sweat over a tray of small pies. "You're not having any fun."

"I don't want to have fun."

"There's enough food out." I took her hands from around another bag of chips. "It'll go to waste."

She extracted her hands from mine and tucked a loose strand of black silk behind her ear. Across the room Eric was throwing peanuts in the air and catching them in his mouth.

"I don't . . . *like* this."

I waited for her to go on. She rubbed her thumb over her fingernails, one at a time, as though polishing them.

"When Doyle got it," she continued, "they came around here. All of them. Talking and questioning and helping and *supporting*. Bringing me frozen meals and comedy DVDs, for Christ's sake. I didn't want them here. I don't want anyone here. This is *my* place."

"Everyone's got their secrets," I chipped in.

She eyed me cautiously. I waited. She didn't bite.

"I'm not as social as Eric. Not to offend you but I was enjoying working by myself after Doyle's funeral. I knew someone would have to replace him eventually but for a while there I was relieved. I didn't have to play the game."

"What game are you playing with me, Eden?" I asked, watching her as I sipped my beer.

She didn't answer. I was about to lean in and lay it on her—tell her that I knew something was off about her and Eric, ask her about the names in her wallet and the picture I was sure I'd seen in a newspaper or on a wanted poster somewhere. But Eric knocked over a schooner glass and it crashed loudly on the glass coffee-table. By the time Eden had cleaned it up and come back to the kitchen she was obsessing over the food again.

"Have you eaten anything?" I asked.

"I ate before you got here."

I leaned against the counter and pulled the top off one of the pies. She stopped fussing for my benefit and sipped her wine, looking nervously at the guests.

"Here," I told her, "let me make you a Frank Bennett special."

I pulled the top off another steaming pie and jammed a slice of cheese into the innards. She watched me scroll a delicate circle of tomato sauce over the cheese before squashing the lid back on.

"That's not how you eat a pie," she said, taking it from me.

"Oh, so there are rules now?" I asked, making myself one.

"Stop that. You're jeopardizing the integrity of the pie by opening it." She smiled a little. "You put the sauce on top. Cheese in a pie is un-Australian."

"Who's wearing the Blues jersey here? You don't get to tell me what's un-Australian."

Eric came up behind Eden, let his hand brush her hip. A look passed between them. Eden took her phone from the counter and retreated to the balcony. I pretended to eavesdrop on the girls talking low in the corner. Eric sampled the snacks spread out before him, mixing dips and getting crumbs everywhere and humming gently to the music. I thought about moving out of the kitchen but a stupid stalemate for kitchen space ensued. Eric sipped his wine and watched me. I cracked another beer and raised it in a salute to him. We stood locked in tension, neither wanting to be the one who moved away from the other.

The pregame coverage began. One of the owls turned up the

sound. People took their places on Eden's long sofa. Empty bottles were starting to accumulate on the countertops and in the corners, and the voices of the guests were rising.

Eden appeared between the balcony doors. She was staring at the horizon as she spoke on the phone. I watched her slide inconspicuously between the guests, around the sofa towards the front door. She disappeared and the room seemed colder without her, as though a window had been left open.

I broke the stalemate and went to the balcony. Eden was talking on the street corner, just beyond the orange light of a lamp.

Eric's voice behind me made me jolt.

"Maybe I was wrong about you being a misogynist, Frank," he said. "You seem pretty attached to Eden."

I said nothing. Eden looked frail in the light, wiry like a spider as she paced by a stone ledge.

"Just remember, the last guy who tried to keep her as a pet got his head blown off."

"Doyle was overprotective?" I asked. "I find that surprising. You're overprotective enough for the entire department."

"Doyle was nosy. Possessive. She's your partner. Out of hours, she stops being your partner."

"I was hoping she would be my friend." I tried to keep a lid on the hatred in my voice but it seeped in like ink. "But you wouldn't know much about that, would you, Eric? You're surrounded by people who are afraid of you."

"You make her your friend and it's a conflict of interest. The job's about being impartial. If someone threatened her, you'd have to be able to watch her suffer for the protection of others."

"Maybe we should be partners." I smiled brightly. "I'd love to watch you suffer."

He sneered. I took a deep breath. I'd let myself be sucked in again, into the pettiness of a meaningless rivalry.

Eric glanced over at Eden.

"Come on, idiot." He cocked his head inside. "You're missing the game."

I ignored him and leaned on the balcony rail. Eden was stationary now, covering the phone mike with her hand as though even the distance between the party and the street, the distance between where she stood and the apartment, was not enough to reassure her that she would not be overheard. She ended the call and stared at the phone in her hand for a few seconds, her face passive and detached as it had been in the Sampson house, and then her eyes lifted and she looked at me, surprised and, if I wasn't mistaken, a little angry. Even from where I stood I could see the muscles in her shoulders flex with momentary defensiveness. I turned around and walked through the balcony doors and almost ran right into Eric. He had the same look on his face.

12

Jason arrived fifteen minutes early. He tried to do this every-where he went. When you came early you caught people off guard, got to wait in their living rooms while they dressed, got to look at the things they had forgotten to put away, read their mail, talk to their kids, play with their dog. He was disappointed to find Sandra Turbot waiting for him just inside the clouded glass of the front door. She had heard his car. She was a small woman, mid-forties, and bent as though she had been scurrying, antlike, under a great weight for many years. Her eyes peered from be-hind thick-rimmed black glasses that she probably thought were in keeping with fashion but reminded him of 1980s politicians in brown suits. She didn't smile when he stepped up onto the porch. They never smiled for him.

A man appeared. Jason felt electric terror surge through him, the impulse followed closely by rage that almost blinded him.

"Who the fuck is this?" he asked as Sandra opened the door.

"My husband, Reg. He knows. He's known the entire time." She shrugged a little, afraid. "It's his money."

Jason sighed and pushed past her into the hall. The husband was another bent and big-eyed creature, a bald top shaved close, leathery neck crisscrossed with wrinkles. Jason had known about the husband but hoped somehow to catch the woman alone. He enjoyed the quiet tension of a woman on her own, the sparkle of threat in the air, the knowledge shared between them of what he could do, what he was capable of. Had he wanted to hurt the Turbot woman he could easily have done so, but the husband made things messier. Jason resigned himself to communicating his disappointment through sighs and sternness rather than violence.

He went to the dining-room table and dumped his things. Sandra and Reg watched him. He began unpacking, clumping things into piles.

"We want to know more about the donor," Reg said.

Jason let out another sigh, long and loud like a hiss, closed his eyes and let his head hang. When he looked at Reg, the man winced slightly.

"Fuck you," Jason said. "Fuck. You. Reg. I don't know who told you you had any say in this, but it sure as hell wasn't me. Your wife and I have made an agreement. There's no turning back now. Shut your fat head and tell your bitch to sit over here."

Sandra seemed to waver between loyalties. Eventually she crept to the chair at Reg's nod and sat down.

"The donor," Jason sneered. "Jesus H. Christ. Who the fuck is the donor to you? What if the donor was your neighbor, Reg? The local priest? The mayor's wife? What the fuck are you going to do about it? You need this heart or Sandra is going to die."

"We were under the impression that the donor would be someone of . . . of suitably low, uh . . . worthiness of life."

Jason shook his head and took a stethoscope from the table. He fitted the earpieces.

"Take off your shirt."

Sandra looked up at him.

"Take it off."

She glanced at her husband, cringed, moved as though in pain as she slipped slowly out of the garment. Jason stood over her, sniggered at her plump brown breasts inching their way up into fat rolls at her armpits.

"You wanted a junkie." He nodded, glancing over his shoulder at Reg. "A prostitute or a violent sex offender, something like that. Sure, maybe I could have gone down that road, and you might have thought to yourself that you were complicit in the death of someone who deserved it or who was probably going to kill themselves anyway out of selfishness, stupidity, greed. What you don't understand, Reg my friend, is that it doesn't matter."

Jason made some notes on a clipboard on the table. He listened to Sandra's back, counted the irregular, half-certain heartbeats against his watch.

"Of course it matters," Reg bristled. "We're . . . we're not . . . *animals.*"

"That's exactly what you are," Jason sighed, pulling a syringe from a box and unwrapping it from its plastic sheath. "You're animals. You think putting on a tie and slipping on Italian leather shoes and waddling your fat arse to your Lexus every morning doesn't make you an animal? You think that because you listen to fucking Chopin you're not an animal?" He laughed. The Turbots listened, each as hard as a rock, watching the doctor's face. In the yard a dog was barking, pawing at the screen door. No one moved to placate it.

"Let me illustrate this for you," Jason said, waving the syringe to accentuate his words. "Couple of years back, on my way into work, I was on a train that hit a man. Terrible thing, you know, I mean here we are, fifty or more people in the carriage, all standing chest to chest and crotch to crotch and trying our best to ignore each other, and someone—some *junkie* probably, some person unworthy of life—decides to run out and leap in front of the train. We knew what had happened, even back in carriage eight. You just *know*, you know? There was a distinct locking of brakes, a pause and then a poetically wet *foomp!*"

Sandra and Reg both screwed up their faces. Jason nodded as he prepared to draw Sandra's blood.

"So when the announcement comes, as it inevitably must, everyone is mortified. There's sorrow in the carriage so tangible you could have bottled it and sold it to Hollywood. People are covering their mouths and saying, "Oh God," and crying—this one woman, she even prayed. Ha! The train sits there while emergency calls are made. No one can get off, of course, because bits of this guy are strewn everywhere and there are pictures to be taken and reports to be written. An hour passes. People start to talk to each other, you know, as strangers do. People begin to look at their watches, sigh, wriggle around. There's no air-conditioning. When another hour's passed, people start to get restless. They beat on the windows and try to talk to the cops, ask how long it's going to be. They swear and they make phone calls. They start bickering with each other, get stuck into their packed lunches, sweat, pick their teeth, talk about what's wrong with society. A fight breaks out. Women cry and babies scream."

Jason capped the blood and plasma vials and labelled them, slotting them into foam cartons. He wrote some dietary instructions for Sandra on a piece of paper and weighed it down with the fruit bowl in the center of the table.

"People care for as long as it's socially appropriate to care," he said finally. "They love and they hate and they share and they feel guilt as long as they need to, and not a second longer. You can switch that off whenever you want to. You can make it so that you don't feel anything at all. You're an animal. *Homo sapien*, that's you. Most evolved primate of the family *Hominidae*. Guilt is not in your nature, Reg. It's not in your DNA. Never was, never will be."

The doctor packed his things away and hefted the bag onto his shoulder. He glanced at his watch and noted the date.

"I'll see you in two days," he said, looking Sandra in the eye and ignoring her husband. "I'll expect you to be alone."

He got too old for them. That was Hades' reasoning for sending them to school when the boy was thirteen and the girl was eleven. He was too old to equip them for a world of friends he couldn't choose, jobs he wouldn't understand, for a world he couldn't protect them from. He told himself these things, though it still hurt when Eden pleaded with him to change his mind and Eric erupted with rage. They couldn't live and learn with him at the dump forever. They would need to live in the real world, even if it meant pretending to be something that they weren't.

He told himself that normal children needed schooling. A long-silenced voice at the back of his mind, however, whispered about the good it might do for their strange ways. Interaction with others their age might stop them, he hoped, from sneaking out and wandering alone at night in the countryside. It might stop them from talking about justice. It might stop them from hurting and hating and planning things.

For weeks the old man waited anxiously at the kitchen table every afternoon for the children to arrive home from school, and for weeks he silently agonized when Eden ignored him on her way into the house and Eric stormed in and slammed his backpack into the kitchen wall.

The teachers told him they were brilliant, calculated and at times almost militant in their work. Their books were immaculate. Their assignments far exceeded expectations. Eden obliterated records on the running track. Eric declined, when invited, to represent the school in boxing championships at a national level.

Hades was pleased.

However, despite these triumphs, they were also quick-tempered, withdrawn and resentful of the other children. Eden spent her lunches in the library. Eric spent his picking fights. Hades held out hope that things would change.

A year passed, then two more. Reports of their detachment continued but the mood of the children lifted. Eden kissed him on the head on her way in. Eric sat down and stole the newspaper from under his fingers. Eric remained a loner, but once Hades heard Eden talk about a girl named Rachael or Rebecca or something, about how the other girl had taught her how to make bracelets out of colored bands. Eric hated the girl, said she was a fat loser who didn't even have the balls to raise her hand in class. Hades assumed that was just jealousy. Eden had a friend, even if it was a shy, overweight girl who hung out in the library with her, and if he held out hope long enough Hades supposed Eric might get one too, some other overconfident, volatile little billy goat he could butt heads with.

The old man supposed that things weren't all that bad.

He didn't see the killing coming.

Hades thought it was a client at his door. The way the footsteps approached with the barely contained urgency of a killer needing help reminded him of the many desperate customers who had appeared in the doorway. A robbery goes wrong and a banker is shot. A small-time drug war erupts and a gang leader is executed. They would appear there, sometimes men, sometimes teens, blood-spattered and wide-eyed.

Help me, Hades. I've made a mistake. I've made a terrible mistake.

When the old man looked up from his newspaper and saw Eden standing there like that he choked on his scotch. She stepped over the threshold hesitantly and wiped her sweat-damp hair back from her temples with bloody hands. Her eyes were wild. Hades rose, in a daze, from his chair.

"Hades," she breathed. "We've made a mistake."

She was still wearing her school uniform. It wasn't unusual for the children to be home late from school without explanation. Hades assumed they'd decided to walk home in the rain. They would arrive, dripping wet and laughing, fighting and shoving each other into walls. The rain brought out the animal in them.

A wholly different animal was looking at him now.

"What's happened?"

"We . . ."

She was lost for words. Eden was never lost for words.

"Whose blood is that?"

She backed towards the doorway, her eyes pleading. Hades wrenched his jacket off the chair and ran after her.

Her rack-thin body disappeared into the dark, slippery like the body of a cat. It didn't matter. He knew where she was going. Hades ran blindly through the rain. The workshop lights glowed in the darkness. The world jolted as his old bones carried him, the square of golden light arriving too fast.

The scene might have looked staged to a novice in the art of killing. Eric stood by the worktable wearing one of Hades' plastic aprons, a long silver hacksaw in his hand. The body of a man lay on the table, missing his legs from the knees down. Blood ran in thin ink streams off the edge of the table and onto the floor, pooling in shapes of marble on the concrete.

There were many things wrong with this scene. The killer was a boy. Beside him a blood-soaked girl stalked guiltily to center stage.

"I told you not to get him," Eric growled at her.

"What have you done?" Hades ran a hand through his hair. He gazed at the body. "What have you done?"

The children were silent. Absurdly, Hades found himself checking the corpse's throat, hoping for a pulse.

"Hades," Eric sighed, gearing up his reasoning voice. "Look . . ."

"No," Hades snapped. "You. I want to hear it from you."

He pointed his stubby finger at Eden. The girl squirmed, unable to decide where she should rest her eyes. That morning she'd braided her long black hair. She gathered it up now, knitting her fingers through the messy weave.

"He's my teacher," she mumbled. "My science teacher. I decided we should take him, not Eric. I waited in the rain by the bus stop. I knew he would drive past. He offered to give me a lift. I led him back here. You wouldn't have had to know except . . . except we couldn't move him all in one piece, and the saw won't go through . . ."

"Great," Hades snarled. "That's great. I wouldn't have had to know. I wouldn't have had to know you'd murdered someone in my work-shop!"

The rage was making him tremble. He found that his throat was closed. Eric fingered the blade of the saw quietly, his expression blank as his nails wandered over the bloodied teeth. The boy glanced at Eden and she sighed and let her shoulders drop.

"I found him with Renee," she said, flicking her head at the corpse.

Hades tried to breathe slowly.

"Who?"

"Renee. My friend. Renee."

"She's not your friend," Eric said.

"Shut up!" Hades snapped. "What do you mean you found him with her? What were they doing?"

Silence fell. Eden licked her lips.

"They weren't . . ." Hades began.

"She told me all about it," Eden murmured. "She said they would do it all the time in the art room cupboard when everyone was at lunch. It's at the back of the hall and you can lock it from the inside. She didn't like it. She said she didn't know how it started but she wanted it to stop."

The words were tumbling out of Eden. Her hands gathered up the cloth of her skirt and squeezed it tight.

"She told me if I said it was happening to me too, then maybe we could do something about it together. She was afraid to do it alone."

Hades waited for the tremors in his body to stop but they didn't. He asked himself if he had ever expected this. He realized that he had, that the dread that he was feeling was a much-denied and long-anticipated thing. He had known this would happen. He had seen it in their eyes, heard it in their whispers.

"This man was a monster, Hades," Eric said. "He deserved to die. It's the right thing. It's justice."

The old man wiped at his eyes, looking over the corpse on the table. They had made an amateur mistake. The children hadn't anticipated the wetness of the blood and the strength of the bones, the way the saw would slide and refuse to cut. An adult body needed a long-tooth saw. The section cuts should try to take in cartilage, not attempt to sever mid-thigh.

"Get out. Both of you. Get out of here," the old man said.

"He was a beast." Eric frowned, confusion and rage mingling in his features. "He was a fiend, Hades. Don't you underst—"

"You don't know what you're doing," Hades panted, his jaw locked. "You're children. You don't get to decide who lives and who dies."

Eric dropped the saw. It clattered on the concrete. Eden was hugging herself, looking over her shoulder at the two as though she couldn't bear to face them. The boy wandered around the table, pausing in the doorway to the rain-soaked night.

"We were never children," he said before he left.

13

He didn't feed her. Martina lay as night fell, thinking about kidnappings, sex slaves and torture, and she decided that if the man was going to keep her for any length of time he would have fed her. A day came and went since she had seen him, she guessed. She sat with her back to the doorway, not wanting to look at the steel operating table, or let her thoughts turn into visions of blades and pulsing organs, pooling blood and her own screams.

Whatever he planned for her would come soon. It would come before she could starve to death. It would be hours, not days. If she wanted to live she would have to get out before he returned. She did want to live. She wanted to live like she never had before.

In the long silent hours and chilling darkness Martina had time to consider what her death might be like for the people she would leave behind. Luckily, she supposed, she was an orphan. There was a string of ex-boyfriends who would feel a stab of regret, a bunch of friends who would sob for her, but sitting there in the dark with nothing of her life to grasp onto, Martina Ducote realized that her exit from the world would be an insignificant ripple on the surface of a large ocean. There would be Facebook tributes and flowers at her apartment gates, speeches and crying and hugging at a church somewhere. But those things go. Those things fade. If anyone ever found out who did this to her she would live on only as a name in a list in a true crime book somewhere, if she was lucky. If not, it was the newspaper archives for her.

Insignificant. No one was coming.

Martina realized in the dim blue of growing morning that there was no one who she could rely on to search for her, to find her, to save her. If she was going to live, it would have to be through her own efforts.

The pain of hunger prevented her from sleeping or lying still and she crawled laps of the cage, trying to find a weak spot. The base was iron, welded to the bars, and the padlock on the cage door weighed a kilo. She pushed her legs through the bars and tried to move the cage along the ground but the awkwardness of the position made her strength useless.

She cried and then growled at herself, furious with how easily she accepted defeat. Wiping her face, she cleared spent sweat and tears from her cheeks.

"Okay, okay," she murmured, breathing deep. "There's a way. There's always a way."

The wall beside the cage looked like drywall. She wondered if she could kick through it with her heels, making a hole to the outside of the house that she could yell through or make a signal.

Martina scooted to the edge of the cage on her backside and fitted her legs through the bars, giving the wall a mighty *whump*. Not only did her heels pierce the drywall but the cage rocked slightly. She looked about her. How much did the whole cage weigh?

She shoved her feet against the wall, slowly this time, testing the tipping weight of the cage. Martina gripped the bars above her and shoved, feeling the base of the cage lift slightly under her backside.

"Come on," she snarled, her teeth clicking as she ground them together. "Come on. Please. Please."

The cage tipped. She threw herself backwards, landing hard on the cage door, her water bowl crunched painfully under her hip. She coughed and gasped, limbs trembling as she rolled onto all fours.

"Yes," Martina shuddered. "Yes, yes, yes."

She rose, her back bent, feet flat on the floor between the bars. The cage seemed to weigh a ton. She shuffled forward away from the wall, dragging the cage two half-steps, and then dropped it, robbed of breath and strength.

As she waddled towards the doorway with the entire weight of the cage braced against her curved spine, the first operating table came into view. She saw the instruments and bottled drugs lined up in the cabinet and stopped to be sick all over her hands.

It felt sinful to be enjoying an almond croissant, surrounded by so much sickness and death. Eden insisted I finish the breakfast treat in the hall outside Cameron Miller's hospital room. She scowled as I moaned and munched, soft almond paste slick between my teeth. I'd offered her one and she hadn't wanted it. Her loss.

She'd been strange, stranger than usual, since she'd climbed the stairs of her apartment block to return to the party the night before. I'd sat down to watch the rest of the game, pondering what had made her so desperately paranoid about a single phone call. The only people I'd ever known to walk off into the distance to take phone calls had been guys I knew who were compulsive cheaters. But from what I could see Eden was single and vehemently refusing to look.

At the press conference, we had announced our dead ends. We'd traced all the public telephone calls to Ronnie Sampson's phone in the days before his operation but couldn't get any CCTV on the phone boxes, and they were littered throughout the city. The toolboxes in the bay hadn't given us a positive ID of the killer—they'd been purchased in no discernible pattern, at different stores, all without video cameras or particularly observant counter staff.

We had identified Courtney Turner and four others but there were still sixteen bodies without names, so every family from Sydney to Madrid with a missing son or daughter who could fit their loved one into the place and time frame in any conceivable way was clogging the department phone lines wanting to line up and see them.

We'd tried to see if a leak in the national patient information database could give us a clue about where the killer was getting the Medicare records, addresses, birthdates and treatment histories of the victims and recipients, but every GP in the country had or could get access to the same information on the office computer, and searches into individual records weren't logged like they were with prisoners and wards of the state. We were running with leads on stolen drugs across Sydney hospitals, but nurses, orderlies and doctors could be sticky-fingered, and some hospitals were giving us trouble bringing in their numbers.

Eden and I had driven to the Prince of Wales Hospital in silence, the weight of our task pressing on us like an unbearable heat.

Cameron Miller's bed was closest to the window where he could enjoy a view of the hospital's decidedly heartless architecture, a courtyard of walls studded with identical windows where the sick and injured stared out. The quadriplegics could stare across the vast empty space at the cancer patients and wonder what it felt like to be in pain. The cancer patients could stare back, imagining numbness. I took my position at the window ledge and felt guiltier still about my almond croissant.

Mr. Miller was dying of pancreatic cancer and had been for some months. We'd received a call that morning saying he wanted to talk. He was still on the list for a transplant. I looked over his anemic and dishevelled body half-sunk in the bed and I wouldn't have put money on his chances of success.

"I've met your killer," he said as Eden sat down. She froze in the red plastic chair, her hands braced on the armrests, her lips parted as she tried to reassemble her thoughts.

"You have?"

I gave a surprised smirk and sunk into the other seat. Cameron's cheeks were so hollow I couldn't tell what expression he had on his face. With yellowed eyes he glanced at a packet of Pall Malls on the counter beside him. I picked them up and extracted one.

"I'll bet the nurses give you flack for this," I murmured as I lit the cigarette for him.

"Fuck "em," Cameron grunted.

Eden took out her notebook and sent a quick text on her phone. Cameron Miller took his time, smoking quietly, his stubble looking blue in the icy light of morning.

"I've been in Critical two months," he began. "Got moved up from General when they stopped with the experimental surgeries. I haven't taken a shit of my own accord in all that time. Cancer's spread to my stomach, you see, so they got to feed me through a tube. Before that it was flowers and live music and library-cart visits, all that crap they go on with down in General to keep your spirits up. The Wiggles. Fucking kiddie pop, every day, like they live here—bunch of skivvy-wearing faggots. Up here on the seventh floor, people are waiting to die. There's no food. There's no music. The best thing they got going around is the jolly trolley and I can't eat anything on it. They don't let the volunteers in because people are likely to snap at you on this floor. They don't like that. Stops the volunteers from coming in, they see a bit of fear and death."

Eden looked at my eyes. The sweetness of the almond croissant was going bad in my stomach and I felt, somehow, that she knew it.

"About a month before I got sent up here I got a phone call in my room," Cameron continued, licking his dry lips. "Thought it was probably my ex-wife. She calls now and then to tell me how bad she feels and how she's spending my money. Half the time I'm so juiced up on painkillers I can't work out how to hang up, so I just listen, you know, until the nurses come back. This time it wasn't my ex-wife. It was a man who wouldn't give me his name."

Eden scribbled a couple of quick notes. I stared at the veins in

Cameron's skinny wrist and tried to guess how old he was but found the task impossible. He could have been thirty, or seventy.

"Do you know the approximate date of this phone call?"

"I don't even know what month it is right now."

"That's okay." Eden nodded. "Go on."

"So this guy, he starts telling me things that get my old heart a'ticking. He tells me he can bypass the organ waiting list and do the pancreatic transplant himself. I think he's joking, so I laugh, which fucking hurts. He tells me he wants to meet with me and I tell him that's fine. I got no visitors, see, and I kind of wanted to hear the punch line. The next morning he turns up here and sits beside my bed, just the way you're sitting looking at me now."

"Jesus," I said. Eden's eyes concurred.

"He told me the deal," Cameron said. "Told me what it would take. Didn't pull any punches, this guy. Said he'd been doing it going on two years with a lot of success."

"Two years," I said. "No way, man. Someone would have refused it. Someone would have reported him."

"I said that myself." Cameron smiled a little and nodded at me. "I said, what if I refuse? Go to the cops? What then? I'm gonna die anyway, what have I got to lose? Then he showed me a picture of my little grandkid, my son's boy, playing in a sandpit somewhere, I don't even know where. The picture was taken on a mobile phone. He said it wasn't worth it. Asked me what I was going to tell them anyway. I didn't know his name or where he'd come from or how I could get in contact with him again. We didn't talk much more about the what-ifs, but I got the idea that people don't refuse him often and when they do nobody says anything. Pretty good at making problems disappear, this guy. Got all his bases covered. Likes things sterile, you know what I mean?"

"So just to be clear," Eden said carefully, "when he made the offer, the man told you he would recover the organs from unwilling donors?"

"He didn't put it so nice like that," Cameron said. "He told me someone would have to be murdered so I could survive and I would have to live with that forever."

The room seemed suddenly smaller. I had been listening to Cameron speak, thinking I was getting to know the guy. Now all that was shattered. I realized I didn't know this dying man in the bed before me. The way he spoke about the murder of others, in his slow drugged tone, was confusing and cruel.

I was holding my breath. Cameron stubbed out his cigarette on the face of a pink Hallmark card that was lying on the bedside table.

"So what did you say?" Eden asked.

"I said, how much?"

Eden exhaled quietly. She stared at her notes for a long time, perhaps waiting for me to speak. I had nothing. I was afraid that if I opened my mouth I would be sick.

"Yeah, yeah. I know what you're thinking right now, both of you," Cameron sighed. "And I'll tell you, it's not only the situation of our physical differences that disqualifies you from understanding. I'm being eaten alive from the inside, see, and you both look like you've been up all night drinking or fucking or talking. Generally enjoying your health. You could leave here and go to the beach, get some sun, breathe in the sea air. You could go out to dinner, have a steak, enjoy a fine glass of Merlot. You could quit your jobs, gather up every penny you have and go live in Rome. I'll never step outside this room again. This is it. They'll wheel me out of here when it's over, straight down the lift and into the morgue, and from there it's the ground. The cold, hard ground."

Eden and I glanced at each other.

"It's not only that, though," he continued. "I served in the Gulf, twice. I'm no stranger to taking life to save my own. You get one life. That's it. One. This guy was going to extend mine just when it seemed like it was up. I didn't ask for this. I didn't do anything to deserve it. If some junkie or some lowlife had to die so that I could live then, hell, what am I going to say?"

"The first body we recovered was an eleven-year-old girl," Eden said, not lifting her eyes from her lap. Cameron didn't speak. He was gazing out the window at the building across from ours like he hadn't heard what she'd said.

"Why didn't you go through with it?" I asked, when a heavy silence had passed. Cameron Miller's eyes slid to mine. He smiled and the flaccid skin around his mouth hardly responded.

"I didn't have the money," he said.

We used the administration office's fax machine to get a description out to all the major news networks and plied the security department for an hour on what we needed from their CCTV. We ended up with minimal slices of his face—a cheekbone here and the edge of a smile there—but he was wearing a cap and seemed to know where the cameras were.

Eden stood on the footpath outside the hospital for a long moment in silence, her skin white and flawless in the sunshine. People walked and jogged and hobbled and wheeled in and out of the hospital around us. A middle-aged woman and a small boy sat on a garden bench in front of the hospital's stone façade. The woman was crying. The boy was drawing shapes in the dirt with a stick.

"This guy does a lot of work to get this gig in order," I said. "A *lot*. He has to know his prospective client is the kind of person who will take the deal. Financially and emotionally. Even if they aren't, he has to know he can hook them in some way so that they won't reveal him. There's so much groundwork. So much preparation. It must all be fun and exhilarating or he just wouldn't bother."

"I don't think it's a question of effort and payoff, Frank. I think it's one of necessity. It's a lifestyle. He just feeds the desire to get to the beginning of the ritual."

"The ritual?"

"I'm only speculating," Eden's eyes darted towards me and then away, "but he's doing the same thing over and over again. It's planned, prepared, orderly. A contained experience between him and his client, him and his victim, in a makeshift operating theater. Imagine standing over the two of them with your scalpel in hand and slowly, carefully, taking life from one and giving it to another. Playing God. I can imagine it's a pretty amazing experience, however abhorrent it is to us. An experience worth waiting for and ultimately something he can't live without. Once it's over the countdown begins until he *needs* to do it again."

An ambulance whooped as it slid into the traffic circling the Royal Randwick Shopping Centre.

"Just speculating, huh?" I smirked.

"All doctors have some kind of God complex. Why would you be one otherwise? The hours, the stress, the years of training, the responsibility. Then you become a lifesaver. A hero. A demigod."

"But his desire is tied up with taking life."

"Yes, what a delicious duality for an unsound mind."

We entered the underground parking lot and slipped into the motor-pool car. Eden's cheeks were flushed like she'd run up a flight of stairs. A silence fanned out in the vehicle as she started the engine, that cold stillness that follows a line half-crossed. I felt ill at ease.

The old man disappeared for six days, telling the children not to follow him. Of course they knew exactly where he was. At sunrise Hades would slip into the dense forest that lined the east side of the dump, a playground of rotting logs, hollowed 200-year-old eucalypts, lantana as dense and unforgiving as razor wire. Eden and Eric had spent much of their childhood nights there, creeping, exploring, hooting and hollering and chasing, having snuck out of their beds the moment Hades began to snore. When Eric tried to follow Hades down to the forest on the second day, he was stopped by the dump workers, who had been warned that if they let him pass they'd pay with their jobs. He noticed other men, strangers, meeting Hades at the gate before sunrise. When he tried to enlist Eden's help in sneaking around the boundary of the neighboring farm, trying to find Hades in the forest that way, she declined. She was too hurt at Hades' silence. The old man hadn't spoken to her since the night they had killed the teacher. When she had implored him to forgive her, Hades left the house and wandered alone in the alleyways and streets created by the stacked bodies of cars, old household appliances, rotting bookcases and bedside tables.

On the seventh night, 168 hours since they had committed their first human killing, Hades looked into Eden's eyes. She stopped inside the hallway, her schoolbag slung over her shoulder, and watched him rise from his chair. Eric had been crashing and rumbling his way into the house with such relief to be home that he thumped right into Eden from behind.

"Leave your things here," the old man said, pointing at the ground. He walked towards them and the children sunk into the wall as he passed.

He didn't wait for them at the door. When Eric and Eden emerged from the house, Hades' squat figure was distant on the path that led through the dump towards the forest.

The children ran. Twenty meters or so behind the old man, they stopped. Eden's breath came in hot whimpering rushes. Her brother's face was set, the eyes locked on the skull of the man in front of him. The bush was swaying with an icy wind that lifted the hair off Eden's brow and burned her lips. She folded her arms against the chill and let her body brush Eric's as she walked, his arm eventually coming around her shoulders and pulling her close.

"He can't take us both at once," the boy said. "We see one other person down here, I want you to go. You understand? I'll take care of everything."

"I don't want to go," Eden whispered. "Eric, please, make it all better, please."

"Hurry up," Hades snapped over his shoulder. Eden fell silent. They entered the forest and followed the uneven trail behind Hades. They passed a pile of disturbed earth, a vast dump of soil that smelled of rain and decay. Ten minutes passed in silence. Above them, the black canopy writhed and swayed against sky lit a dull orange by the dump's sodium lamps.

Hades waited for the children at the edge of the path. They stopped three meters away from him. Hades thought that they looked afraid. He was glad. A cat moaned somewhere, gearing up for a fight, the sound causing Eden to jolt in the frame of her brother's arm. Hades let *them sweat under his glare for a minute or so. Eric held his glance while Eden shifted stones with the toe of her shoe.*

"This is where you'll be spending your days from now on," the old man said, gesturing behind him. The children looked, squinting into the dark. Hades walked up onto the porch of a house, the steps seeming to materialize beneath his feet from the night, as though he had willed them there. Eric let Eden go and wandered forward, taking in the roof of the tiny bungalow, the recycled corrugated iron and mismatched pillars that held up the porch—one oak, one painted pine, one ornate wrought iron. Hades unlocked the front door, a heavy mahogany thing he had been saving for some time, fitted with stained glass, like something from a confessional booth. This is what you've been doing your whole life, he thought as he entered. Collecting the waste of others. Gathering the unwanted to you. Building your life from it.

The newness of the things inside the house was stark against the used scraps and bits that made up its exterior. In the first room, two large L-shaped desks, the barcode stickers still on them, polished black and inlaid with glass. Huge lights hung over them, ambient bar-lamps. Two great bookcases lined the back wall, stacked with volumes. Eric went to the shelf nearest him and ran his fingertips over the spines. Some were leather-bound, inlaid with gold, as thick as bricks. Some were paperback textbooks, covered with clear contact paper. They were categorized by subject, date, relevance. On the upper shelves Vesalius's De Humani Corporis Fabrica, Philosophiae Naturalis Principia Mathematica *by Isaac Newton. On the lower shelves titles like* Hematology in the Technological Age, The Science of Ballistics, Autopsy: Finding Justice for the Dead.

Eden was standing in the middle of the room, her shoulders rising and falling gently as she panted. There was something like a heartbroken relief in her face. She let her eyes wander over the things arranged on the desks—the sleek silver laptops, one each, the stacks of note-books and paper, the jars of pens. Under the window a reading place—two couches facing one another, a wide coffee table.

"I've enrolled you both with Monash," Hades said quietly. "Distance education. I had to pull some hefty strings. Eden, you're going to focus on the physiological side of things. The body, the mechanics of it, the ins and outs of disposing of it. Autopsy. DNA. You're also going take a major in criminal law. Eric, you're going to concentrate on the practical side. Ballistics. Bloodwork. Physics. You're going to take sociology and psychology as electives. This isn't going to be like regular university. You get perfect scores or you start again. This isn't about getting an education. It's about arming you for what you will become."

The children stood like mannequins, limp-armed, silhouetted against the sickly orange light outside, barely above blackness.

"I've already withdrawn you from the high school. You start here tomorrow."

"We're not old enou—"

"You are now." Hades took a thin stack of papers from one of the shelves above the desk, slapped them on the glass. The gold foil on Eric's new passport glinted against the light as Hades' body passed. He moved through the short hall. One door led off to a tiny kitchen, another to a bathroom. Eden could smell the fresh paint on the walls as she followed. She watched the old man heft a hidden trapdoor up from the bathroom floor, the edge aligned with the foot of an old pink toilet she recognized from the sorting center. Hades disappeared into the hole. She followed, Eric holding the shoulder of her shirt as she placed her feet on the rungs.

A concrete room. Against the care and consideration that had been put into the upper rooms, this place was painfully empty. A steel table, bolted to the floor. Bare shelves. Hades stood looking at his blurred reflection in the table as Eric landed on his feet at the foot of the ladder with a thump. Eden thought about going to the old man. Putting her hand on his. She didn't. The three of them stood in silence.

"I won't give you the things you require for this room," Hades said. "When I come here to teach you, I'll bring my own tools. I'll give you the basics, the necessities of the craft, and nothing more. When you're capable, I won't come to this place again."

He watched them, and noticed in quiet horror how young they looked in the light from the overhead lamp. Perfect skin. Bright eyes. He thought quietly that Eden was at the age now that she should be getting a woman's shape about her. She wasn't. The muscles of her upper arms were curved and toned, like a teenage boy's, her chest flat and her feet and hands long. Animals, the two of them. Built for running. Built for killing. Caught in time like spiders suspended against a mighty wind. A twinge of pain rippled through his chest, an old warning instinct, and then was gone.

"Why are you doing this?" Eden asked.

"Because I love you," the old man said. It was the first time he had said it. "Don't you understand that? I've loved you from the first moment."

And that was how it was when all was said and done, no matter what he saw when he looked at them—the way Eden could look like an angel and feel like a child when she was in his arms, the way Eric could be such a stupid boy, strutting around and puffing his chest out, desperately imitating a man, full of hidden terrors and needs. No matter how much Hades fantasized about the two of them being children, moldable and teachable and eager for love, they had stopped being children the night they were given to him, the night their parents were killed. Hades had fallen in love with two chimeras, two monsters in disguise, incapable of feeling the way he felt, of loving the way he loved. The horror they had experienced had cut a hole in them *and they would be driven in vain to fill that hole for as long as they lived. Dogs with a taste for blood, enslaved to the need.*

But he loved them anyway. He loved them with a complete and undeniable love, the love of a father. The best he could do was try to turn their killer instincts on those other monsters out there in the night who deserved it, and in a twisted and sickening way maybe they would be making the world safer from the same darkness they each carried. The best Hades could do was try to help them understand how to do it right so that they fed their needs without causing unnecessary suffering, which he knew would only grow new needs, and without getting themselves caught, because he didn't know how he could ever deal with that.

The old man drew a breath and sighed, let his eyes finally leave those of the girl.

"Just because I love you doesn't mean I won't kill you both if you do wrong here," he said. "I planned to bury you that night, the night I found you. I had a place picked out. It's not something that's beyond me. I'm not sure you know right from wrong yet but I'm hoping it's something you can learn. This is a place for the evil ones and never for innocents. Never for innocents, you understand?"

He stabbed a stubby finger into the surface of the table. The steel shuddered, made a thundering sound. The children nodded, mouths closed. It was the confused and wide-eyed nodding of the hopelessly wicked.

The old man walked back to the hill shack alone.

Martina didn't know how long it took to get to the door. The time passed in furious heartbeats and now and then stopped completely when she was sure she heard tires on the gravel outside the house or the beep of a car horn on a distant highway. He was coming. He was coming. Martina would freeze and wind her arms through the bars of the cage and grip on, determined not to be removed from it. It was hard to breathe. Sometimes the terror was so strong that noises warped into voices, the creaks and groans of the old house becoming cackling laughs and scraping boots.

Come on, baby. Let's play.

Martina got to the door and shoved the cage through, centimeter by centimeter, only to howl with despair as it came to a stop, wedged at an angle between the doorframe and the corridor wall. She gripped the frame with her fingernails, pulled, twisted, rocked back and forth, knocking her elbows on the cage. Nothing.

Endgame.

Martina sunk to the bottom of the cage and cried breathlessly for a long time, surprised by her own noises and her inability to stop them, the moaning and the howling and the chattering of her own teeth.

Fuck you. Fuck you. Fuck you.

"No, no, no, no, no," she murmured, dragging herself up to her knees. "No. Not yet. Not yet."

She looked around her at the hall. There was nothing but bare space, a window boarded up at the end before a door to another room, piles of dust and animal hair crowding along the baseboards like grey waves. Near the door to the room she'd escaped from was a wooden broom leaning against the wall covered in spiderwebs. Martina stared at it. She couldn't move the cage farther down the hall because of the frame of the bedroom door. It was only a wooden frame. A wooden frame keeping her from staying alive. She pushed her shoulder into the bars of the cage, reached out as far as she could reach, knocked the broom over and dragged it towards her by its bristles. Trembling, bumping the broom against the walls and cage bars and her own limbs, she maneuvered it into the cage with her and grabbed hold of the handle outside the cage, bending it back with all her might. The broom handle began to crack. Slowly. Martina squeezed her eyes shut and pulled. The broom cracked more. She rocked and pushed, her hands sweating and sliding on the unpolished wood, now and then breaking into sobs.

The broom snapped, and just as it did she heard a car door shut outside somewhere. Martina gripped the bars around her, fought the urge to be sick again. Long, slow deep breaths shuddered over what felt like holes in her lungs, painful muscles straining in her chest against the urge to lose control. No footsteps followed. Had it really been a car door? Martina hugged herself for a moment, gripped her hair and pulled her legs into her chest. No sound. Her face was wet, tears and sweat and snot, hot like a mask. She swept back her hair and slid the broken broom handle into the cage, twisting it apart.

Yes, yes, yes.

Just as she planned. The shorter section of the handle, from the split to the rounded top, had broken away from the base with a nice sharp edge. Martina turned around, pushed her arms through the other side of the cage and slid the sharp edge experimentally into the tiny gap between the doorframe and the wall, knocking chips of paint onto the floor. She levered. The frame moved. Martina pushed the broom handle farther into the gap, bashing it with her palm until the bones in her hand ached, as she levered and levered until the outer section of the frame was slightly askew. She extracted the broom handle and wedged it into the gap again, higher this time.

"Please," she whispered. "Please, God, please."

The doorframe cracked, wobbled on its long thin nails as she rocked the broom handle back and forth. With clawing fingers she dropped the handle, ripping at the frame as it hung by the very tips of the nails holding it to the wall. Martina screamed as the frame tumbled to the ground. She pushed the cage forward and giggled hysterically.

One more doorframe and she could fit the cage into the room that held the steel-top tables. The key to the cage had to be in there somewhere. If it wasn't, there was no hope.

14

I was in a foul mood the morning after our meeting with Cameron Miller. The kind of mood where having to part your lips to mumble hello to someone is enough to piss you off. I felt stale all over standing at the coffee station trying to figure out how to use the machine. The mug I had grabbed was stained at the bottom and read "Only Gay in the Office!" I'd left the station at 1AM and had only driven home because the very sight of the place was making me furious. I'd showered, watched some early-morning religious programs that told me how my soul was going to burn in hell and returned worse off after a fevered half-snooze at the kitchen table.

Eric, wearing Armani and smelling of Boss, slapped my shoulder so hard and so suddenly that the sugar was launched off my spoon and across the counter like a spray of glass.

"*Good morning, Fran-kie,*" he sang. "*The world says hell-o!*"

"There are guns in this place, you realize," I said. "They're everywhere."

"Well, if you're going to go on a shooting spree, friend, let me know. I'd love the recognition of bringing you down."

He slapped me again and wandered away, whistling. I was about to spew some abuse over my shoulder when I noticed Captain James standing by the door to the smoker's balcony, admiring our apparent camaraderie with a moustachey smile. Things seemed on the up-and-up when I sat down at Doyle's desk and picked up the glossy funeral booklet sitting there. Eden and I, it seemed, had been invited to celebrate the life of Courtney Turner.

The booklet actually made me feel a little better. It reminded me of how trivial my lost sleep was in the scheme of things. I was flipping through the booklet when Eden walked in, wearing black jeans and a pair of heeled boots you could cripple someone with and a grey hoodie with the sleeves rolled up. She looked tired too. The braid down the back of her head was crooked.

"Another day in paradise." She yawned as she passed. I grunted in response and burned my tongue on my coffee.

The booklet was artfully presented. There were photos of Courtney opening Christmas presents and proud on her first day at school, her arms behind her back and her birdcage ribs thrust out. The back page was dedicated to a class photograph surrounded by messages written by her classmates.

We love you Court. We'll miss you. We know you're watching us up in heaven.

I sighed and kept flipping. There was a picture of Courtney and Monica sitting together on a bed with their arms around each other. Monica was slightly older and her hair slightly darker, but otherwise they were almost identical. Crooked smiles and big, glowing, excited eyes. Monica was holding a caramel teddy bear under her arm. The bear was wearing little green scrubs, a bouffant cap and a stethoscope. Doctor Bear.

I tipped my head and held the paper a little closer to my nose.

Monica's feet were bare and the bed was unmade, white sheets pulled back behind the girls.

"Eden," I said. She wandered over holding her booklet in one hand and a mug that read "World's Best Dad" in the other.

"Hmm?"

"Where do you reckon this picture was taken?" Eden sipped her coffee and turned to the page I was on. Her eyes were bloodshot. I kept a finger on the photograph.

My heart began to pound. Eric was leaning back in his desk chair with his hands behind his head, feigning sleep. Eden's coffee was frozen in the air, inches before her lips.

The sensation growing in my stomach was like that of something forgotten, some important thing that I knew needed to be recognized, now, before chaos erupted. My mother had called that kind of feeling *the hoo-has*—the unaccountable knowledge that things were not as they should be. I had *the hoo-has* bad.

I got up and wandered over to Eric's desk. He let one of his eyes open to a small slit and watched me pass like a snake eyeing a mouse.

"Has anyone seen Monica since Courtney went missing?" I asked. Eric frowned. I paced in front of his desk, waiting for him to answer. He let his hands drop down from his head and crossed his legs on the desk before him.

"You're actually talking to *me*, aren't you?"

"Cut the bullshit for just a minute," I said, thoughts snapping together in my brain. "Has anyone from the department seen her?"

Eric looked past me for a second, frowning.

"There's not really been any need to. She's at her grandmother's place all the way out in Richmond. I think someone's conducted a phone interview with her but she's a kid. She doesn't know anything."

"No one's *seen* her, though."

"No."

"This picture's not that old. It doesn't look more than a year old," I tapped the booklet. "Look at this picture and tell me those two girls aren't sitting on a hospital bed."

"This doesn't mean anything necessarily," Eden said. "She could have visited the hospital recently for anything."

She sat on the edge of my desk while I picked up the organ transplant waiting list. My hands were shaking. I flipped through, looking for Monica's name. There was only one Monica, and her surname was Russell, not Turner. I felt the air rush out of me. Eden smirked.

"Jeez," she said. "Heads would have rolled if we'd missed a thing like that."

"Yeh," I sighed. "It was a stupid idea."

I scratched at my chest. My shirt was suddenly irritating me. Eric went back to snoozing and Eden wandered away. I tried to get on with checking the list of leads, running through my emails, fixing up the reports I'd written. But I couldn't sit still. Quietly, I picked up the phone and got onto the front administration desk, got them to call through to Dr. Claude Rassi.

"Oh good, you're back," I said.

"Just got in this morning. How can I help?"

"This is going to sound pretty stupid," I told the doctor. "But I didn't know any other transplant specialist to call. I'm just curious. I've got a weird feeling. I want to look at the medical history of a girl named Monica Turner. Have you got access to that national database thingy?"

I heard Dr. Rassi's leather desk chair groan as he shifted in it. His breath crackled on the phone.

"You got all her details?" he asked.

"Somewhere." I shuffled my papers around.

I fed the doctor the details. He was silent for a long time.

"My national database thingy doesn't have a Monica Turner with that birth date in it. Which either means she's never been sick or she's changed her name, and she's not Turner in our records."

"Changed her name," I murmured, slowly rising out of my chair. "What, so you can have one name on your birth certificate and one name with Medicare?"

"No," Rassi said. "Your name with Medicare has to be the same name that's on your birth certificate. Your legal name. That's the law. But you can *assume* a name, start using it, signing things with it, going by it, long before you change it with the registry—there's nothing illegal about that. She could have been using Turner for a year without us knowing about it while her real name is something else."

"Could she have changed it unofficially at school?"

"As long as she had her parents' permission."

"She just started a new school . . ." I stuttered. "So all her new friends would know her under Turner . . ."

"Sorry?"

"So if her mother *didn't* change her name with Medicare, if she'd never been Turner on her medical records, they'd all still be under her former name."

"That's ri—"

I dropped the phone on the desk and ran into the kitchen. Eric watched me go. I skidded to a halt behind Eden as she stood looking into the fridge. She yelped when I grabbed her arm.

"What's Eliza Turner's maiden name?" I asked. She stared at me. "What is it?"

There was a cold, electric tension in the car on the drive back to the Turners' house. Though we were in an unmarked car, passers-by somehow seemed to sense our dark purpose. It felt like they were staring.

We had run out of the office, leaving Eric to get the warrant organized by the time we got to the Turner house. Eden's body was rigid. Her hands, illuminated on the steering wheel by the glow of early-morning street lamps, looked white-knuckled and hard. She had barely cut the engine before she was striding up the concrete path towards the porch. I passed her in a sprint as I let the full force of my anger surge through my leg, into my foot, through my boot and into the door.

The door exploded open as our backup pulled into the drive. From the porch, I saw Derek Turner jolt violently in his chair at the kitchen table and Eliza leap up with a scream.

"Police!" Eden snarled, shouldering in beside me and covering Eliza. "Get on the *fucking* floor!"

"Oh Jesus!" Derek howled, crawling numbly off his chair. "Oh *Jesus!*"

There were two plates of scrambled eggs and toast on the table. The smell of roasted coffee filled the room.

"Mr. Turner," I said. "I'm going to ask you once where Monica Russell is. You don't tell me, I'm going to put a bullet right in the back of your skull."

I already felt like I was burning up, my body thumping with exhilaration. There was sweat on the back of my hands. Eliza

Turner was screaming. She stopped abruptly when Eden pressed a boot down on her neck.

"Please. Please. I don't know what you're talking about."

Eden threw down the printout she had rolled up and stuck in her back pocket when we left the station. It was a copy of the waiting list. On page four, three from the bottom of the list, was Monica Russell.

Female. Age thirteen. Chronic glomerulosclerosis. Two kidneys required.

Monica had become very sick. Her family was visited by a tall handsome man with a big leather bag one dark night while the two girls were supposed to be sleeping. Not long after the family had moved houses. Monica had become sicker and sicker as the months passed but she'd still attended a new school with a new name. They'd pretended everything was fine, all according to plan. One night Monica was taken by the man with the bag to a house somewhere and given a needle to make her go to sleep. Monica lay on a steel-top table next to her sister, Courtney, who had smiled wearily and held her hand as the other girl was put to sleep too.

The rage in me was so heavy and so hot that I felt out of control, frightened by what I might do. I could see Courtney against the back of my eyelids. I crouched over Derek and slid my fingers into his hair, wrenching his head up as I knelt on his spine.

"You organized the murder of a fucking *child*."

"Derek," Eliza sobbed. "Don't say anything."

"We didn't have a choice. Monica was going to be on the list for years. There was no time."

"You had Courtney killed to save Monica." Eden was shaking her head. "Why? Why? They were both yours."

Derek started crying. I shoved his face into the floor.

"*Why?*"

"Derek, don't."

"Because I wasn't going to have that *bitch* live over Monica," Derek said, tears dropping off the edge of his jaw. "Courtney was so fucking spoiled. Monica didn't deserve what she got. One of them was going to die anyway. One of them was going to die. We didn't do anything wrong. We didn't kill anyone else's kid. We just switched them, that's all. We just switched them. They belong to us and we can do what we goddamn want with them."

The backup officers filled the room. One of them took Derek from me. Eliza struggled in Eden's arms as she was cuffed. Eden stood and covered her mouth as the patrol officer took over, her eyes wandering across Eliza's body like she didn't know what the woman was.

"Detective Bennett," one of the officers said, putting a hand on my shoulder. "We found the girl."

I stepped outside with Eden and paused by the back door of the house. There was an old green-and-yellow swing set by the fence, its legs submerged in unmown grass. We were both huffing, pacing, wiping our faces in the cold morning air. I couldn't get my heartbeat down.

In the car on the way to the house I'd hoped that I was wrong, that somehow there was another Monica Russell out there suffering, dying, that the Turners' daughter really was at Derek's mother's place. But Derek's eyes as they lifted to mine in that moment when the door had slammed open confirmed I was right. I followed Eden to the aluminum shed at the back of the yard and slid open the glass door.

The sun on the heavy curtains was weak. There was a female patrol officer sitting beside Monica's bed, holding the girl's hands.

I let my eyes wander over the machines that surrounded her—the heart monitor and the respirator and the stand holding the intravenous. Monica looked small and frail. Her hair had thinned down to a limp curtain of chestnut brown that hung about her bony shoulders. An oxygen tube was taped under her nose.

"What's wrong?" she asked me, her eyes wild and black. "What's happening?"

"It's okay, baby," I said, a sour taste dancing on my tongue. "You're, uh, you're going to be out of here in just a minute."

"Where's Courtney?" the girl asked, looking at Eden and the woman beside her for guidance. "Are you going to take me to where Courtney is?"

15

I caught some sleep at my desk while Derek and Eliza Turner were processed. It had been an awful rush at the Turner residence to get the parents into the paddy wagon, secure whatever physical evidence we could from the scene and remove Monica. The worst thing that could have happened would have been for the press to turn up while we were there, to discover what Derek and Eliza had done, to leak this to the world before we could use it to our advantage.

Within the hour, the Turner house was shut up, the phone disconnected, the curtains drawn. Neighbors, who had gawked from their windows, quickly lost interest. When I woke around midday there were no journos on the front steps of the station. If we were lucky, we might have pulled it off without the country knowing what had occurred.

As I slept, Eden took her rage out on the treadmill in the station gym. I found her in the hall outside the glass doors to the cardio section, towelling down her neck and breathing through her mouth.

"You feel better?" I asked.

"No," she replied.

I didn't either. We were both angry. I had spent many restless hours thinking about Courtney, about her parents, about what it must have felt like to have a child ripped from your life. I felt sick now thinking about how they could have set up the killing of Courtney in Monica's place. Had they allowed the killer to abduct her right off the street, as he seemed so skilled in doing, or had they taken her and Monica to the door of his chop shop? *Come on, girls, we're going for a little ride.* Had he even taken them anywhere? Had he conducted the operation right there in the garden shed? I wanted to hurt Derek Turner. I wanted to twist his bones. All the tears, all the heartache, now seemed like a personal insult to Eden and me. Maybe the Turners had been hurting. Maybe they had genuinely felt something about the situation. I understood favoritism happened in families—particularly with stepparents. Hell, I wasn't that naive. But to murder one child for another? How much trouble could Courtney have been?

I followed Eden to the ladies' changing rooms and stood outside while she showered and slipped back into her clothes. She came out and walked right past me, pulling her long inky hair up into a ponytail. We didn't speak as we entered the interview observation room. Derek Turner was sitting at the table with his wrists cuffed, his wide hands clutched around a half-empty paper cup.

"Someone gave him coffee?" Eden asked.

There was silence from the men and women who stood around the observation room, watching the man through the mirror. No one admitted to giving Derek Turner a coffee. It might not have seemed like a big thing to anyone else, but I felt, as I was sure Eden did, that the coffee cup should have been rammed down the man's throat.

I followed Eden through the side door into the interview room. We sat down. Derek looked at us, expecting something, but I didn't speak and neither did Eden. It was hard to know what to say. Eden was looking at her hands, straightening her fingers to examine the nails.

"I haven't asked for a lawyer," Derek offered.

"Were you there?" Eden asked without lifting her eyes. Derek seemed to tremble. He drained the rest of his cup of coffee and let out a great long sigh.

"Were you there when he put her to sleep?"

"No," Derek said, his voice already straining. "No, I wasn't there."

"Weak stomach?"

Derek shivered and rubbed at his nose. His breath was steadily increasing, seeming to catch in his throat as he talked.

"One of our children was going to die, okay? You understand that? We'd already come to terms with the fact that she was going to die. She had a rare blood type and aside from that she was way down the donor list. A man came to us and told us he could fix it. He said it would take him some time but he could find us another kid to take her place. We didn't . . . we didn't like the idea of killing someone else's kid. Courtney was giving us so much trouble at the time. She was such a fucking bitch. She was just . . . she could be unbearable."

There was silence on our side of the table. Derek wiped at a tear and sighed again.

"Courtney had never liked me, ever since she was little. She was just like her idiot father. She was always wild. When Monica started getting sick, she started abusing teachers and skipping classes and throwing tantrums at school. The head teacher asked us to get her assessed, you know, for being mentally ill or something. I knew she wasn't mentally ill, she was just a fucking brat. She was . . . I don't expect you to understand."

"Good," Eden said. There was a long moment of silence. Derek seemed to be off in his own world, staring at the coffee residue staining the bottom of his cup.

"It was his plan, all of it," Derek trembled. "He told us to get the girls out of their school, move away, change their names but don't do it with the registry so that they wouldn't find her on the list. Wait—so people would forget us. We weren't a very social family anyway. We waited as long as we could. Monica was really sick. He called and I told him we couldn't wait any longer."

"So months of planning went into this," Eden said.

"Yeah."

"*Months*," I said.

"Yeah," he murmured, scratching his neck. "Look, we didn't kill anyone else's kid. I don't know why you can't see that. He told us he could find us someone and we'd never have to know who it was. But we didn't want that. We didn't want to hurt anyone."

"*Je*-sus." I laughed madly, covering my face with my hands. I felt like I was watching a terrible joke unfold. Like some serious hilarity was being attempted and was failing dismally before my eyes. Maybe I was tired. Hacking laughs erupted out of me. I ran my fingers up through my hair, scratching at my scalp.

I guess Derek was confused by the whole situation. He'd probably seen interrogations on television where the cops talk a lot, insinuating things, threatening things, leaning over the accused and pointing their fingers in his face. Eden and I sat still in our chairs and looked at the ground. I didn't know about her, but I almost didn't want Derek to confess. I didn't want to hear what he'd done or what he felt. I just wanted to jump across the space between us and punch his teeth in.

"So, um . . ." he said, trying to spur some reaction. "So this is where we start talking about some kind of deal, isn't it?"

Eden's face snapped towards Derek.

"A *deal?*"

"Yeah, you know, like a deal for my, um . . . for my confession and all that?"

"Oh no, no, no. Honey, no." Eden laughed. "No, Mr. Turner, you're going to prison for a long time, there's no question about that. A *long* time. It doesn't really matter what the sentence ends up being. In a year, you know, maybe two, someone's going to come into your cell in the middle of the night and put a sharpened toothbrush handle through your neck. That's what *happens* to people who kill children, Mr. Turner. They don't cut deals."

"But I can help you." Derek shuddered, tears falling unchecked down his wide cheeks. "I can help you find him. I know what he looks like."

"Yeah? So do we. He's a handsome prick."

"He'll call me. He said he would call, on the first of every month after the operation for six months, you know, to check on Monica. I can make him come to me. I can help you trap him. You have to cut a deal with me. You have to."

Eden stood up from her chair so fast it skidded out from

under her legs and hit the wall behind us. I remained sitting while she tugged Derek Turner forward by the collar of his sweat-stained shirt until his nose was inches from her own.

"What you have to do, Mr. Turner, is pray. You better pray to God you have the chance to help us and that I give you something, anything, in return, because from here on in you're going to have to beg for everything you ever get. You're going to have to beg for . . . Every. Last. Breath."

16

It was the third coffee of the night for Santi, and the last he would ever have. He stood at the Bean-Man espresso machine in the middle of the 7-Eleven and watched the brown foam rise in his paper cup, dreaming of being at home in his bed. It was always at this time, the third coffee and the eighth hour of darkness, that he would begin to think of home. The clean slide of his bare legs into the cold sheets. The tick of his wall clock. Three hours to go. The night shift was a long one but there were fewer people to watch, to cater for, to fear. The man by the magazine stand was the only person to come into the store in the last hour and he seemed satisfied with an impersonal nod from under his plain baseball cap. Santi took his place behind the counter, ran a hand through his dark hair to bring feeling back into his scalp and settled down for another hour of reading John Connolly's *Every Dead Thing*.

The woman came into the store and stood in the middle of the entrance between the grocery stand and the counter. For a moment Santi was so engrossed in the book that he didn't lift his eyes to her. When he did, the book under his fingers tipped and slammed itself shut. He looked at the sheen of sweat on her bronze skin, the black stain of rope marks on her wrists. She was wearing a torn black dress that barely covered the curve of her backside and a set of heels that Naomi Campbell would have had trouble walking in and that were caked in thick clots of mud. Santi lifted his eyes to hers and recognized the cold animal terror there, the kind he had seen in the eyes of his co-workers during holdups.

"Help me," she said softly. Santi felt his mouth drop open. "What . . ."

The last sound to leave Santi's lips was a muffled *chugh* as the bullet met his skull. Martina jolted at the sound, turned and looked at the eyes of the man who had put her in the cage. He was standing in front of a rack of magazines, one of them rolled up in his fist, the other hand letting the gun lower from where it had dispatched the counter clerk. The man shook his head at her, his jaw set with rage.

"How the hell did you get out?"

With two long, angry strides he seemed to have crossed half the store. His hand encircled her bicep with room to spare. Martina remembered his touch. She felt her lip curl as her hand reached out, taking in the shape of whatever it was that was nearest to her with a crushing grip.

Later, when the security tapes were analyzed, twelve officers would watch as a grainy image of Martina Ducote took the pickle jar from the grocery stand and swung it up and over like a hammer into the killer's head. The sound of the impact could be heard outside, where a woman was filling the tank of her Mitsubishi. She would say later that she thought it was a second gunshot.

"Get *away* from me!"

Martina's voice would sound like a cat screech on the tape. The killer took the blow heavily, his head snapping back, body limp as blackness momentarily closed over his eyes. Martina stood paralyzed in the entrance of the store as the man who had abducted her recovered, got to his feet, stumbled through the automatic doors. The woman who had been filling her Mitsubishi watched in confusion as the killer took off in a blue Ford with no plates. In the artificial light of the store Martina Ducote sunk to her knees on the pocked linoleum and began to cry.

I caught a glimpse of myself in the rearview mirror as I pulled up at the hospital, my face lit only by the pale blue of predawn. I didn't recognize the haggard, sleep-mussed man who looked back at me. I was surprised, therefore, to find Eden in the hall dressed immaculately, hair pinned up so that it was off her neck, a cup of coffee in her hand. It made me wonder if she had been up already when we received the call about the woman named Martina Ducote. I glanced at my watch. It was 4AM.

"This is it." Eden grinned uncharacteristically. "This is our Big One."

All cases have a "Big One." It's the colossal mistake, the underestimation or oversight that killers make to break the case. Most homicide cases have one. Ted Bundy was pulled over for failing to stop at a routine traffic check and a search of his car revealed a ski mask, a crowbar, handcuffs, garbage bags, a coil of rope and an ice pick. Critical oversight. Jeffrey Dahmer's last victim punched him in the face, escaped and led police back to his apartment, where they found a human head in the freezer and photos of the mangled victims on the walls. Devastating underestimation. From the telephone conversation I'd had that morning, Martina Ducote had got herself out of a dog cage, walked six kilometers through bushland and turned up at a 7-Eleven on the side of the Pacific Highway. Better yet, she'd run into the killer and conked him on the head with a jar of pickles. Colossal mistake. I'd driven to the hospital with sugarplum fairies dancing in my head. We probably had the killer's blood on the jar, his face on the 7-Eleven CCTV, a description of his car. The killer might have touched something in the store, which meant we could lift his prints. The store clerk, some poor Indian student who took an extra shift on his night off, had copped a bullet in the head. Unless it was hollow point, Santi Verma's bullet would lead us to a gun. This was most certainly our Big One. I was anxious to see Martina Ducote so I could hug and kiss her for saving us so much work.

Somehow I hadn't expected the woman to be in such bad shape. A person who could break herself out of a cage, scramble through the bush to safety and fight off her abductor with nothing more than a glass jar seemed, in my mind, someone who was impervious to injury. But Martina was roughed up bad. She was sitting on the edge of a hospital bed while a doctor treated blisters on her feet that were so large and gruesome they looked like acid burns. Her arms, face and neck displayed the telltale nicks and scratches of the bush. Her short black hair was sticking out at odd angles from behind her ears, and the little black dress she was wearing had given up on the left-hand side, revealing the edge of her round breast. She was deeply engaged in one of the two basic emotions victims of crime display: anger.

When Eden and I walked in, she looked up at us with a chilling, silent fury that could have shattered the windows. I could see it wasn't personal, however. The doctor copped it too.

"Miss Ducote," Eden said, "I'm Eden Archer. This is my partner Frank Bennett."

Martina reached out and shook my hand. I noticed the rope marks on her wrist.

She saw my grimace. "They're not as bad as they look."

"I don't think we have to tell you you've done an incredible job." I smiled. "From what I've heard you really kicked ass."

She sighed. "Yeah, well, unless he's collapsed from delayed cerebral hemorrhaging, he's halfway to Perth by now."

"Doesn't matter. You've provided us with some crucial evidence. There'll be nowhere to hide, not when we know who he is."

Martina nodded and licked the split in her bottom lip. The remains of smeared makeup under her eyes made her look even more exhausted than I'm sure she was. I noticed the heels she had been wearing on the bedside table, already evidence-bagged. The straps had worn red grooves of raw flesh into her ankles.

"He talked about my blood type and he said I had a working heart," Martina said, watching the doctor wrap her feet in bandages. "I saw a news story the night before I was taken about a . . . about a man who was stealing people's organs. In the room where I found the keys to my cage there were two operating tables."

No one spoke. The doctor had stopped what he was doing and was crouching, looking up at the woman on the bed. Martina gazed at me, and for a moment I felt like the only other person in the room.

"He wanted my heart, didn't he?"

I nodded. Martina opened her hands and stared down at her

palms where the skin had been torn from tripping and breaking her fall on something rough. Three of her manicured nails had survived the ordeal.

"I think I can take you there," she said.

Eden stirred beside me and I felt my heart twist in my chest. "Where?"

"Back there," Martina said, tucking her hair behind her ear. "Back to the place where he kept me."

They were very different learners, the two of them. For Eric, it was all about locking himself in the house in the forest, back bent and head down, frowning under the light, hours and hours spent in the same rigid chair. He needed to memorize, summarize, make lists, color code and organize things on calendars. The shack was always dark, silent, immaculately clean, the windows closed against the wind that threaded and wound through the trees.

Eden was his opposite. In the winter months she liked to sit in the sunshine that filtered through a bottlebrush tree at the bottom of the hill, her hair pulled up into a bun with a ribbon, her mouth and nose submerged in a grey wool scarf as she flipped through the pages of the monstrously large book on her lap. Hades would watch her through the front screen door, see her lift her head and stare off into the distance as she linked concepts and came to conclusions, her lips gently murmuring words.

They needed no encouragement, the two of them. They fell into a routine of studying, writing, planning, reading, from the light of morning to the shadows of dusk. When he tested them, Eric sat in the kitchen chair, upright, unblinking, like a hound waiting for dinner. Eden liked to do things while she recited her answers, stirring a pot on the stove, filling in a crossword puzzle, braiding pieces of her long hair. Now and then when he was wrong Eric would erupt into violence. Eden was never wrong. When he gave her the scores she would shrug and go back to her work.

In their second year Eden came to the shack and presented him with a paper he had not asked for, placing it on top of the novel he had been reading. She went to the fridge while he looked at it, adjusting his glasses on the bridge of his uneven nose.

"And this is?"

"It's a correction," she said, sitting down across from him with a glass of milk. "For the textbook. They're wrong. I thought they should know about it."

Hades looked at the paper, lifted the first page and frowned.

"Protection of intestinal epithelial cells from clostridium difficile toxin-induced damage by ecto-5-nucleotidase and adenodine receptor signalling?" he asked, lifting his eyes.

"You betcha."

"What do you want me to do with this? It can't go anywhere under your name. You're supposed to be seventeen."

"I thought maybe you could hand it in anonymously." She licked the milk from her lips. "You know? Like a letter to the editor?"

The old man nodded thoughtfully and watched her go into the sitting room, flopping onto the couch with her half-empty glass. He put the paper aside and didn't think about it for days. When he posted it to the contact who had allowed him to enroll the children in the course, a gambling addict he had occasionally enslaved over the years, the man offered Hades twenty thousand dollars in order to publish it under his name.

After some consideration, he decided to tell Eden about the offer. Unlike Eric, he knew she would deal with the news humbly. She was always embarrassed when he praised her and he enjoyed it. He went to the front door and opened it, stopping on the first step when he saw Eden sitting at the bottom of the hill on her favorite tree stump, her back to him.

There was a boy sharing the stump with her, the space barely big enough for two backsides and the careful distance a girl of fifteen required from the opposite sex. Hades felt his jaw tighten. Making his way down the hill, he recognized the long curly hair that ended at the nape of a thick bronze neck, the wide shoulders of the Savage boy. Elijah Savage had been working for Hades for thirteen years as a dump-truck driver. His son had the same wide, calloused bricklaying hands and seemed to enjoy the same cheap cigarettes. Hades felt a mixture of blinding rage and fatherly joy. The Savage boy was a good boy, wholesome and forgiving like his father, with the kind of gentle good humor that characterized well-raised men. Hades stood behind the youths and listened. The boy's cigarette leaked smoke over his shoulder.

"A biochemical catalyst?" the boy was saying. "Is that, like, some kind of explosion?"

Hades was surprised to hear Eden laugh.

"You're going to be the catalyst for a murder investigation in a minute, Savage, you keep slacking off," Hades said.

The boy leaped off the stump and backed away from Hades a step or two, his dirty boot rolling on a stone by the side of the road.

"Whoa, yes. I gotcha, Mr. Archer." The boy saluted.

"Uh huh." Hades watched him go, taking the seat he had occupied. The Savage boy let his eyes drift to Eden for half a second before he turned and jogged back to the gathering of men near the sorting center. Eden closed the book on her lap and drew her legs up into the lotus position, one of them hanging over the old man's lap. They looked at each other and she broke into a rare grin that filled his heart with light before her eyes flicked away.

"You don't even have to say it," Hades sighed. "I'm, like, totally lame. Right?"

17

Displacement. Wandering. Jason felt as though the world had somehow been tipped and not righted correctly so that he was walking on slanted tiles, trying to keep his balance between leaning walls. It wasn't just the blow to the head. He couldn't return to the apartment. It had been risky to even contemplate as the news reports kept increasing and his blurry, half-formed picture kept appearing on the screens around him. And the house at the foot of the mountains was a loss now. There was no center to his world, no axis on which to pivot. Where were the mice? What would happen to them? He imagined them, pawing the glass, padding at surfaces they could not see.

The light above him in the public toilet was flickering, coughing to life an electric purple that made his eyes in the mirror look black. Outside, a train rumbled into the station, didn't stop, went squealing away again like an angry child. His hand trembled as it held the tweezers. Glass in the sink, spotted with his blood. He turned his head and felt the wound, winced as the instrument scraped against bone. He still felt pain. That was good. The naturalness of it made his limbs warm, made the crooked purple world seem a little righter. He washed his hands and raked his fingers over the hole, trying to feel any glass that might remain. He hadn't even thought about the woman yet, the one who had escaped him. He was afraid of the fury, of what it would make him do.

Jason had pulled two stitches into the gash in his head when the man entered the bathroom. He was not in a position to look, holding one end of the thread through his skin between his teeth, the needle above him and to the left, almost out of sight. He heard shuffling footsteps and felt the air leak in from outside. A lanky, halting figure appeared in the mirror beside his own, long hair and a leather jacket, huge gaps between narrow nubs of grey teeth. Jason had seen him outside on the bench, waiting, making a young woman sitting there uncomfortable with his close, loud talking. Some mentally ill homeless nobody creeping around the earth being a problem to everyone he encountered. Shadow person. Man of smoke.

"What you doing?" the man asked. His voice was high-pitched, cronelike, the voice of an elderly woman. "You hurt yourself?"

Jason let the air escape his lungs slowly, gently, between his teeth. The wound was bleeding again. He had only just managed to stem it before the homeless man entered. The air smelled of urine, nearer and more immediate than it had been before. Jason slid the stitch from the wound and stood there half-sewn, his hands gripping the sink to stop the shake.

Before he could open his mouth, the man spoke again.

"Can't get a bus. Nope. Not at all." He shook his head. "Bus strikes all over. Reminds me of the Whitlam days. The bad old days. I've called my mum. Maybe she could get you to a doctor on the way home, if you want. I could ask her. She's nice. She'll probably do it."

"You called your mum, did you?" Jason's voice shuddered from between his lips. The rage was pressing at the back of his eyes like fingers trying to worm their way out of his tear ducts. He looked at the man. He had to be forty. "You live with your mum?"

"Off and on. Can't stand her cooking. Can't cook for shit, my mum. Heh. Heh. Can find better stuff on the streets, yes sir. Don't have to clean my room up none neither. Don't have a room, do I?"

The man's head bobbed slightly, eyes hungry for approval. For friendship. Jason gripped the handle of his bag tightly, heard the leather groan, the buckle pop open.

"I know you," he said.

"Really? We've met before?"

"Oh yes." Jason licked his bottom lip, felt the stitches in his head pull tight. "You've been wandering around the edges of my life from the moment I was born. You, the un-right, the slightly off, the occasional rarity. Sick one. Damaged one. Runt who should have been pushed from the litter and starved but was not because of the stupid rules we make, because of the laws we write, because of the continuous unreasoning idiocy of it all piling one on top of the other until all we're doing is walking around in one huge, disgusting hallucination. You, the over-hugged, over-soothed, over-supported. You're a walking problem. You're this." He pointed to the hole in his head. "You're a wound that no one's got time to close."

"Hey." The man half-frowned, uncertain. "That's a mean thing to say."

"Parrot, that's what you are." Jason stepped towards the man, into the cloud of his urine smell. "Parroting the words you overhear. The Whitlam days. The bad old days. You got any fucking idea what you're talking about? You can't even manage to get from point A to point B. You can't even manage to shake off your own dick."

Jason was trembling from head to foot. His lips stopped moving but the words still came. Parasite. Leech. Burden. Sucker of teats. Bag of skin. Useless, useless creature. Just another example of the world's lack of instinct, of the will to simply close his mouth and nose and remove him as methodically and as effectively as the amputation of a rotting limb. The world was so full of these unnatural creatures wandering, bumping into each other, fumbling in the dark. Inside them were organs, blood, bones, plasma to feed the strong, nutrients that should have been returned to the earth from whence they came to fuel trees, grass, plants. The circle interrupted, bent out of shape. User of good air.

The man was sucking it in now under Jason's hands on the floor of the bathroom.

Drawing it into his mouth as he drew it into the wide, gaping slash in his throat.

Jason felt blood on his face as he worked. It was not all his own.

"You," he grunted, slicing and slicing, hacking away wet flesh. "You. Are. Unworthy."

18

Martina Ducote had wandered into the Grose Vale 7-Eleven at the base of the pristine Blue Mountains, off Bowen Mountain Road, a main arterial to the nearest signs of civilization. The killer had driven her, unconscious, a good two hours west from the city. Eden drove us up the sloped driveway of the gas station and parked beside two patrol cars. I could see four Grose Vale police officers leaning against the hoods, smoking.

Martina had been quiet for most of the journey, staring out the windows at the bushland rolling by, rubbing the bandages on her wrists. She had fixed her hair, and now it hung dead straight in a neat bob that framed her face. She was exotically beautiful despite the bruises and scrapes that lined her jaw. Big eyes and lips, a wondering look about her all the time, like she was trying to decide whether to up and leave her entire existence, shut the door on who she was and disappear. One foot in life, one foot out. She hadn't even let the hospital keep her overnight, nor had she let us put an officer in her place. She seemed determined to get on with things. All of that could have been the rigid determination of a very strong woman or it could have simply been shock—a refusal to acknowledge the horror and instability that would, very soon, push its way into her consciousness and drop her like a stone.

In a way it was more helpful if she did go home, though we'd never have asked her to do it. If the killer ever went after her again we had her apartment covered by patrol units 24/7.

When I picked her up that morning she was dressed in a white top and jeans, and there were no friends or family to accompany her. I didn't ask why.

We got out and did the characteristic chest-puffing and belt-adjusting with the Grose Vale cops, talking about the chill of the morning in the shadow of the Bowen Mountain. Martina stood by uncomfortably, watching as forensics officers wandered in and out of the crime scene in the store. The cops seemed to recognize her from the newspaper photographs. One of them whispered something to another about her looking better in the clothes she was in now than she did in the famous party dress that had been all over the news. I felt sickened by the sleaziness of it, even though I agreed.

"Okay." The lead cop clapped his hands loudly. "Let's get moving, huh?"

Martina led the way awkwardly and uncertainly, pausing by the wall of bushland at the side of the road, trying to find a way in. I held back some brush and let her through. We fell into a rough line, the Grose Vale cops at the rear, Eden in the middle, Martina and I up front. Eventually Eden got sick of the progress and went ahead, jogging and sliding sideways down the embankment like a mountaineer. Martina watched her disappear, one of the few times she lifted her head to look beyond her own feet. She must have tucked her hair behind her ear a hundred times as we walked together down narrow animal trails. The light was sparse, hitting the forest floor in small golden pools.

Martina's hand brushed mine and we both apologized at once.

"It's, uh," she swallowed, "it's totally different out here during the day."

"Must have been scary, scrambling through here in the dark," I said.

"People have asked me if I was scared he might chase me into the bush. I didn't even think about seeing him again until I got to the gas station. I was more worried about getting lost out here. I didn't . . . I couldn't know how far it was."

She seemed a little breathless suddenly, like she wanted to sit down. There was nowhere to do so.

The Grose Vale cops passed us without interest, splitting up at the bottom of the embankment and taking two paths winding in the same general direction.

Martina crouched for a minute or two, then rose up beside me, hanging on to my arm for support.

"My feet hurt."

"If it was just you and me I'd probably carry you," I said. For a moment she looked like she didn't know whether to take me seriously or not. "I can't be doing stuff like that with other men around, though. I'd make them look bad. They might hurt me."

I shrugged helplessly. She cracked a half-grin.

"You couldn't carry me with those bitch-ass arms."

We walked for a long time in silence. When it got awkward we spoke briefly about stupid things. Whether it was too cold for snakes. The terrain. Why old people like bushwalking. She always seemed ready to laugh. I've never really been "the talker" in my job but I sure as hell knew Eden wasn't going to do it. Sometimes talking rubbish with a victim could spur memories they didn't know they had.

When the local cops lost their way they let us lead again. Martina stopped and squeezed her eyes shut, breathed for long moments, oblivious to the noise as Eden reappeared through the bush to our right. She looked up at a ridge of mountain above us, turned around and seemed to judge its relation to another distinctive peak where the rock jutted through the canopy like a broken tooth.

"That way." Martina pointed to the north.

"She's right." Eden nodded ruefully. "There's a farm up there, two hundred meters or so. I'm pretty sure it's the one."

"How do you know?" I asked, but she turned and jogged away. Everyone else followed. Martina stumbled and gripped me hard, and through my shirt I could feel her hand shaking. We were alone again.

"You all right?"

"Yeah."

"Sure?"

"He's not here," she said, sounding as though she was struggling to believe her own words. "He wouldn't come back here."

The smell of smoke became overpowering, stinging in my eyes and throat. As we approached a break in the bush I noticed the leaves were coated in wet ash. We emerged into the long grass beside a barbed-wire fence.

A property sprawled before us, bleak and abandoned. Half of the grass was dead and shrunken against the earth and the other half was waist high. A small house had stood in the middle of a large field. Now it was a blackened carcass, ribs of charred beams reaching towards the grey sky. There was a fire engine sitting by the remains of the building, as well as a patrol car. Two female officers leaned against the hood, one writing a report, the other taking photos. I looked around for Eden and the others but they were already halfway across the field.

"You were wrong," I told Martina. "He came back."

She nodded. The female cops were surprised to see us arrive.

"So you guys couldn't put two and two together?" I gestured towards the house.

"You're not in Grose Vale anymore," the lead male answered. "We're in Kurrajong's jurisdiction now. I'm sure if they'd known they'd have let us know—right, girls?"

"You're Martina Ducote." One of the Kurrajong officers pointed at Martina with her pen. "So this is . . ."

We all looked at the house. Firemen were walking around the black and wet innards, kicking things over, stomping on embers.

"Yeah," Eden sighed. "This is the chop shop."

He had done a good job of destroying the house. The heat had been so extreme that the cage from which Martina had escaped had melted and bent and was now a surrealist appropriation of its former self. The room with the operating tables had taken the explosion of several gas tanks. Parts of the table were embedded in the field fifty meters away, with pieces of scalpels, knives, saws and syringes. What remained of the defibrillator was a melted pool of beige plastic. I walked among the ruins with Martina, picking up pieces of burned paper and the broken halves of chemical bottles and slipping them into evidence bags. There were remnants of a couple of pieces of jewelry that had survived the fire: a gold hoop earring and a man's watch.

Eden came over and walked beside us, told us that a check of the property's deed showed it was government-owned land and that the house had been scheduled for demolition years ago, but hadn't been a priority. I watched as Martina broke away and crouched in what must have been the living room, reaching out and coating her fingertips in ash from the floor.

I should have been looking for evidence. I should have been feeling something for Martina, a woman who had survived an entanglement with a monster, who had returned to the place where he had attempted to take her heart. But my mind was elsewhere. I hugged my jacket against the wind and looked out at the Blue Mountains.

A news van came into view, rumbling down the narrow service road towards the front of the property. There was no way of knowing if they were simply trying to cover the fire or if somehow they'd got wind that this was the killer's chop shop. Two of the police officers were on their phones. I started walking, hoping to stop the reporters before they defiled the crime scene.

"Hey!" one of the Kurrajong officers cried from the other end of the field. "Hey! Hey! Come here, quick!"

I stopped in my tracks. Not only was she screaming so that her voice could reach us, but it had risen more than a few octaves. She sounded afraid. I turned and ran with Eden into the mess of grass behind the house. The cop was standing by a squat stone structure in the far right corner of the field. My boots crunched on glass and debris, even as I approached the barbed-wire corner of the property.

The structure was a well. Officer Sanders of the Kurrajong Police had gone right ahead and shoved the concrete lid halfway off the well. She'd stopped vomiting long enough to call us and that was all. I scooped up the end of my shirt and pressed it against my mouth, shading my eyes as I looked down into the dark.

The well was about six meters deep. I could see one dead milky eye staring up at me in the crescent moon of grey light. From the smell I could tell there were many more.

19

Cops become callous. It's a story as old as time. Those over-exposed to death and cruelty stop believing in the general goodness of the human heart and all that greeting card crap, and they look upon depravity and murder as being common to the human condition. They stand by, smoking, joking about the dead, moving off topic and speculating about the weekend's football. They sigh and trudge in the grass and whine about their work in a manner identical to a thousand other professions.

For the cops who arrived to empty the well of bodies, a job that would last long into the night, the killer's evil was more of an inconvenience than an abhorrence against humankind.

So when Martina Ducote decided to stay and watch, I felt a twinge of concern in my stomach. Not only was she about to witness what she might have become but she would, no doubt, see the disrespect of the dead that comes so naturally to cops.

I kept an eye on her as night fell and two forensic officers were lowered by harness into the well to photograph, fingerprint, take samples and the like. They were rushing some special forensic anthropologist in from the city by helicopter, having called her at home while she was making dinner for her kids. What a job. A bunch of patrol officers were trying to move the camera crews and pretty journalists back from where they'd set up, blasting light onto heavily made-up faces and setting up mikes.

Eden wandered around with her arms folded, thinking. I lost myself in thought as well, probably coming to the same conclusions. Why well bodies and bay bodies? It seemed like he was conducting operations here and this was the most convenient way to dump the corpses, and those he dumped in the city must have been from another operation site near the bay. Did he have a city apartment?

Within two hours the first of the bodies was removed, carefully extracted from the tangle of remains like a piece of a puzzle sculpture, lifted out of the darkness using a stretcher and a winch. It was a man, curled on his side in a fetal position, eyes closed. Martina watched the body hover above the well with no expression on her face. Her cheeks were lit with the flashes from the press who had spotted her standing there beside me. Someone made a crack about the dead man sleeping on the job and people sniggered. I put my hand on Martina's shoulder.

"Haven't you got anyone worried about you?"

"No," she said without looking up.

"Can I give someone a call?"

"No one who won't be surprised to receive it." She smiled a little at my efforts. "I don't really have anyone close enough to be 'the one' I would call in a crisis."

I stood there for a moment thinking how sad that sounded before I realized I was in the same position. It seemed that Martina and I ran the same kind of lives—unattached, coasting through circles of acquaintances, intimate only with strangers. I lived that way as a destructive self-preservation technique I'd long grown accustomed to. Martina Ducote didn't seem old enough for that. I realized she was watching me and smiled awkwardly.

"This is going to be an all-nighter," I told her. "I saw a Hungry Jack's at the bottom of the hill on the way in."

"I love Hungry Jack's," she said. Someone started singing "We're Sendin' Our Love Down the Well" to a chorus of laughter and I blushed, ushering Martina quickly towards the car.

I don't know how long it had been since Martina had eaten something, but she gave me the impression of someone taking the chance while it was safe to do so. She backed up her burger with onion rings and a Coke, which she sipped retrospectively, staring out the window at the cars pulling off the highway on their way up the Blue Mountains or back down. The restaurant workers, who were all teens, kept darting out from behind the counter when they had the time to frantically wipe tables, their cheeks rosy and shimmering with sweat. My first job had been a fries boy at McDonald's. I took a moment to appreciate how awful the job was and the fact that I was sitting there eating and not engaging in it.

"You want a sundae?" I asked Martina, kind of hoping she would want one so I could have an excuse to get my own.

She snorted, folding the corner of her burger wrapper.

"Thanks, Dad."

I brought back a strawberry and a chocolate. She took the strawberry one. It was very feminine of her, I thought.

"You deal much with this sort of thing?"

"With what?" I asked, putting my arms on the table.

"I don't know. Kidnapping victims. People who . . . people who were almost . . ."

"No." I stabbed my sundae with my spoon. "I generally try to get the reports and leave it at that. To be honest, victims don't usually hang around the way you have."

"I don't feel safe," she admitted, keeping her eyes locked on the cup. "Funny things make me want to run and hide. Lights. The feel of cold metal. The sound of the wind."

It hurt to hear her talk about the niggling desire to dart right out of life. I'd experienced it after Louise's baby died. Our baby. The sound of a female voice on the phone. The sight of a pregnant woman. The color pink. These things had made me nauseous and flighty, right on cue, for months. My second wife, Donna, I'd found and married pretty swiftly to try and force myself back into the women-and-babies lifestyle, like a kind of immersion therapy. Bad idea. She'd got wind of my weirdness and coldness and "emotional unavailability" within months.

"They got a name for that," I said. "That's why you shouldn't be hanging around with us. You should be sitting on a couch somewhere trying to feel better."

"I feel better when I'm with you," she said. She let the words hang in the air, punctuated only by the crash of fries baskets and the yelling of order numbers in the kitchen. A couple of truckers took a booth behind me and Martina followed them with her eyes, scratching unconsciously at her temple.

"I know he probably won't come back."

"He won't," I said. "You're not the only escapee. He tried to drown a junkie off the harbor the morning we found the bodies.

By all reports he was happily finding Jesus with a bunch of other NAs in Darlinghurst last night."

Martina listened to my words carefully, dissecting them as the ice cream melted before her. She took a couple of spoonfuls and sucked them thoughtfully, her big eyes hidden behind her black lashes.

"Someone was in line for my heart," she said quietly. "There's someone suffering somewhere, waiting to die. Someone who's sick and weak, maybe. Someone who believes they didn't deserve what they got. I've seen his face, the surgeon, but I haven't seen the face of the man or woman who was supposed to lie in the room with me. I could pass them in the street. They could be sitting here with us now."

I couldn't help looking around. There was a family sitting in the booth behind Martina, a mother straightening a paper crown on her toddler's head.

"You never get them all," I sighed. "Evil is like a disease. It rubs off, scrapes off, gets airborne and breathed in. It gets picked up from living hard or from being hurt. It comes from need. Everybody needs. The person lined up for your heart had a need. You can't punish all the evil in the world. You wouldn't get any further than yourself."

"You sound like you've been doing this too long."

"I have." I was glad to see her smile, even if it was only the lifting of one corner of her mouth.

"What have you done that needs punishing?" she asked. The sounds and smells of the restaurant seemed to have dissolved. My hand was near her hand on the table, looking gnarled and old next to her smooth fingers.

"I was cruel to my first wife," I said. "I was unloving to the next one. I didn't like my former partner because she was one of those loud and outgoing and cheerful and chubby people who get around making everyone's business their business and handing out annoying compliments. I ignored her and pushed her away when I should have been someone she could rely on. She shot herself."

There was a nonchalance to the voice in my head that formed the words coming through my lips. It was an unfamiliar thing. I wondered if I was tired, or if I simply liked Martina, liked the way she considered my words for long seconds before deciding on her own.

"I hurt people to make myself noticed," she said. I watched her sculpt her ice cream into a round pink hill. "It began when I was seven. I was adopted by a large mixed family after my parents died—a combination of half-brothers and half-sisters, adopted brothers and adopted sisters. You couldn't raise an eyebrow by screaming but you could make them look at you by being vile, by being removed and bad. I liked it. I liked being the one that no one loved."

She glanced up as two cops entered the restaurant and strode to the counter. They were ordering dinner for the crew at the crime scene. The girl attending them seemed to shrink as the order went on and on, her finger weakly jabbing at the plastic panel before her.

It was as I was letting my eyes roam over the restaurant, avoiding thoughts about how much Martina reminded me of myself, that I noticed the newspaper on the table beside ours. I spent long moments reading and rereading the headline. The picture on the cover meant nothing to me. It was a grainy black-and-white shot of a man in his forties holding a baby, his face turned to look down into the eyes of the infant.

It was the name that zinged energy through my bones, making them ache for a moment as I sat still at the table. Something about the name made my insides burn.

NO RESULTS IN SEARCH FOR
MISSING FATHER JAKE DELANEY

Martina, the one who no one loved, was watching me. I pushed the tray aside and stood up, grabbing the newspaper from the table and tucking it under my arm.

"Come on," I told Martina. "I'll take you home."

20

Derek Turner had spent five days in protective custody at Long Bay, separated from the general population of inmates to avoid word getting out about his arrest. The guards, however, had come across information about his crime—the way that guards do, through whispers and murmurs in hallways, through innuendo and sightings of official documents left lying out in the open. You can't keep anything from prison guards. They're a needy, paranoid, curious bunch. It comes from years of skepticism and watchfulness, the universal understanding that an inmate's job is to keep secrets from the institution, and the institution's job is to discover those secrets. A prison guard's need to gossip is fed by hours of wandering empty halls and standing in spotlit courtyards, feeling time pass. A rumor or a mystery can keep a man entertained all night. When Derek Turner showed up and the guards were told that his presence was secret and his crime unknown, well . . . it was a mystery that could make the minutes tick by like seconds. It was a secret that simply had to be uncovered.

Eden and I pressed into Derek's tiny concrete cell. I stood by the wall while Eden took the only chair, a steel-framed, backless thing that was bolted to the floor. The place smelled of disinfectant and felt damp. Derek was covered in a thin film of sweat, and probably would be until someone could be bothered escorting him to the shower room where he would wash, swiftly and in cold water, in front of four guards.

"They've been flicking razor blades under the door," was the first thing Derek Turner said. Eden and I turned and looked at the tiny slit beneath the iron door to the cell. Down the hall, someone was screaming and banging on the walls. Eden glanced at her watch.

"Yeah." She nodded, bored. "They'll do that."

There was no telling who was giving Derek Turner the means to kill himself but my guess was it was probably the guards. A child killer is a common enemy to inmates and guards alike. The guards would encourage him to kill himself for the good of everyone involved. The inmates would not be as merciful. The arrival of someone like Derek Turner into the system would cause a sensation at Long Bay. They would begin talking about what they were going to do to him the minute he set foot in the yard. My first case as a fully fledged homicide cop had been over at the John Morony jail investigating the in-house murder of a guy who'd strangled his ex-girlfriend's little boy. He'd had his throat slit open with the lid of a tuna can by his cell mate. Took the guy half an hour, apparently.

The Long Bay boys would be ready for Derek Turner with their buckets of scalding water, their braided sheets, their shivs.

Eliza Turner would likely be getting the same treatment over at Silverwater women's prison.

"I'll do whatever I can to help you," Derek mumbled. "I want to testify against Eliza. I know what we did was wrong. I knew it all the time, but she . . . she was so strong, and . . ."

"That's really funny, Derek, because we've spoken to her and she wants to testify against you. So you can spare me the blame toss, okay?" Eden held up a hand. "I want to make this quick. Because I haven't had breakfast yet and I'm not good when I'm hungry. You need to agree to follow a script when you receive the call from the killer tomorrow. His usual first-of-the-month call. You need to run through this script a couple of times with one of our specialists."

"I'll do whatever you want."

"Officers are going to arrive tomorrow morning to prep you for the phone call. It's a long shot that he'll even make contact with you. This story is everywhere. But if you carry on like normal, like you've not been found out, he'll be banking on the fact that you want your daughter to live and he'll want the money you owe him. If he's as addicted to the danger as we think he is, he'll enjoy the risk. If you warn him in any way about what we're trying to set up, I'll make things worse for you. They can get worse, Derek. You might not think so, but believe me, they can."

The man who had been Courtney Russell's protector, her mentor, her family, burst into tears, nodding as he did. Eden got up and brushed her pants off as though trying to remove scum and mold she had picked up from the room. Derek's face was crimson and bloated as I banged on the door to announce our departure.

"Please." Derek sniffed, "I just want one thing. Can you just help me with one thing?"

"What?"

Derek cried into his hands. I stood watching him as the guard opened the door, Eden sliding through the gap and walking down the hall.

"They whisper to me at night," Derek sobbed. "The people out there in the hall. They give me the blades and they whisper for me to do it, do it, end it now. Make them stop, please. Just make them stop."

I stepped through the door and watched the guard lock it behind me. He was a thickly built Indian man with bright pearly teeth. When our eyes met I knew it was him and his friends who were taunting Derek Turner. He grinned and nodded up the hall.

"This way, Detective," he said. "If you please."

The older he got, the harder the waking became. Hades thought that one of these nights the coma sleeps he fell into would consume him utterly, swallow up his life like glossy black mud. When he dreamed, he dreamed of the children, and they were always black and white and sharp against the backs of his eyelids. They were never within his grasp. They were always laughing and he was helpless to know what spurred this evil noise.

When he woke under Eden's hands he did so with a yelp, her fingers spread over his bare chest, thumping down as though trying to resuscitate him.

"Wake up!"

"What? What?"

"He's gone. He's gone. He's gone after Travis!"

Nothing made sense. Hades lolled out of the bed like a heavy fish and began drawing on his jeans, the girl frantic, scrambling over the bed, throwing clothes at him.

"Hurry, hurry, please, Hades!"

Hades picked up the book lying beside the bed, shook his head like a dog, set it down again and picked up his car keys. His heart was thumping in his cheeks and neck. This was what a heart attack felt like. He thought about all the bacon he had consumed over the last month, the cigarettes and iced coffees the workers brought him. The scotch, God, the scotch. Eden was pushing at him. He was at the car.

Only in the light of the sodium lamps did he wake fully, notice that she was crying. He gripped her face.

"What's wrong with you?"

"Eric's gonna kill him," she moaned. "Eric's gonna kill Travis."

On the road leading through the forest the car skidded in the gravel, the engine thrumming under his bare foot. It was early morning he guessed. Rabbits hurtled across the path of the car, zipping into the bush like furry rockets. Eden's crying was unfamiliar, a frightening sound. She cried like a girl, softly and brokenhearted, into her hands. In time it subsided to sniffing and he gained the courage to look at her.

"He caught us," she said, feeling his glance. "A week ago. Travis and I. Near the creek."

"Doing what?"

"Aw Jesus, Hades," she whined. He nodded, focusing on the road. He knew she had been going with the Savage boy. He'd known it that day, two years before, when he had seen them together on the tree stump in front of the hill. He knew it from the quiet tension that rippled through Eric's body whenever she talked about the boy, always minimally, always playing down her relationship with him. The boy went away for months at a time with his father on trawler jobs in the Top End and Eden carried on like he'd never existed at all. Hades had kept an eye on the situation, dropped a few quiet threats to the boy of grievous bodily harm should he decide to touch his daughter. After a while, the old man lost interest. Who was he to interfere in these things? Eden was clever, mature, deeply assured of herself. If the boy messed with her, she would eat him alive. She seemed like a cat to Hades, curious and amused by a creature she barely understood but who she knew instinctually was no threat to her. The boy was dreaming, every minute a bonus, borrowed time.

The old man hadn't considered Eric's stance on the situation.

"We were supposed to meet," she sniffed, "at the wattle tree on the west fence. Just for a walk, you know? He never came. When I got back Eric was gone. He'd left a note."

"What did it say?"

"It said he was sorry."

Travis Savage and his father lived on the flat lands that nestled behind the national park, a good ten minutes from the dump. Sparse modern-day farms that produced nothing more than dry grass, rusted machinery, car bodies, and here and there a dope crop. Hades and Eden fell into silence. The street was wet with newly fallen rain and lit by a thousand orange reflections. A patrol car was sitting on the corner by the intersection at the Utulla city limits. The officer in the front seat waved a handful of McDonald's fries at Hades as he turned. A girl sat up in the passenger seat, indignant.

Hades stopped the car outside the broken wire fence but didn't turn it off. It was clear that the boy was not there. The lights in the house were out, the carport empty. Eden dashed from the car before he could stop her and did a circuit of the house, peering helplessly in the window, her hands cupped to the glass.

"He's not here."

"No shit. Get in."

She drew her legs up to her chest as he drove away, spraying gravel. His hands were wet on the steering wheel. This was his fault. All of it. He hadn't even thought about Eric. It was like forgetting to check an old boot for spiders before slipping your bare foot in. He was there, waiting, a constant figure of watchfulness, of burning hatred.

There was too much on. The dump was prosperous. The old man had simply let the boy slip his mind.

They didn't speak as the car wound through the empty streets behind the city of Camden, into the industrial area that housed a plastics factory, some importation lots and the local RSPCA. Tall white gum trees lined the road between the huge fenced-off lots. They both knew the only other place that Eric would be. Hades had received plenty of calls from the school and the local law enforcement complaining of the children hanging out in what was once a Singer sewing machine factory, smashing windows and running some of the old machines. It was the one place away from the dump that the children liked to hang out. They weren't welcome with the other teens at the city mall or cinema because of their disagreeable, confrontational natures and Eric's exhaustive history of fistfights.

It was clear when they pulled the car into the factory's loading dock that someone was inside. Hades could see the shadows of machines moving against the ceiling through the high shattered windows, the shadow of skeletal arms and strings and pulleys reminding him of an old black-and-white horror film, the kind he had loved as a child. The machines inside the warehouse were squealing and grunting, unoiled and in protest at this new mission. The old man reached over and grabbed Eden's arm before she could slide out of the car.

"You stay behind me, girl," he snapped. His eyes were enough. Eden shrunk in her seat and nodded. Hades got out of the car and left the door open, light-footed in the gravel as he moved towards the door.

The scene inside the factory reminded him of some of the Renaissance paintings he had come across when teaching the children, of the rendering of primitive torture chambers and prisons. There were broken parts and machinery left over from the factory in its prime—sewing-machine bodies, racks of tools, ancient mechanized arms above conveyor belts, their cog-and-wheel insides exposed. There were polished worktables and reams of rotting cloth, spray-painting machines dripping black and bubbling at their rusted seams and washers. Above him, chains and hooks lifted electrical cords above the floor, banding them together like veins and running them down the length of the factory to the power station. One of these chains had been disconnected, spilling wires. A body hung from it by the wrists.

Travis Savage was hooded and gagged. From the edge of the hood blood ran thick like honey down his bony chest and rib cage, artistically bright in the light of a single lamp. Over his chest and belly and naked thighs several dozen small teaser wounds had been opened like almond-shaped red eyes, each weeping more blood down his naked figure. Eric was standing nearby, holding the implement that had inflicted all these gaping holes—a short fat blade Hades had often seen him with.

Hades made some sound of anger, a grunt or huff of outrage he did not plan to make, and Eric turned towards him like a dog with a rabbit in its teeth—shocked, defiant, prepared to run to save his catch. Hades felt Eden behind him. She put a hand on his trembling arm and then pulled it away when she felt the fury pulse in him.

Eden tried to run to Eric but she got no farther than the outreach of Hades' hand. It encircled her and threw her aside. Hades strode forward and knocked the blade from Eric's fingers, grabbing a fistful of his hair and dragging him through the door. The boy did not resist. Hades slammed his face into the hood of the car and held it where it landed.

His mouth and jaw were so tight that words barely escaped them. He had to lean close to the boy in the night wind and force himself to speak.

"He hear you? See you?"

"No."

"He have any idea who you are?"

"No."

Hades held the boy's head against the car a little longer, panted as *the anger coursed through him. Now was not the time to let it consume him. Now was the time to be controlled, not furious. He let Eric's head go and grabbed ahold of the back of his shirt, opening the car door and shoving him inside. Eden stood, wrapped in her own arms, in the doorway. Hades thumped past her, went to the Savage boy hanging from the chain and cut him down, letting him fall into a sobbing heap on the factory floor. He picked up the knife and pocketed it, wiped all nearby surfaces with the edge of his shirt. The old man left the boy there, saying nothing.*

It was only in the kitchen of the little shack, the door closed and the curtains drawn, that Hades let the rage take over. Eric let him beat him. In some ways, it was a lack of resistance that made Hades angrier. The boy simply accepted his punishment, taking the punches with humble silence, raising his hand only to wipe the blood from his mouth when Hades had finished. Eden also did nothing. She stood in the door to the hall and watched, her hands pressed together as though in prayer and resting on her closed lips. When it was done, Hades rinsed his bloody knuckles in the sink, his back teeth still locked, aching. Eric sat on the floor in the corner, wheezing with what was probably broken ribs, a red tongue probing, exploring, at a missing tooth.

Long minutes passed. Hades leaned on the sink and looked at the patterns in the curtain in front of him, letting his body cool. His shirt stuck to his chest with sweat. The scrapes on his knuckles reddened again in time, weeping blood.

"You leave here tomorrow morning," he said eventually, pushing the curtain open before him and staring into the night. "I want you packed and ready to go by six. I'll call a cab. I don't want to see you."

For a long time, there was no response. The boy lay slumped in the corner, one hand covering his already swollen eye.

"Where will I go?"

It was not a helpless question. Hades knew it was genuine. Eric would go wherever he told him to go. He was his slave. His sick and violent dog, obedient despite his nature.

"I've got a friend in the city who will take you. When you're fixed up you're joining the police force. Goulburn, like we planned. It'll be the last place someone would look for a monster like you. You'll be pulled into line there. You'll learn more about the game."

"Eden?"

"No." Hades looked at the boy for the first time, feeling his jaw clench once again, an involuntary muscular tightening. "She'll follow you when I say it's all right. For now, you need to be on your own."

Eric's eyes wandered across the kitchen to those of the girl, rested there a moment or two before dropping to his hands. Hades' breathing gradually returned to normal. The beating had done him some good, burned some of the energy out of his throbbing veins. He rinsed his hand again and wrapped it in a clean dish towel. In time Eric dragged himself to his feet and went into the bedroom to pack.

21

I didn't like sitting at Doyle's desk. It was like lying in his grave.
Even though it was bare and the drawers were filled with my
meager belongings, there was the presence of a man I didn't know,
his fingermarks on the chrome frame, his thoughtful scratching
at the cheap paintwork. Around me, the men and women of the
station were going through their third briefing about the operation at the Turner house. It seemed a fairly simple operation on
the face of it, but hours of planning, sketching, calculation, argu-
ment and barely contained panic went into it in a boxy room at
the back of the station that could comfortably hold three people
but had been crammed with thirteen. With the help of logistics
men, operations specialists, computer geniuses, criminal lawyers
and negotiators, we'd managed to get Derek released into our
custody for the night so he could be taken back to his house in
Maroubra and held there in anticipation of the killer's call. We

had carefully scripted a scenario for Derek to read, asking the killer to come and visit Monica to treat what seemed to be a cold but that could well threaten her fragile post-op state. We'd have the place surrounded and would jump on him when he arrived.

I saw a million things wrong with it. Everybody did. But media pressure was forcing our hand, and we needed to get a shot happening, even if it was a long one.

I sat slumped in my oversized flak jacket and bulletproof vest like a bored kid at a wedding, moving things about on the desk in front of me. More unsettling than the feeling of Doyle's ghost and the impending crazy plan to snare the killer in a trap were the images Cameron Miller, Martina Ducote, Derek Turner and Eliza Turner had put together with the help of a sketch artist. I had them laid out on the desk before me.

The Body Snatcher, as some of the press was calling him, cut an imposing figure at close to two hundred centimeters tall, with chiselled features and large brown eyes. He had a lion's pride and audacity about him. No discerning marks, scars or tattoos. Thick muscled frame. Short-cropped chocolate hair. Not the desperate, hunchbacked ghoul everybody had been expecting. This guy was downright handsome. Something made me wonder whether the image of his soulful eyes would increase the public hatred or lull it. All the attention would put extra strain on the possibility that he would call Derek, that he would dare to turn up at the house in Maroubra when called. But if there's one thing I've learned in all my years in this job it's that the kind of narcissism and self-grandiosity required to kill and maim and torture other human beings over a long period of time meant that you couldn't count our psychopathic friends in on the normal rules of behavior. I'm no psychologist. I've just known a lot of bad people in my time. Bad people don't like to be told they can't or shouldn't do something that they want to do because it mightn't be "good" for them. Even if the killer sensed that something was up he might come for a look at the fanfare he had created. It was all about ego with these people.

Eden was off helping other cops suit up, but her brother sat watching me with little interest from across the room, perched on the edge of his desk by the window. I glanced at him occasionally, hating myself every time that I did. Eric rolled a cigarette between his thumb and forefinger, licking his canine teeth. I wrenched open the top drawer of Doyle's desk and shuffled things around in it, trying to alleviate the burning sensation between my eyes as I squirmed under Eric's gaze.

It was then that I saw the piece of Masonite. Doyle had cut the thin sheet of wood so close to the dimensions of the bottom of the drawer that it sat almost flush against all sides. When I wrenched open the drawer it shuffled the few millimeters' distance, alerting my eyes to the inconsistency. I cocked my head as a tingle began to grow at the nape of my neck. I pushed my pens, pencils and pages back from where the sheet of wood met the front of the drawer, picking at the tiny crack with my fingertips.

I took one of my pens and jammed it into the crack, my heart-beat increasing. The board was so closely cut to size that it wouldn't lift. I picked up a ruler and carefully inserted the corner into the gap. Eric was frowning at me. I ignored him. In moments I had jimmied the false bottom of Doyle's top drawer up, revealing the photographs underneath.

The first thing that struck me was the blood. So many of the images contained blood. It spilled from noses and dribbled over eyes, smeared reddish-brown on wrists and thighs. The first layer of photographs depicted three different women, bound and beaten, crying. In some of them I recognized Doyle from his "In memory of" photograph in the foyer. His hand was woven viciously in strands of a woman's black hair. His fist, knuckles scraped, clenched as he looked over a woman cowering in a corner of an empty room.

I had stood up sharply without realizing it. The sheet of Masonite fell closed over the photographs as though they had never been there. I stood in the middle of the bull pen staring at a perfectly normal-looking desk for a long moment, my breath frozen, unsure about what I was supposed to do.

Halfway to Captain James's office I realized I hadn't brought the photographs with me. I swivelled on my feet, took two steps back towards the bull pen, then realized what I had seen was potentially evidence. The drawer, the false bottom, the photographs probably contained Doyle's prints and perhaps the prints of others. I swivelled back around and jogged to Captain James's office. He was on the phone, probably calling in sky support for the sting, writing on a notepad as he listened.

"Barker Street," he repeated to the caller. "That's what I said."

"Captain James?"

He scowled at me before continuing to write. I nodded apologetically and dawdled in the doorway until he put the phone down.

"Phone, Bennett," he said.

"Of course, sir, I'm sorry." I leaned in the doorway. "Can I borrow you for a minute? It's really important."

James grabbed his coffee cup as he maneuvered around his desk. Somehow I doubted he would be refilling his cup on the way back. He lumbered behind me, fatherly and simmering, as I led him to my desk.

The drawer was closed. I had left it open. I stopped and James scraped the back of my shoe with the tip of his.

"Sorry, sir." I cleared my throat.

"What's the issue?" he grunted.

I tore open the desk and felt for the Masonite board. It was gone. Lifting the entire drawer out of the desk and dumping it on the surface proved only to make a mess of my stationery. I pulled out the two remaining drawers and rifled through them. Captain James stood by, scratching the back of his wrinkled neck.

"As unlikely as it might sound," he said, "mysteries are not my thing."

"There were some photographs here, *seconds* ago, belonging to Doyle. They were . . . compromising photos, sir, of a criminal nature." I struggled, looking at the mess on my desk. "I . . . I just . . ."

Captain James's drooping bulldog eyes surveyed mine. I let my hands drop by my sides.

"Uh huh." He finally nodded, tapping his coffee mug with his index finger. "No more coffee for you, Bennett. We're about to undertake a major sting operation and you're worried about missing happy snaps. Wise up, will ya?"

I went back through my drawers as he walked away. I even flipped through the papers on the desk, absurdly convinced the photographs had been found by someone else and misplaced. I heard Eric's laughter from the smokers' balcony and looked up to see him exchanging stories with one of the owls. He turned, stubbed out his cigarette and grinned at me through the glass doors.

My advance towards the doorway frightened the owl into the corner of the balcony. He gripped the steel rail as I ripped open the door and stepped out, slamming it behind me.

"Why?"

"Why what?" Eric smirked.

"The photographs," I said. "Why did you take them? What have you done with them?"

"Naw. You're talking in riddles now, Frankie. How cute."

I grabbed the front of Eric's flak jacket in my fists and shoved him into the balcony rail. The owl slurred a panicked excuse and dashed inside the office. Eric's smile didn't falter. He looked at me in an almost sympathetic way. I could feel my pulse ticcing in my neck.

"What was I going to find?" I asked. "Was your face a feature in those pictures?"

"I told you you'd have to be quicker, Frankie." His voice dropped, became unfamiliar and chilling. "I told you you were running with wolves."

I released him. His smile was rigid. The morning air felt painful in my lungs.

"Why would you want to protect a man like that?"

"I think his undertaker would agree that our mutual friend Doyle is far beyond my protection."

I seethed. Some of the owls were watching us from inside the bull pen, their novelty coffee mugs frozen in their fingers with phrases like "Hands off my Inflated Ego!" and "I've got PMS and a handgun . . . any questions?" emblazoned on them. Defeat prickled in me. Eric smoothed out his jacket. He knew I wasn't going to hit him, not here, and there was doubt in my mind that I could make contact even if I tried. The force of the slap he had given me in the men's room of The Hound was at the forefront of my mind. He could move fast. Faster than an old man like me.

"Get ahold of yourself, will you, Frank?" Eric shook his head as he walked inside. "You're putting everybody on edge."

You can't prove anything, I thought as I pulled my car into the lot behind the Liquorland on Malabar Road, five hundred meters from the Turners' house. I wedged my car behind five or six other unmarked police cars and turned off the headlights.

You can't prove anything.

What did I really have, if it came to the moment when I would stand face-to-face with Eden and Eric and accuse them of covering for Doyle's sickness? What did I have even then, other than my own assumption that they had serious reasons for not wanting anyone to know what Doyle did to those women? Maybe Doyle had been a monster. Maybe Eric had discovered it. Maybe he had stepped in when I had been about to expose this information to the captain of our station and inevitably to the world. It could have been nothing more than a desperate gesture to preserve a dead man's dignity. Maybe it was more than that. Maybe the photographs had something to do with Doyle's death.

Why would Eric want to hide anything relating to Doyle's death? Whatever it was, without the photographs themselves I had nothing to go on. I was beginning to wonder if I had really seen them in the first place.

I stood outside my car in the dark, just beyond earshot of the gathering of patrol and SWAT officers at the back door of the Liquorland. I didn't hear Eden approaching, her boots soft on the gravel.

She didn't say hello. I lifted my eyes, and she was simply there, looking at me, waiting for me to speak.

You can't prove anything.

"You know what's important, don't you, Frank?" Eden said softly. In the distance I could hear the crunch of waves on the beach and for a moment the sound seemed to rattle in my chest.

"I know what's important," I said.

"We're going to catch this killer tonight, aren't we?"

"We most certainly are."

Eden held my gaze for a long moment, saying nothing. Then she turned away, heading back towards the gathering of cops. The breath rushing in and out of my mouth left a mist in the night air. Eden wanted me to keep my mind on the job. How had she known it was wandering?

With a thundering heart I followed Eden towards the group. The Velcro flap at the back of her flak jacket was up, a single word in fluorescent white letters read POLICE. Across the circle of men and women I saw Eric, who had already caught sight of me. He was grinning in the light of yellow flashlights, shadows dancing under his cold blue eyes. He pulled a dark cap over his hair and I watched as his eyes disappeared. Now I couldn't tell if he was watching me or not. A hollow feeling crept through my stomach, pressing at the insides of my ribs. Eric mouthed some words and I jolted when I worked out what he was saying.

Want to play a game?

"As soon as any car pulls into the street I want it caged by checkpoints here and here." Captain James, standing at the center of the circle, pointed to a map he had spread out on the hood of one of the cars. "Feed the registration check directly to me. The code word for our boy is 'Chopper.' The code word for central command is 'Bird.'"

My face was already burning, the sensation spreading down my neck like a bushfire on a hillside. My black cotton shirt was sticking to my chest. I pulled my cap down low over my eyes and glanced at the map, hardly taking anything in as the captain gave directions to each of the teams. There was a slow, sizzling energy in the men and women standing around me in the dark. They were shuffling on their feet and clapping their hands together softly, drawing ragged marks in the gravel with the heels of their boots like bulls awaiting the opening of a gate.

Eden took her pistol out and loaded a mag. Then she slipped her pocketknife from her belt, snapped it open, and examined the blade in the flickering beam of the flashlight.

You know what's important, don't you, Frank?

I closed my eyes, drew a long breath and let it out slow.

What's important is catching the killer before he takes more innocent lives, I told myself. *That's my job. That's what I'm here for. I'm not here to chase ghosts. I'm not here to follow hunches. I'm here to protect innocent lives.*

My eyes snapped open as Eden shouldered past me. I followed her around the side of the Liquorland and into the main street, darting between shadows, on her heels, the faint perfume she always carried with her, of shampoo and incense, filling my nostrils. I tried to keep pace, but every time she arrived at a corner or crouched by a small stone fence I was two steps behind. The sensation of not knowing where Eric was in the dark streets sent chills snaking up my spine. I glanced around and saw the silhouettes of other officers, but when they stepped into the light it was never him. Eden took her position behind a car across the street and one house down from the Turner residence. I crawled into the shadow behind her, crouching so that my chin was level with her shoulder. I sat in silence for a full minute before realizing my earpiece was hanging by my neck. Sweating, I fitted it into my ear.

"Bird to all units," a voice in the earpiece called. "Status report."

"Ground Unit One, set."

"Ground Unit Two, set."

"Ground Unit Three, set," Eden whispered. Her voice inside my head felt like an intrusion, a slow taking over of my mind.

The checkpoint units and sky unit called in. Now and then I could hear the dull beating of helicopter blades, but it was keeping well off, doing laps of the coastline until called to avoid scaring the killer away.

We waited. Somewhere, someone was having a barbecue. The smell made me suddenly ravenous. It was an hour and a half before anything happened. Eden crouched, rigid as a stone, staring at the Turner house, where lights burned behind the drawn curtains. I squirmed in the silence, shifting my feet on the gravel, sinking down to my knees to try to relieve the tension in my ankles. It seemed to me that Eden was hardly breathing. Her silhouette was as motionless as a statue and for a moment I thought of reaching out to touch her, just to be sure she was really still there.

"Checkpoint A, we have a suspect sighted."

"Ground Unit Three checking registration."

"Roger," Bird confirmed.

I rolled up onto my haunches and turned towards the checkpoint. A bronze Toyota van had pulled into the street. The ground unit, stationed in the next street with a mobile patrol unit, began looking up the registration details of the van.

"Negative on that one. Registration checks out, Bird."

I watched the car turn into a driveway three doors down. Two children leaped out of the vehicle and ran to the front door, while a man and a woman began unloading plastic shopping bags from the trunk.

Another hour passed. A huge black cockroach circled us curiously for a while and then disappeared. Shadows moved in the Turner house. I felt sweat rolling down my calves, catching in the hair, tickling in my socks. I wanted to talk to Eden but I was unsure if she would even answer. Her words rang between my ears, zinging in the silence of the street.

You know what's important, don't you?

The voice in my earpiece sent electricity through my chest.

"Checkpoint B, we have a suspect sighted."

A small green car, possibly a Kia, had rolled into the street from the other end. The windows were tinted almost black. Numbness prickled in my feet as I got up onto my heels. Eden shifted slightly, watching the car as it rolled towards us.

"Ground Unit Three to Bird. This isn't his street. Car registered to a Michael Dalley, Chatswood."

"Bird to all units, we could have Chopper. Get ready, guys."

Eden slid her gun silently out of the holster on her belt. I did the same, flicking the safety off. The green Kia rolled past us quietly, pulling along the side of the road outside the Turner house. The lights on the car flicked off but no one exited. Trembling, I pressed a hand into the pebblecrete driveway I was crouching on, steadying myself in preparation for dashing forward.

"Steady all units," Bird murmured.

Another minute. I counted the seconds as the car remained still. The sound of the door popping open echoed around the street like a gunshot. A man exited, tall and dark-haired, wearing a faded orange cap down over his eyes and carrying a black shoulder bag on his hip. Eden rose swiftly and began to run as the man moved towards the door. Suddenly, I was surrounded by running people. A cop from Ground Unit Two got there first, crash-tackling the man to the front step as he reached for the Turners' doorbell.

"Get down! Get down! Get down!"

"Police! Get on the fucking ground!"

A howling voice, the scrambling of limbs. The radio was a wash of voices in my ear.

"Chopper is being subdued, call for patrol unit."

Eden shoved aside the nearest cop and grabbed the man by the collar of his shirt.

I looked down at my feet as I recognized a smell. The bag the man had been carrying was crushed under my foot. The toe of my right boot was submerged in what I knew intimately to be butter chicken on jasmine rice, accompanied by what appeared to be Peshwari naan bread. One of my bachelor cuisine favorites.

"Christ!" someone yelled. Eden pulled the cap off the boy's head. The logo on the front read CURRY 4 U.

"Please, please, don't hurt me," the boy sobbed, his hands shaking visibly in the air. A wave of panic rippled through the people around me. The Turners' door opened and three officers tumbled out onto the porch, guns drawn.

"It's not him."

"Bird to all units. Withdraw. Withdraw."

"We've fucked it," I seethed. "All of it."

I turned. At the south checkpoint, an unmarked car had been drawn out onto the road to block any attempt to escape. This was now unmanned, the officers having sprinted towards what was almost certainly Chopper, lying on the porch under the hands of fifteen men.

Beside the checkpoint was a single dark figure sitting astride a motorcycle, watching the commotion. As I spotted him, he turned and kicked the engine into life.

"Come on." I grabbed a fistful of Eden's jacket. "That's him, come on!"

Eden beat me in the sprint to the patrol car parked at the checkpoint. I threw myself into the passenger seat as she began to pull away, the tires screeching as they momentarily failed to grip the wet road. I tugged the microphone out of my collar, grabbing the roof with my other hand to steady myself as Eden swung the car around a corner.

"Ground Unit Three to Bird, pursuing Chopper on Malabar Road heading south."

Nothing came back to me. In the tense moments while I awaited a response, Eden leaned forward over the wheel, knuckles white in their grip. I was so wired that I jumped in my seat and smacked my skull against the roof of the car when a hand touched my neck.

"Isn't this *fun*, comrades?"

Eric laughed and spread his arms over the backseats as though enjoying a carriage ride in the park. I had not heard him get into the car at the checkpoint. I wondered if he had been sitting there already when Eden and I climbed in.

I couldn't think about Eric's presence for long. Eden cut across a flat roundabout, screaming through a set of lights after the motorcyclist, who breezed between the cars on the main road. The patrol car flew over the hill towards Maroubra Junction. In the windows of a dozen tiny salt-sprayed apartments, people were watching television and sitting down for dinner. Eden blasted through another intersection, the red of the lights reflected in the rain on the road.

"Unit Three, we're backing you up. Hang tight, keep the reports coming."

Two marked cars, lights flashing, appeared on the road behind us. Eden gained and then lost ground on the motorcyclist. The man on the bike cut between two passing trucks, causing her to slam on the brakes. She followed at a distance, the red eye of his taillight blinking between the passing cars as we entered and then left the motorway. On Botany Road, the rider seemed to decide where he was going, leaning forward on the bike and gunning it between the cars waiting at the lights.

"Fucker," Eden growled. She let out a short, hard sigh. "He's heading for the airport. He'll lose the helicopter out there and we'll lose him in the crowd."

"Ground Unit Three to Bird, Chopper is heading to Sydney Airport via Botany Road."

I could almost hear Captain James swearing on the other end of the line. If the killer got into the airport, it would be a nightmare trying to find him.

"We'll try to cut the entrances off before he gets there. Stay on him."

"No chance." Eric laughed from behind me. "He's going to make it with room for an espresso."

Eric was right. The red taillight of the motorcycle zipped right across an intersection of nine lanes of traffic, gliding down the domestic terminal lane like a kid on a bicycle. Eden wove and screeched into the intersection, leaning on her horn. By the time we reached the lineup of taxis waiting to pick up new arrivals the black helmet and leather-jacketed shoulders of the rider were bobbing through the traffic a hundred meters ahead of us. Eden threw the car into park and jumped out, dashing ahead of me. I sprinted onto the road, running between the cars.

"Police! Get out of the way!"

Ahead, the rider abandoned the bike and helmet and ran through the automatic doors into the terminal building. The crowd waiting at the taxi rank scattered as I approached, my gun hanging by my side.

I glanced behind me to try and find Eric but he was gone. There were five hundred or so people in the check-in area. No one was running. Fat elderly men in Hawaiian shirts. Young ladies in pantsuits. Army guys lugging duffel bags. The stairs to the food court were loaded with people laughing, talking, carrying plastic trays.

A plump airport security guard, already sweating, wobbled up to my side, his pistol in hand. I flashed my ID, barely looking at him. In a glance I saw clear pale skin over rounded cheeks, eyes pinched at the corners by fat. I dropped my eyes to his name badge, hardly aware of his presence in my tangled thoughts.

My name is Chester and I take jokes about airport security very seriously.

"You got comms to all units in the building?" I asked.

"Sure do," he nodded eagerly.

"You're looking for a white male, six foot something, wearing a black biker jacket and jeans."

The security guard grabbed his radio and gave the report. Without waiting for him I ran off toward the restaurants, stopping at the top of the stairs to scan the hundred of diners.

If he had not been looking right at me, I might not have noticed him. The killer was standing at the far side, by a large blue fire door. As soon as I turned towards him, he slammed the silver bar on the door down. A great screeching alarm erupted through the dining area, causing every single person to freeze.

The killer disappeared through the fire escape. I ran down the stairs, sensing Eden as she fell into step beside me. On the way across the dining hall I knocked over a man standing with a tray in his hands, watching in numb shock as we approached. The alarm whirred overhead, buzzing in my ear canals.

The fire escape opened onto a loading dock. The killer was nowhere. Eden and I split up, taking two different sets of stairs to the bottom of the dock where pallets of frozen french fry boxes were waiting to be lifted up onto the next level.

To the left and right, dozens of similar loading docks stretched into darkness. I jogged uncertainly to my right, sweeping my gun around the next dock, glancing behind me as Eden appeared in the street, working her way down the left, her figure disappearing between the glowing circles of orange streetlights.

Don't leave her, I thought, an impulse that had no meaning. *Don't let her get away.*

I tried to shake the thought out of my head. Eden's report crackled in my ear as she reached the other end of the building with no success. I opened my mouth to give my own report when all that came out was a howl. I didn't even know I'd been hit. My mouth didn't work and then my legs gave out, the oversized bulk of me in my bulletproof vest and flak jacket slumping to the ground.

I blinked away the lights in the corners of my eyes. I tried to move my arms but they were useless. The commands in my brain seemed to fizzle out. Two boots appeared beside my face before a hand seized my collar from behind.

"There's no gratitude anymore, is there, Detective?" a voice sneered.

The man in the biker jacket rolled me onto my back. He was huge. As the feeling slowly returned to my legs and arms, I lay beneath him, panting. My gun was in his fingers. I could feel warm blood running down the back of my neck.

"You try to do people a service," the killer smiled, his blue eyes glinting in the orange light, "and all you get is trouble. People don't understand. This isn't life. It's survival. We're forgetting where we came from."

I had no idea what he was talking about. The gun was pointed at my face. I drew short hacking breaths as the killer lifted a boot and pressed it against my upper chest, the toe resting on my Adam's apple.

"Don't," I said, trying to think of a way out and coming up blank. "Just don't. You'll only make this worse for yourself. Drop the gun and run."

The killer laughed. The back of my head felt wet on the concrete. When he spoke again, they were practiced words. I could hear him saying them to me, and at the same time I could hear him saying them to men, to women, to children he had strapped to a steel operating table. His voice carried through my ears to the ears of waitresses, university students, council workers, business brokers. A mother. A father. A schoolgirl. His victims, gone and yet present with me at the same time, reliving their last moments as I was living mine.

"My name's Jason Beck." The man above me smiled. "I'm the last human being you're ever going to see."

Beck levelled the gun between my eyes. It bucked in his fingers, kicking upwards with a flash as the bullet cleaved into the concrete ten centimeters above my skull. I looked up in time to see Beck double in pain, clutching his shoulder. I blinked and he was gone, and the steel beams of the loading dock ceiling receded into the dark green mist of my fading consciousness.

I opened my eyes to a furious pain in my nose. Chester's chubby fingers were crushing the cartilage in anxiety, his other hand holding my mouth ajar. I bucked wildly as his mouth descended towards mine.

"Holy Jesus!" I yelped, scrambling away from him. "I'm alive, goddamnit!"

Chester breathed a sigh of relief. There was sweat dripping from the line of his round jaw.

"You weren't breathing," he panted. "I just finished my certificate IV in first aid. You were in the right hands."

Men and women appeared around me. Someone lifted me to my feet and my head began to throb. An ambulance buzzed and flashed its way through the street between the loading docks, the paramedics shoving aside cops and security guards to get to me. Eden and Eric stood in silence by the pallets, watching the fray with detached interest. A sickness brought on by their stares, as well as the blow to the head, pounded through my stomach. I retched but there was nothing in me.

"I can see the headlines now," someone said as Captain James made his way through the crush of bodies. "Deadly Doctor Winged by Rotund Rent-a-Cop."

There were a few snickers. These cops had jumped in from the airport station and had no investment in the obvious humiliation of losing the killer when we had him right in our hands. I looked around and saw my own people. None of them was smiling. Chester, who looked like he was bordering on a heart attack, was sitting in the back of an ambulance, sucking gratefully on an oxygen mask.

"I've never used my weapon before," he was blubbering, his voice muffled by the mask. "I . . . I . . . I've never used my weapon before."

"Hey, hey, hey, be careful," someone else laughed. "He takes jokes about airport security *very seriously*."

Jason Beck was long gone but the general consensus was that he had taken a bullet. There was blood on the concrete, not all of it mine. The press were arriving at the end of the street where more guards were setting up barricades. A couple of reporters slipped through and began to jog towards us through the spots of lights. One of the paramedics had walked up to where I sat perched on a milk crate and was unclipping my bulletproof vest. In my daze, I hadn't realized she had worked my jacket off my shoulders.

"Hang on," I said, coming to my senses. "Hang on a sec."

"You've been clubbed with a crowbar, sir. You're going to need to come with me."

The woman pressed a sterile pad against the back of my head. The contact stung. I stood up too fast and tried to push her away. Eden and Eric looked at each other. It seemed that in slow motion they moved, turning at the same time, wandering through the fire door.

"Someone get a photo," one of the street cops yelled. "I want Frank and the rent-a-cop arm in arm with a caption: My Hero, the Kiss of Life Saves Sydney Detective."

I groaned and let the paramedic lead me to the ambulance.

22

The crowbar to the head afforded me the rest of the night off, despite my wishes. We had a name and that was enough to light a fire in me, one that drowned out the low-level mockery about Chester trying to give me mouth-to-mouth and the double black eyes that were emerging on my face. I was dropped home to pace my apartment in a near fury. I took a shower and tried to stave off all thoughts about Beck and what approach we should take now that we had a name to put to his face. Sucking on a beer as the sun rose, the circuit of names pounding in my head brought me around to Jake DeLaney.

I still had the newspaper I'd taken from the restaurant with Martina. The nagging sensation that Jake DeLaney meant something to me crawled beneath my skin. At 5AM I had rifled back through all my previous cases—I filed the cover sheets under my desk—but found nothing to hint at him. The newspaper reported that Jake, a divorced father of two and casual labor-for-hire man, had gone missing after leaving a bar in Coogee. He had been gone three days, with only his wallet, keys and phone, the clothes on his body and a box of Tic Tacs. Three days wasn't long by any means, but his lack of activity since the point of disappearance was worrying people. He had placed two bets on a football game and won a total of $63.23 but had never claimed his winnings. His phone and bank accounts had not been activated in the time he'd been gone. He had not been spotted at train stations, bus stops, airports or rental-car lots. No taxis reported picking him up from the bar. The tides were calculated and water searched to no avail. By all accounts Jake DeLaney had waved good-bye to the usual Sunday afternoon crowd on the ground-floor sports bar of the Palace Hotel, walked out the side door onto the street by Coogee beach and disappeared into thin air.

It took me until 7AM, lying on my back, staring at the ceiling and wondering how many minutes I had before Eden called me, to realize where I had seen the name.

In Eden's wallet.

I grabbed a sheet of paper from the notebook beside my bed and a pen from the water glass behind it and wrote down the name Jake DeLaney. I remembered another name, the only other one that hadn't been crossed off the list, because the man's last name was the same as a girl I'd dated for two weeks in high school.

Benjamin Annous.

I don't keep a computer at home. Never have. Aside from reporting or looking up databases on inmates or probationaries, which I only do at work, I don't have much use for one. A short walk from my apartment brought me to the Biz-zip Internet

Café, which for two dollars an hour offered me Internet access, free cups of chilled water and a view to the busy highway. Schoolchildren dawdled on their way to the bus stop and construction workers were marking out sections of road to tear up. I took a computer against the window and ordered a double-shot coffee from the lady behind the counter. She looked like she knew as much about making coffee as I did about computers.

As I sat down my phone began to chirp. Eden's name flashed up on the blue screen. I ignored the call. The sound of the phone had made me jump, like I'd been caught doing something perverse. It felt wrong to be questioning my partner as my mind inevitably began to do, picking around my memories of her that night in search of something about her words or behavior that explained a missing man's name in her wallet days before he had gone missing. I remembered the furry feel of the edge of the paper, worn soft from months, maybe years, of rubbing and scraping against her jeans. If she had kept his name on some kind of list for so long, why had he only disappeared now? I tried to remember the names before him, those crossed and recrossed by the ink of different pens, but they'd never been fully snapshotted into my mind.

Jake DeLaney had slowly evolved into a working-class hero from days wallowing in the primordial ooze of petty crime. I pulled up his criminal record from the police database and scrolled through a list of assaults that had been recorded—from a mass that probably hadn't. The man had a short fuse and a shorter reserve of willpower. He had been ordered to undertake six weeks of rehabilitation as a part of his parole for smashing a car into a dress shop window on a coke binge. The more serious of his convictions included attempting to hijack an armored vehicle with two other men outside a Westpac bank in Bankstown, an underestimation of police resources that cost him five years of his freedom.

I wrote down the names of the two other men convicted of the failed hijacking. Richard Mars and Geoff Gould. I put these names into the criminal file search engine and found similar records of low-level mischievousness leading to a catalyst crime. I decided it was possible Eden had worked on their cases at some point, but when I dug deeper into the case files I found that she was not listed anywhere, probably because she had been a baby at the time of their prime achievements. When DeLaney, Mars and Gould were released from Long Bay, Eden would have been four. I sipped my sour coffee and licked it off my teeth, staring at the image of DeLaney's plump face filling most of the mug shot on the screen.

Mars and Gould. I couldn't remember whether or not their names had been on Eden's list. I looked at my watch and realized I had thirty-five minutes before we were due to meet to prepare for the briefing. With a growing sense of guilt, I put Mars's name into a public search engine.

I knocked over my empty coffee cup when the first article appeared. Mars had gone missing two years earlier in Thailand, the case put down to a murder-robbery or a purposeful disappearing act to escape conviction for a crime the cops had not yet discovered. He had last been seen at the Indigo Pearl Resort in Phuket, walking down the beachfront on his way to the taxi rank. He was reported missing by his girlfriend, who had flown there with him to enjoy some cheap shopping. His loss was lamented by few others. With nervous, aching fingers I minimized the articles I had been reading and renewed the search engine, ready to type Gould's name.

My phone buzzed in my pocket. The counter attendant looked up as I answered.

"Yeah?"

"You're late," Eden said.

"I know," I rose from the desk. "I just, uh . . . lost track of time."

"You want me to pick you up?"

"No." I plonked some coins on the counter and pulled open the sliding door of the café. "I won't miss the start of the meeting, I promise."

When she was a child, Eden liked to stand in the hallway and watch Hades sitting at the kitchen table reading novels and newspapers by the light of a dusty antique lamp. She liked to watch his hooded grey eyes moving over the printed words and remember the night she'd first met him, the way his eyes had scanned her bloodied face and hands with a fatherly pain she had thought gone from her life. She liked to stand just beyond the reach of the light and close her eyes and feel the old man's presence before her, dream about letting him put his arms around her and hold her as he did sometimes. She hoped that one day the feeling of being held by him wouldn't make her feel itchy and frightened and small. The frantic moments when her real father had held her while the kidnappers burst through the cabin doors had ruined all physical contact for her.

It was seven years since she'd laid eyes on Hades and he had not changed. She hadn't wanted to come back until she could show him somehow that his work had been worth the effort, that she was becoming someone powerful, someone meaningful, that she had taken what he had given her and used it to grow. Oh, they'd spoken on the phone. She'd sent him things. Letters. Books. Trinkets that reminded her of him. But she'd never gone back, not until she was ready to show him her new self. Full of justice. Full of strength. Ready to begin her real work.

As she stood in the dark before the screen door, she felt as though she were looking in on the past, the perfect stillness interrupted only when Hades lifted and turned the thin paper, rested his stubbled cheek on his thick hand. Eden raised her fist and knocked on the edge of the door. Hades' eyes lifted, picked out her silhouette.

He said nothing. The screen door gave a loud creak as she opened it. The thud of her boots was out of place on the unpolished boards. She sat down beside him. She was wearing the fitted coveralls of the street, navy blue and pinched at the waist by her huge gun belt. A black police baseball cap shaded her face. He let his eyes wander over the uniform, the badge, the rank slides on her shoulders. It was the first time he had seen her wearing the uniform and the last time she would. From then on, it would be the suits and plain clothes of the homicide department. The old man and the young woman examined each other silently. In time she placed a hand on his hand where it lay by the edge of the paper, curling her fingers into the warmth of his palm.

"You look tired," Hades said. Eden felt a smile creep over her lips and she nodded, her eyes set on the paper. The old man, wary of how much she hated being touched, lifted his hand and tucked a strand of her fine black hair carefully behind her ear.

"You look beautiful," he said. "But you were always beautiful."

There was sadness in his voice. Eden closed her eyes. She could feel his eyes moving over her hands, wondering what agonies they had wrought.

"I've missed you," she said. "In every street. On every corner. In every room. I never stopped missing you."

A silence stretched between them. The night birds, who were so familiar to her, did not call tonight.

"Where's Eric?"

"In the car. I wanted to have you first."

Hades nodded. He closed the newspaper absentmindedly. He seemed afraid to look at her. She squeezed his fingers but he didn't turn.

"I've been afraid all these years that you might have regretted what you did that night," she said. "I've worried that you might be here thinking that if you'd known what we would become you would have just . . . you'd have taken the money and just . . ."

"I knew what you were and I never stopped loving you," Hades said. "I knew that first night."

Eden licked her lips.

"It's not your fault you are what you are," the old man said. "I didn't do it to you either. One of the men who made you this way is dead. I buried him the night that I was supposed to bury you. The five others, well, they're still out there. I always planned to wait until you were ready and then tell you who they are. I think you're ready. I think that's why you're here."

The old man stood and Eden began to see now that, though his appearance hadn't changed, the way he moved had. She watched him shuffle to the cupboard above the sink and retrieve a small enve-lope from where it stood against the inside wall of the shelf. He ex-tracted from this envelope a piece of notebook paper. Eden felt a tremor rush through her body as Hades slid the piece of paper across the table to her. She moved her hand away to avoid touching it, her eyes frantically scanning the names.

"The one who brought you here told me it had been a mistake, all of it. I was merciful with him. I hope you'll treat the others the same way."

"We're always merciful," Eden said. She let the paper rest on top of the table for a long time, unable somehow to find the strength to take it. Eventually she took out her wallet and tucked it into the notes sleeve. A little of the paper poked out, as though trying to escape.

"Some of those others," Hades said, pausing with the difficulty it caused him, "I've watched them over the years. They have children."

Eden felt tears spill finally from the edge of her long lashes. She forced herself into the old man's arms and gripped at the back of his shirt. When Eric arrived at the screen door he found Hades holding Eden tightly as she cried.

23

I missed the start of the briefing to the media by ten minutes. Everyone noticed. Eden told the press that the department was employing all possible means of finding Beck and asked the public to contact the police if he was spotted. I stood against the wall of the conference room and watched as she read from a list of what we had so far.

"Jason Beck, thirty-nine, is wanted on a number of charges including murder and abduction relating to the discovery of bodies at Watsons Bay and Kurrajong, and for related offenses dating back over the last two years. Beck is believed to have studied at the University of Sydney in 1999 and worked as a medical practitioner in a number of overseas locations between the years of 1999 and 2003. Beck's whereabouts from 2003 to the present are not known. It is not believed he practiced licensed medicine in Australia at this time.

"What we have been able to discover about Beck is that he has been a committed and talented student and a valued and responsible employee. Our interviews with his former colleagues and co-workers reveal that he was a quiet, socially limited and well-mannered person, and we have no reason to believe that anyone who has interacted with Beck in the past anticipated such abhorrent action by him or indeed acted to assist him in any way. His behavior has come as a shock to many. Consistent interpretation of his actions by the people we have interviewed suggest that Beck's behavior might have something to do with his immutable beliefs about nature, Darwinism, natural selection and the like. But we're only speculating at this point. Our real priority is getting him in custody.

"I'd like to make it abundantly clear that at this point we have no reason to believe that Beck has ever acted in partnership with anyone, nor that anyone we have spoken to from his previous employment has known about his actions. We believe more will come to light about Beck's motivations in the near future, but until then we can't say much more. The Sydney Metro Police Homicide Squad again warns the public that at no time should the suspect be approached if identified in public."

From the report that Eden had compiled during the night, it seemed that Beck had established himself as a one-man travelling GP in Uganda, where he had received government funding to work at refugee camps and small villages. It seemed the perfect training ground for the kind of unorthodox methods Dr. Rassi mentioned, those required to chop and change medical procedures to successfully perform transplants on his own, and not as a team.

As soon as Eden stopped talking the questions erupted from

the crowd. She answered them stoically, her hands folded on the tabletop before her.

Cameras flashed and journalists yelled as Eden finished answering the required amount of questions and stood. She left the table and walked towards me. Her gaze was exhausted and irritated as she passed me without a word.

I was achingly aware of Eric's movements around the bull pen. He and two other officers had been assigned to help us sift through the public tip-offs we received about Beck. He sat with his feet on his desk, tossing a blue rubber ball up in the air and catching it behind his head. As I tried to keep my head down, I was startled by the ball bouncing once, hard, on the paper in front of me before landing in my trash can. Eric slapped me on the shoulder as he passed.

"Sorry about that, mate."

"No probs." I smiled. "Let me know if I can help you find a place for that thing."

Eric wandered over and bounced the ball a few times on Eden's desk, looking down at her as she worked. He leaned over and whispered something in her ear and she frowned and glanced around her at the room.

"It's too soon," she murmured. "You know that."

I leaned on my elbow and watched Eric making restless circuits of the room, unable to keep my mind off the disappearances of Jake DeLaney and Richard Mars. Between shifting through the stacks of useless tip-offs to the *Crime Stoppers* show, I treated myself to five minutes—no more—to address my obsession with DeLaney and his associates. Watching Eric's progress back and forth,

I opened the lid of my laptop and logged into the criminal database.

Geoff Gould's profile came up with a flashing bar beside a grainy mug shot. I placed a paperclip between my teeth and chewed it as I stared at the blinking red text.

WHEREABOUTS UNKNOWN—SEE MPR 06/02/95

I clicked on the missing persons report link and got a bunch of text and another picture of Gould, this one strikingly similar to the photo of DeLaney holding a baby on the cover of the *Herald*. Gould, however, was grinning at the camera.

Mars, Gould and DeLaney. All criminal associates. All missing. Were they all on Eden's list?

It was only by sheer chance that I closed the laptop lid as Eric's ball sailed towards it. I caught the rubber ball against my chest and stood. One of the owls was stepping through the sliding door to the smokers' balcony. I pegged the ball through the gap as it closed, the shiny blue orb gliding over the rail and into the empty space below without a sound.

Eric watched the ball disappear with his hands hanging by his sides. Emotionlessly, he opened the top drawer of his desk and extracted an identical one, smiling cheerfully at me as he bounced it on the surface of his desk.

"Fucking incredible," I sighed, sinking into my chair. The telephone on my desk started ringing.

"Frank Bennett."

"Detective Bennett?" A woman's voice. "This is Gina at the front desk. I think you should come down and see me, please."

Immediately the sense that I was in trouble for something. It reminded me of my days at school, when I would be called to the principal's office via the PA system.

"Okay," I said. "I'll head right down."

Gina Shultz, a woman I passed on my way to the bull pen every morning, was standing by the front doors of police headquarters. I had never seen her out from behind her desk before. Not only did she have legs, but they were muscled and tanned like something out of *Playboy*. Delicious. I approached and stood beside her as she stared out at the rain.

She seemed to sense me there and nodded towards the front steps, the pouring rain.

"Friend of yours?" she asked.

Martina was standing on the third step, her arms wrapped around herself. I felt my smile fall.

"Why didn't you bring her in?"

"I tried," Gina said.

I jogged out into a torrential sleet of icy water, cowering as it battered my ears and slid between my shoulder blades. Martina was drenched through to the skin, a black T-shirt and jeans hanging off her like an extra skin. I went against all my professional instincts and wrapped my arms around her as though I could protect her from the weather. She gripped my shoulders like a cat, pushing her face into my chest. I could feel sobs wracking her entire frame.

"I'm not okay. I'm not okay."

"No." I squeezed her shoulders. "Obviously not."

I walked Martina inside the building and stood at the door with her. Her sneakers squelched and squeaked on the marble tiles.

Gina stood by, holding a standard-issue Windbreaker, something I'd worn dozens of times beating the pavements of Sydney in the winter. I wrapped it around Martina's body. It fitted like a blanket.

As Gina retreated quietly, Martina struggled to swallow sobs. My whole body felt hot from her touch. It wasn't a sexual sensation. It was something more primal, like a fitting together of pieces, a coming home from a long time away. I felt renewed by the feel of her, awake and exhilarated. I didn't worry about the men and women moving through the foyer around us, curiously tossing glances our way. I wiped back the wet hair stuck to her cheeks and pulled the collar of the jacket up around her neck.

"Silly woman," I said. "Look at you."

"You're probably busy."

"I've got enough time for you," I said. "Come on. It's warm in here."

The café to the side of the foyer was for the exclusive use of those in the building yet it didn't have the usual tinny, stale feel of work restaurants. Taxpayer money had been used to fit it out with immaculate red leather booths and modern chrome and glass. A goldfish pond, artfully incorporated into a black hexagonal pillar, dominated the center of the room. I took a booth at the back, facing the doors. I was surprised when Martina slid into the seat beside me. Her thigh pressed against mine. I ordered two coffees while she patted down her face with a napkin.

"I told you you needed to be seeing someone," I said when the waitress was gone.

"I'm seeing you."

I was struck dumb by that for a minute or two. The waitress came and deposited our coffees. Martina massaged the sugar inside the paper packet, breaking it down into the individual granules with her fingernails.

"How do people keep going on?" she asked, looking around the room. "There's a monster out there. He's making monsters of other people. Men and women and children are dying. Why hasn't everything stopped?"

I followed her eyes. Two women were sitting by the windows, laughing and sniggering behind their hands. Outside in the street commuters billowed out of the train station, running under tilted black umbrellas across the street and under café awnings. The rain kept falling, on and on in hammering waves. No one had stopped. Life was churning away while the woman beside me struggled to assemble the pieces of her own. She had forgotten her umbrella. She had forgotten her coat. She had forgotten how confused people were when they saw a stranger crying and shivering in the rain. The rules of her life had been destroyed. How was she supposed to respect these simple normalities when another human being had put her in a cage?

"No one understands this thing but you," I said. "No one else can feel it. To them, it's a passing interest in their lives. This darkness is yours alone. All pain is like that, you know?"

I didn't know if she understood what I meant. Her eyes were fixed on her hands. I was thinking about my ex-wife and the baby whose death I hadn't been there for. Even when I had arrived at the hospital Louise's agony had been untouchable. I couldn't help her. No one could. I was helpless to understand what the child meant to her, what losing it really felt like. The world kept going on and on then, as it did now. People laughed and joked and went to work. The weather was reported on the news. Other babies were born in other rooms of the hospital. Nothing stopped. Time was careless. I forgot how to eat and sleep. There was no one who felt my wretchedness, no one to share the burden of it. It was unrelenting. The guilt. It was a poison in me.

Martina took my hand suddenly. I looked down at her fingers. Her nails were pink and perfect, unreal next to mine.

"It's going to take forever, isn't it?" she said. "It's going to take forever to remember how everything works."

"I'll be here," I said. A tiny smile crept over Martina's lips. The sobs that had been shuddering gently through her had stopped. I still felt the heat that her body had given mine, the indescribable energy that came off her, as though my body was recognizing hers. I didn't know how to treat this strange new desire for another human being. I wanted to spend every minute with her, but not in the way I'd been attracted to women before—the longing for ownership, domination, compliance. I didn't *want* Martina like I'd wanted to win women before, remove them from their lives, call them my own. I felt like I would be happy to observe her in her little world forever, maybe link that world with my own. Stupid thoughts were running through my head, one following the other like train carriages. She made me ashamed of myself, this woman. Ashamed that she could touch me, and all that I was.

As much as Martina protested, I called around and soon found out that the closest person in her life was her landlady, a fussy Italian woman called Issa with a squat frame and huge breasts who occupied the apartment above Martina's in Randwick.

When I walked Martina up the stairs towards her door, Issa was standing with her hands on her hips in the doorway, babbling sternly in Italian. She gathered up Martina's cheeks and squeezed and shook them in a gesture of half desperate love and half disappointed fury. Martina stiffened like an unfriendly cat.

Issa hugged and kissed her before disappearing into the apartment, picking up clothes strewn on the floor and straightening furniture like a scolding parent.

"You speak Italian?"

"Not a word," Martina mumbled.

"She speak English?"

"Nope."

"I've organized a counsellor to visit you tonight," I told her. "But I don't feel right leaving you here alone. Not when you're this upset."

"I won't be alone." She smiled weakly. "Issa won't leave now that you've got her started. She's going to stuff me full of meatballs and scrub my kitchen all day."

I nodded. The sounds of pots and pans banging were already coming from inside the apartment. I knew this was the time to leave but instead I stood reluctantly in the hall, the stairs at my back.

"I'm fine." Martina sniffed. "Just go, Frank, please. I've embarrassed myself enough already."

"Christ, don't be embarrassed."

She smiled a little and put a hand on my shoulder. I was about to speak again when she kissed me, softly and insistently, on the lips. It was hardly anything more than a peck but that instant or two beyond friendly left me shaken. I watched, my throat burning, as she walked inside. After the door had closed I stood there dumbly, trying to remember which way I had come.

Eden and Eric sat in the rental car for a long time, watching the apartment block where Martin Vellas lived. It seemed to Eden that sitting there, with the distant presence of the man behind the lit window, was enough. It was enough to imagine him wandering in the rooms of the third-floor apartment, enough to see a flash of his shadow against the kitchen curtains as he washed the dishes and put them away. Enough to know that he existed, that retribution for the death of her mother and father was possible. She breathed evenly and as she sat looking through the darkness she heard Eric's breathing synchronize with her own.

"Do you remember?" Eric asked. He didn't need an answer. She remembered every moment. She remembered the heat of the room and the strange blue of the summer night outside the cabin, the way the sun still seemed to glow in the glassy water of the lake long after it was gone. She remembered her father's cotton polo shirt and the feel of it against her cheek, his fur-covered arms, his fingers in her long hair. She remembered the soft sound of the television, watched by no one, and all of them just sitting there on the leather lounges and being in the presence of each other. Being together for the last time.

She remembered the busting glass and the way the footsteps had made the French doors shake. She remembered shouting so slurred and so rapid that it sounded like explosions. She remembered her father's arms tightening around her, the yank in her shoulder joints as she was pulled away and thrown on the floor. The ripping sound of duct tape as it came off the roll. Eric's face beside hers on the polished hardwood floor, blood on his teeth, the only person in the room who wasn't screaming.

She was five years old. She was a child then and never was again.

"I remember their faces," Eric murmured beside her. She looked at him finally, finding his eyes in the dark car. They were lit by the gold squares of Martin Vellas's kitchen windows. "People say you're supposed to forget their faces first, but I've never forgotten. The way the air sucked out of her as they came through the doors. Her crumpled look."

Eden felt her jaw tightening. Her fingers followed, pressing into her palms, tighter and tighter, until she felt her own blood pool on the skin. She took out her wallet and extracted the list of names, looking at Martin Vellas's name, second from the top.

"Martin Vellas," she whispered.

Eden closed her eyes and slipped the paper back into her wallet.

Eric moved slowly, as though he were drunk, taking the latex gloves out of the packet kept in the center console and pulling them on. When Eden tried to do the same the sweat on her fingers stuck on the rubber. Eric rolled his balaclava down neatly over his face. She was panting now, the wool already matted to her face.

"We're supposed to be merciful," she whispered quickly, struggling to get her seat belt undone as Eric slid out of the car like a collection of smoke.

"We're supposed to be merciful," she said, catching his arm as he *advanced across the road. Eric took her fingers in his, squeezed them so that she could feel the heat of his body through the rubber. He grinned under the woollen mask, flashing his harsh white teeth in the light of a neon sign hanging above the car.*

"We'll be merciful," he murmured, nodding. "Eventually."

24

I did something I told myself I'd never do again, and the shame coursed through me like electricity. I stood outside a woman's door with a meal in my hand, this time a big meaty pizza, and I began a dozen stupid opening lines in my head. Oh, the indignity. I leaned my forehead on Martina's door and sighed. The pizza was getting cold in the box on my palm. I mumbled some profanity at myself and pushed the doorbell with my thumb.

When she finally opened the door, all I had going for me was an idiotic grin and the word, "Hi."

"Hi." She smiled back. She looked at the pizza in my hand. I brought it to my chest and then thrust it at her.

"I didn't think you'd want to cook."

And I didn't know if your landlady would, but I sure hoped she hadn't, and I just wanted an excuse to come round here and see you and hear you and know if you were okay and . . .

What does that even mean?

"You're right," she said. "I didn't."

Martina took the pizza box from me and held open the door with her bare foot. I slipped inside and stood awkwardly, looking around her apartment. The place was narrow and bricky, with a stainless-steel kitchen and posters on the walls like a teenager's bedroom. I immediately thought of how much younger she was, the kind of dickhead I had been in my mid-twenties and what the hard times since then had taught me. There was a perfumed candle burning somewhere and an acoustic guitar on the long, boxy couch. I chewed my lip. Martina put the pizza on the coffee table and went to change out of her pale pink satin robe.

What are you doing here, idiot breath?

I went to the couch, changed my mind, stood by the balcony doors and looked out. The longing for a cigarette pumped through me, an impulse I hadn't had since I was married to Donna. The street was empty. I'd told the patrol boys outside they could go. They'd snickered knowingly, stopped when I frowned. The next patrol would arrive at midnight. I turned when I heard her coming in from the bedroom. Martina emerged in jeans and a black singlet. Her shoulders were brown and smooth like caramel.

"This is probably really inappropriate," I said for some reason.

She smirked. "I won't tell anyone." She brought two wineglasses to the dining table by the balcony doors. I sat down and swallowed half of my wine in one gulp. I'm good at knocking wineglasses over. Do it all the time. With this awareness firmly in my mind, I put the glass down carefully and slid it away from me between sips.

A grey cat lifted its head from where it lay curled in a basket by the door. I hadn't noticed it there.

"Who's that?" I asked, nodding towards the animal.

"Greycat."

"You named him what he is?"

"Sure did."

I smirked. The cat went back to sleep.

"How are you feeling?"

"You know." She shrugged. I didn't. I waited while she extracted a slice of pizza, pulling the strands of mozzarella free with her fingers. "I keep going on. On and on. Can't help it."

She wanted to talk about the case. I chose my words carefully. The wine helped. As darkness closed in around the apartment, I felt my limbs loosen. She lit a lamp that hung over the couch and nothing else. People returned from work and wandered the hall outside her apartment, greeting each other, taking dogs out for an evening walk in the light rain.

I've been thinking about you, I thought.

"I've been thinking about you," she said. I turned my wine-glass on the tabletop. The pizza was half gone. I felt tired. Martina's hand reached out and touched mine. I opened my palm and let her trace the lines on it with her fingers.

This is not how I work.

The realization made a heat run through me. I'm not this man. I'm the sleaze at the bar. I'm the biggest and strongest of all the jerks left in the pub at midnight. I'm the most confident. I'm the quick-witted one. I don't say "love". I don't pay for cab rides home. Feminism will do that to you—leave you alone out on a doorstep in the blazing morning light with the memory of my body already fading from your mind. I'm not this man, this embarrassed, love-hurt, longing man.

Martina moved to my lap, straddling my legs. I gave a terrified sigh, the kind I hadn't made since I was a teenager. I slid the right-hand strap of her top down over her arm, listening to the sounds of a piano play from an apartment across the street. Beautiful, beautiful. Martina wrapped her arms around my head and held me to her heart. I closed my eyes and listened to it beating for I don't know how long.

Jason leaned against the lamppost with his hands in his pockets and looked up at the sky, appreciating the distinct bars of colored light trapped between the city buildings, purple and pink, a layer of almost-yellow before the heavy grey of impending night.

Randwick was a hilly suburb and a resistance tugged gently against his chest and he imagined himself tumbling down the asphalt towards the street below him, raking off skin and pounding bones, the world finally tipped too far. He rolled his wounded shoulder, felt the hole where the bullet had been—pull and twist, the stitches' tug. He longed for more pain, rich and deep-cutting pain that would assure him of his presence on the earth, of occupation of one moment and then the next, of the decisions he made. Yes, there were choices now, plans to make, resources to be gathered, because in the end he was a decision-maker, unlike the mindless ones in the houses and apartment blocks around him droning along in their meaningless lives. Pursuing junk to fill their nests. Comparing their junk with that of others.

Jason was like a fox preparing for the winter, knowing in his very bone marrow that what was to come would be violent, merciless, phenomenal. He would hunt now, and then he would hide and be born again when the darkness had risen and all the world was anew.

He let his eyes drift to the apartment with the lace curtains high above him, his fingers idly finding the stitches in his skull and pulling them so that the skin burned.

A lamp was lit near the window so that he could see the white stucco ceiling. A grey cat wandered out onto the balcony, peered down through the wrought-iron rail as though it had always known he was standing there.

Jason smiled and waved.

Beck's apartment had been swarmed long before Eden and I arrived. It had been a big tactical event more suited to the special ops guys, so we'd met in a café across the street with all the neighbors the team had been able to muster up and started conducting interviews. The café owners, an old Greek couple, seemed a little unnerved by their incredible luck at becoming the informal base of operations. The chiefs, tactical officers, patrol officers, forensics teams, body-handlers, journalists, neighbors and voyeurs had all ordered something from their little cluttered counter while they waited for the apartment to be secured. People were spilling out into the street drinking coffee and squinting at the chalkboard menus. From my table I could see the owners' teenage son in the kitchen trying to toast fourteen ham-and-cheese croissants at the same time and just about crying with the pressure.

The neighbors gave us nothing. The only people in his building Jason had ever spoken to had been a couple on the floor below who had a pair of little boys who would traipse around the staircases at all hours playing hide-and-seek. All James and Kat could tell me was that the doctor in number eighteen was a quiet, handsome guy whose place smelled bad. James had borrowed a power drill from him once and caught a glimpse of what he thought was a snake tank in the hall inside the door. The guy never had any visitors and he never made a sound.

It was mid-morning when Eden and I were called forward. I'd barely spoken to her and a wave of embarrassment swept over me at the idea that she might somehow sense that I had been with Martina the night before. I'd gone home that morning and showered and changed in that stupid daze men get when their world is filled with a woman. Unable to organize my thoughts. I'd walked all the way to the car without my keys. I'd left my watch on the bathroom counter.

We slipped on our fuzzy booties and latex gloves and stood ready for the forensics guys to give us the all-clear and the photographer to sort out his equipment. As we headed up the stairs to Beck's apartment, I found myself thinking about her again. Her long, slender fingers. The way she twitched now and then in her sleep, wriggling closer to me, her nose and mouth against my arm, her face hidden in the shadow of me. I'd wanted to see her again that night but she'd said she was going somewhere. A relative's place. I wondered who. I slapped my cheeks and Eden turned and cocked an eyebrow at me.

"Tired," I said.

"Try sleeping at home."

I scoffed. It was the wrong thing to do. I felt sweat on my ribs.

"I slept at home."

"Did you?"

"Yes."

"Really?"

"Leave me alone."

She gave one of those special, infrequent laughs and walked

into the apartment ahead of me. My face was hot. I was glad for the distraction when I hit the wall of reek that enveloped Jason's apartment. The stench was hanging just inside the door like an invisible curtain. One second I was breathing the slightly musty air of the corridor and then my lungs were full of a rank wetness, like a tropical jungle throbbing with heat and urine. I coughed and hid my face in my elbow. Eden was breathing the air like it was ocean spray, unfazed, standing at the end of the hall in the tiny living room and looking around her.

"What is that?"

"Mice," she said.

The mice were just the most prominent of all the animal smells here because they had escaped the little tank on the dining room table and taken over the house. There were mouse droppings among the papers and empty coffee cups and medical instruments strewn everywhere, on the plates on the kitchen counter and scattered over the carpet like pepper. In the corners of the room a bigger animal had defecated over a long period, something accustomed to using a litter tray but not provided with one. Clumps of dry black feces, smears and claw marks on the walls, no sign of the beast itself. The tanks James had spotted inside the door had indeed housed snakes, but these animals were gone too, only their skins remaining like leftover chocolate wrappers. I stood by the kitchen counter and blinked, my eyes stinging from the ammoniac fumes. There was no option about opening the windows. If there was evidence here, even something as small as an eyelash, we could ruin someone's chance of finding their missing loved one dead or alive by disturbing it.

Eden was flipping through the papers on the table. A photographer came in, looked her up and down and darted into another room. I moved around Eden and checked through the books lying in a great pile by the windows, looking as though they'd been unceremoniously dumped out of a bookcase that was no longer here. Medical textbooks and encyclopedias, thousands of copies of *National Geographic*. Everything felt abandoned. Sad, used, redundant. Rain had come in at some point and started a patch of mold under the bedroom window. The bed looked cold and damp and unslept in.

"Moving in or moving out?"

"I don't get the feeling he's moving anywhere," Eden sighed, opening the kitchen cupboards. They were bare. "He's partly here, partly in the old place where we found Martina. Partly out there, in the never-never. Doesn't have a home base. Running a bit wild, I think."

"Pretty disorganized guy. Aren't doctors supposed to be really anal?"

"I don't think it's always been this way," she said. "He's . . . falling. Going down the rabbit hole. It's always a battle to keep that other instinct in check, that dark thing that keeps trying to pull them out of reality and into the fantasy of the hunt. They only cover their tracks so carefully because they're still connected to reality, still worried about the consequences of getting caught. It's when they start losing that connection with the real world that they become like this." She gestured at the table before her. "Disorganized."

A couple of techs came in and she told them what to bag. I felt empty, watching her. I didn't like the way she talked about Jason's work as if it were an instinct, something emotionally detached and working on its own like a machine somehow implanted in him, pulling his limbs on puppet strings. There was choice in this. I was sure of it. Free will and cruelty and that unique brand of human evil. I had to believe that, because if I couldn't blame what Jason had done to all those people on something I could understand, I didn't know how I was ever going to get over what I'd seen. Their faces. Their limp, lifeless limbs. The way they'd all curled together at the bottom of the well like maggots. Human maggots. How could he have done what he did to Martina without knowing it, deciding on it, enjoying it? You knew everything there was to know about Martina before she had spoken a single word. You knew how she hurt, how she feared, how she loved, simply from the look she gave you, her breath, her laugh. She was an incredibly natural creature. I was certain Beck couldn't have ignored the fact that he had broken something in that woman forever the moment she woke up in that cage. I felt angry, standing there in Jason's mess and filth, his cave of madness. There was no excuse for what he had done.

Eden came over to where I was rifling through a Tupperware bowl of jewelry that had been placed in an armchair by the television like a bowl of popcorn. I picked up a black novelty watch and squeezed its buttons, watched it glow in the dankness of the apartment. It was emblazoned with the image of some action figure I didn't know. I guessed it belonged to the teenage boy we'd found in the bay with Courtney and the others.

"Gotta get this fucker," I said.

"We will."

"Really, now. We've got to get him and hurt him. We've got to make sure we can pin him somehow alone for a couple of hours before we make the official arrest so we can give him a good squeeze."

Eden seemed to watch my face more carefully for a moment,

as though trying to decide on something. In time she forgot it and fumbled in the bowl and picked out a wedding ring. She dropped it and pinched at something on her arm.

"What is it?" I asked.

"Flea."

"Aww, Jesus." I dropped the bowl and brushed off my arms.

"You got one on your neck."

I swiped at my neck and throat. Smiled and walked away.

25

I went for a drive at around 2AM. I'd been in and out of light sleep dreaming about Beck's apartment and had become frustrated with it. I felt as though my eyes were pressing against the bones in my eye sockets and that electricity was buzzing between my temples. Wired. I let my fingers dance on the wheel, taking a tour through the city to look at the lights on St. Mary's Cathedral, warm and bright as they curled into the intricate nooks and crannies of the building. Shadows of the homeless wandered and warped over the sides of the church, giant men lumbering. I stopped at the traffic lights and watched a group of drunk naval officers walking home across the park and muttering to each other, sullen-faced.

Martina had shaken my life. Picked it up and dropped it. Things were leaning in, broken, out of their place. The air tasted different. I found myself strangely repelled by her, by the power that she could have over me, by the changes she could make to my belief system. She was like a flame. I had to get away in order to understand how I really felt about her, what I wanted from this helpless attraction. You have to do that, get away from women in order to think about them. Close up, all you are is a slave to their rich fresh skin, to their honey voices, to the irresistible safety of their company.

I was driving towards Eden's apartment before I knew where I was going. In some way I suppose I wanted to talk to her about Martina. I wanted another being to confirm that this was happening, that it was all right, that Martina could love or want a man like me. Eden knew I'd been out the night before and I supposed it was only a small leap to tell her who I had been with. Dating victims of crime was something that occurred now and then in police ranks, and though it was probably written somewhere in a manual on a shelf that it wasn't supposed to happen, you share something with each victim, a mutual trauma at the crime, a united desire to put things right. This had happened to me at other times. I'd chased a burglar out of an elderly man's house in Coogee in my early days as a street cop and had visited him every Friday night afterwards on my patrol to talk football with him until he died. We'd faced a common enemy, the two of us, and something like that is never forgotten.

I pulled into Eden's street and slowed the car to a stop outside the loading dock coffee shop. No lights were on. Unsure what I had intended in the first place, I was about to pull out when I saw two dark figures moving rapidly across the street.

Eden and Eric.

My senses sharpened, like an animal on point, though I couldn't have known at first what it was about their appearances that seemed strange. I was accustomed to seeing them dressed in black—it suited the two of them with their sharp features and dark eyes—but Eric was wearing a watch cap turned up over his ears. He glanced around the street and pulled the door open for Eden. I watched as he got in and opened the engine up immediately, barely checking the street before he pulled out.

It was the sharpness of their movements, their determined strides, I suppose, that helped me decide that I was going to follow them. I could believe that Eric would wear a watch cap despite the mildness of the weather, and I'd known Eden not to carry a purse but rather to keep her essential items in her pockets like a man. But there was no joviality to the way they walked, none of that comfortable swagger they both had now. It was a walk of pure focus, which made me believe they were on their way to something that was important, something I should bear witness to. In a flash I thought of the photographs of Doyle with his tortured victims, the names of the missing men on the list in Eden's wallet, the murmured words, stolen over Eden's desk, that were meant for no one but her blood brother.

It's too soon. You know that.

Was it still too soon?

I kept at a distance, pulling onto the southbound highway a good four or five cars behind. There seemed an inordinate amount of street lamps flickering and blinking, as though the electrical current running through the city had been disturbed somehow or was overloaded. I told myself it had probably always been this way. My exhaustion seemed to give a sharp edge to everything, to create extra shadows and give added brightness to the reflections of light in the water on the road. I risked edging closer and noticed that Eric had rolled down his window, his elbow resting on the sill, fingers drumming. As we pulled off the highway into the streets behind Mortdale, Eric wound his window back up and seemed to hunch over the wheel.

The distance between us stretched. The car ahead rolled slowly down the main street, past a Chinese restaurant with tables and chairs on the footpath by the street, fairy lights strung between the trees, empty and dark inside. I let the distance creep as far as I could until I could barely catch them turning each corner. When I pulled into Pickering Avenue, Eric was switching off his head-lights. I parked behind a blue sedan and switched the engine and lights off.

Through the windows of the sedan, I could see Eden and Eric's silhouettes in the car. Both pointed, angular faces were in profile. I followed their glance to the house across the street, where a sin-gle light burned in what looked like a kitchen window hung with curtains. Aside from a flowering Christmas bush, there was no vegetation around the place. A beaten-up prefab dump, similar to hundreds of others that littered the western suburbs. There was a small truck in the driveway but I could not make out the com-pany logo on the side panels of the cab.

Eden and Eric didn't move. I squinted, trying to decide if they were talking, but both seemed as inanimate as statues, watching the house. I looked back at it and tried to understand what they were watching, what they hoped to see. Nothing moved.

A coldness began to spread through my limbs. I waited but the two figures remained unmoving as minutes ticked by. I realized I was holding my breath. Dread, thick and tight, was flooding through my chest.

The car doors opened. I gripped the wheel as Eden and Eric's shadows met on the road.

My phone went off, the high-pitched musical peal of an antique phone. I jolted and cringed as adrenaline prickled through me. I always have my phone on the highest volume, the most obnoxious sound, so I never miss it. When I had found the thing in my pocket and shut it off, I looked up and saw that Eden and Eric had paused in the middle of the road.

They were staring in my direction. I sunk slowly behind the wheel until I was eye level with the dashboard. Like two cats, Eden and Eric had frozen at the noise, silhouetted against the light, their bodies stiller than I would have thought possible. Though I couldn't see their eyes, I could feel them exploring the shadows around the car, the blank windscreen, the doors and windows. They couldn't see me. I was sure of it. They wrestled with their instincts in the dark.

Eden, in time, reached for Eric's hand, touched it softly and wordlessly with her own. They climbed back into the car and drove off.

26

As usual, her call woke me. My heart raced. I was panting before I had begun to talk, sitting up in bed.

"We've got a body," Eden said. "Be there in five."

There was silence when I got into the car. Eric had taken the driver's seat beside Eden. Two owls sat in the back, both gripping their lab bags with their fingernails, looking like they were bring driven to the gas chambers.

"Where's the party, fellas?" I asked. Neither of them moved.

"Utulla," Eden said as the car pulled away. "At the dump."

Her words sent electricity through me. At that time, I didn't know why. There was something about the Utulla dump that rang in my ears, something that made me wary. I told myself that it was probably because Eden and Eric were from Utulla that was sparking my recognition.

"Home country," I said cheerfully. "We should stop by your old place, relive some childhood memories."

Eric's eyes watched me in the rearview mirror. Eden shifted uncomfortably in her seat. There was a bike marathon on in the city and traffic was diverted back and forth across the Inner West. On Woodville Road a drunk stood pissing between two parked cars as we pulled up at the lights, his hips rotating slowly like a water-skier. When we finally reached the highway the tension in the car had risen to an almost painful altitude. The owl beside me sneezed and the other jolted like he'd been electrocuted. Eden leaned her elbow on the windowsill and watched the city roll by like she was leaving it and was glad.

I fell asleep against the window and when I opened my eyes the car was rumbling down a wide unmarked road cut through dense bushland. The owls were just about eating their own hands with anxiety. I wiped drool from my lip and sat up in my seat.

A sign made from assorted pieces of trash flew by the window. Pipes and bottles and discarded bits of wire had spelled out the words "Utulla Dump."

Eric parked at the bottom of the hill and began to walk up without waiting for the rest of us. Eden was a little more patient, but only just. I stood beside the car, under the shade of a huge fig tree that must have been two hundred years old. I could see flying foxes writhing and swinging in its crown. That was not what captured my attention, however. Beneath it, two massive horses grazed, their bodies made entirely from discarded pieces of junk.

"Will you just look at this," I gaped. Eden walked up behind me and tried to move me on. I wandered forward through the wet grass, reaching up and touching the underbelly of the huge animal. On closer inspection, an intricate welded frame of cogs, wheels, pipes and tubes made up the animal's body. There were pieces of engines and frames of machines that I recognized from my boyhood as a failed apprentice mechanic. Eden snapped something at me and, in turning to answer her, I spied other trash animals lining the roadside—a gazelle rearing on its hind legs, two oversized possums scaling a living tree.

By the time I got to the top of the huge hill, I was like a kid in an amusement park, my mouth hanging open, my eyes eager for each new marvel. When I arrived in a small clearing of the trees, I realized what had been agonizing Eric and Eden all the way from the city. They stood, Eden looking decidedly uncomfortable and Eric with his arms folded defiantly, on either side of the stocky grey-haired man from the picture in Eden's wallet.

Heinrich Archer.

Hades. The Lord of the Underworld.

I had been right about where I had seen his face before. In the 1970s and '80s, Heinrich "Hades' Archer had graced many of the city's newspapers and evening news reports in just the manner I'd remembered, walking out of courthouses, fleeing the press, his hand up to shield his face from the cameras. Hades Archer was a "fixer," a handler of delicate situations for some of the country's most notorious criminals. He had defended himself in more than a dozen court cases, accused of disposing of bodies, making unclaimed shipments of drugs disappear, silencing large wars that broke out over territory or women in Western Sydney drug and biker gangs. He was never convicted of anything because he was professional, discreet, ingenious. When people had a problem, they went to Hades. When they needed a calm, knowledgeable, authoritative mediator, they went to Hades. When they made a mistake, they went to Hades. He could clean up after the most devastating messes, make profit from the most incredible gambles, salvage the most unsalvageable relationships. He left victims and perpetrators alike smiling and thinking they had come off best.

I had heard some pretty unbelievable stories about Hades in my time as a cop. He'd killed for the first time, it was said, out of self-defense at the age of ten, a street kid preyed on by a hustler. His earliest appearance in court was at age twelve for being involved in revenge attacks against a rival drug-running crew. I'd heard he'd bitten off a man's finger for making moves on his girlfriend. I'd heard he had shot five major crime personalities at a crowded party as part of a takeover bid for the local muscle-for-hire scene. Hades Archer had been accused, in his time, of some of the most incredible feats of criminality. None of this had ever been successfully addressed by the law. Powerful people in the upper ranks of the police department, those old box-headed chiefs and superintendents, seemed very familiar with Hades—whenever he was on television Hades referred to these dinosaurs of justice by their first names. No police corruption inquiry had ever gotten close to indicting him. Hades always conducted himself in public with the calm, quiet, fatherly authority I was seeing now, and his stoniness of character seemed to buffer even the most brazen of attacks.

He was standing before me, his heavy body buckled, leaning on a cane. He looked ancient and lethal at the same time. The man had the thick square head and shoulders of a Bordeaux hound and the same kind of malignant potential. I glanced around at the wastelands that surrounded the hill. This place had been searched for bodies dozens and dozens of times. Nothing was ever found. Not a finger. Not an eye. Nothing. And yet everyone knew what

Hades was doing. Everyone knew what he was capable of. His stories had filled my dreams in the academy.

Heinrich Archer.

Eden's father. Eric's father.

The old man offered his hard chubby hand to me. I took it and felt my bones grind as he pumped it.

"I'm Heinrich." He nodded. "My associates call me Hades, as I'm sure you're aware. It's up to you."

"Frank." I smirked at his candidness. Eden and Eric turned and began walking away, whispering rapidly to each other.

"If you'll follow me." Hades motioned forward. I began walking. Ahead of us, Eric and Eden's heads were close together. Eric glanced back. The path down the hill was well worn by heavy feet, a track that zigzagged between sandstone blocks and more of the impressive trash creations towards a workshop at the beginning of the dumping grounds. In the distance, I could see a number of workmen and women standing around a small pit beside a large mountain of garbage. The air became stale and sour, seagulls and crows hovering overhead.

"You built all these things yourself?" I asked Hades, gesturing to the animals. We passed a glass and wrought-iron dingo inlaid with triangles of gold and yellow glass. Hades nodded sternly.

"I don't like waste," he said. "Everything has potential. You have to be forgiving of the imperfections of things and find new life for them."

My mind was wandering, zinging connections together. Eden's art. Her skilled, strong hands. The darkness in her paintings. The old man I had seen there, swirling in oils, sparks glancing off his shoulders as he welded in the dark. This was the place where Eden and Eric were raised. I stared at the trucks rolling and bumping along the horizon, the black smoke curling from their exhaust pipes. They began their lives in trash, in disease, in darkness.

"I don't care much for the police, you know," Hades said. "The law and I have had a checkered relationship since long before a kid like you was born. I feel it's my civic duty to report a thing like this though. I don't want my reputation sullied by such callousness."

He gestured into the pit before me. I walked forward and looked down on the body lying there. The junkie's back was arched awkwardly over a crumpled jerry can. He had been stripped of all his clothes. In his chest a great long cavity had been carved and, though my anatomical knowledge was limited, I was willing to bet some pieces of him were missing. This wasn't surgery though. This was rage. Blind, violent fury. Jason was coming apart. The ritual was changing. He was losing it. The junkie's foot was still casted from the breakage at Watsons Bay. I turned away and caught my breath, pushing through the dump workers who hung about, shocked and numb. Hades stood at the back of the crowd with his hands in his pockets, his elbow resting on the cane. I watched the owls rigging up a tape barricade around the pit.

"I got a couple of my managers together trying to figure out where the body would have been dumped," Hades offered. "Seems to me, from experience, he would have been city trash. Lotta fast-food containers in the same pile. Too many for a suburban skip."

"Darlinghurst," I shuddered. "He was staying in Darlinghurst while he completed an NA program. I gotta call Martina . . ."

I let my voice trail off and jogged away from the gathering. Martina's voice was sleepy. It hurt to undo all the assurances I'd given her that the killer wouldn't come back, that the junkie being alive meant that he wasn't interested in tying up loose ends.

"Do you think I'm in danger, Frank?" Her voice was low, serious.

"I don't know."

"What am I supposed to do?"

"You've still got a patrol car at your apartment block. Stay there," I told her. "I'll come around tonight."

My words rattled in my brain. *I'll come around tonight.* Was it my intention to spend the rest of my nights protecting her, worrying about her, holding her? Days earlier I had been alone, the way I liked my life, utterly in control of everything that I cared about—my body, my career, my stupid possessions. Suddenly my concerns had doubled. There was a whole new human being to consider now. I felt shaken with fury at the idea that something might hurt her. My hands were trembling as I put my phone away. *This is how husbands feel,* I thought. *This is how I should have felt when Louise called me all those years ago from the hospital and asked where the hell I was.*

"You should shut down the premises," I told Hades. "The place will be crawling with press if you don't."

He appreciated me silently, his eyes narrowed against the sun, causing the leathery skin at his temples to bunch. It seemed absurd, in that moment, that I was to stand there and carry on the façade that I didn't know this man was my partner's father, that I was to keep on pretending that the origins of Eden and Eric's menace was not all around me, in the very ground on which I stood, in the air that I breathed. I could feel them watching me, though my back was turned. This was the game they had trained everyone to play—the captain, the owls, the headquarters staff. This was the game they had to play. Innocent until proven guilty. What good was my knowledge of a childhood guided by one of our city's darkest men if there was no resonating effect to point to? What good was my knowledge of a man and a woman sitting in a darkened car outside a stranger's house if no crime had been committed? What good was a list of names, scrawled on notepad paper, in a wallet I shouldn't have been looking in? I closed my eyes and focused on Martina. *You know what's important, don't you, Frank?* What was important was finding the man who had slain the junkie in the pit, who had been responsible for so much meaningless depravity.

Eric laughed at something, drawing my attention back to where he stood by the edge of the pit looking down at the junkie's twisted figure. His right hand unconsciously flicked the ash off his cigarette and into the trash at his feet.

In the end, I couldn't help myself. I walked halfway up the hill and called my old station, standing in the shade of a giant panther made from thousands of discarded black iPhones. Anthony Charters answered. My old bull pen neighbor.

"I need you to run an address for me," I told him, after the mandatory chitchat. "A place in Mortdale."

She stood in the heat and watched the water run down her fingers, thin and glistening like streaks of lightning onto the tiles at her feet. The heat, on the edge of pain, calmed her crawling skin. It was always this way before one of their kills, before the death of a man whose injustice was their own. She didn't eat. She didn't sleep. Like a woman in waiting for some unknown terror. Like a soldier in the waking dawn before battle. Eden felt the moments ticking away around her as she towelled off, and the sensation of unsated power, of being able to stop time, flickered through her. She lifted her arms and pulled her long black hair into a bun, twisting the strands tightly into the elastic. A smile, rare and painful, lifted the corners of her lips. Soon it would be over. Soon the killing that was so much a part of her life would be blessedly distant and not something that played with the springs and cogs and wires in her brain.

The last man on the list. The last time it would ever be personal.

Eden had never enjoyed killing. What she enjoyed were the moments after the kill had been completed, the body lying still and peaceful on the table, feet bare and pointed outwards, toes that could be touched and limbs that could be squeezed. She liked the emptiness of a soulless thing. Liked to look at it as Eric put the tools away. It seemed clean. Neat. An exorcised body. A monster removed from the earth. There was a certain satisfaction in that. So very many times she had stood in the company of a corpse and felt that satisfaction wash through her, loosening the muscles around her joints, making her feel tired. The world was a little bit safer for sons and daughters, mothers and fathers sleeping and laughing and holding each other in millions of houses in millions of streets all over the world. One fiend at a time, over and over, Eden and her brother had made the world a little bit safer. The job made it so easy to find them, to pick them out and examine them like the lice they were, to choose them and crush them before they were safely bottled. Child molesters, wifebeaters, pimps and psychotics and thrill killers. Snip, snip, snip. She was cutting away the ragged edges of a neat and wholesome world. It wasn't enjoyable but it was so easy. Tonight would be the last night her playtime, and Eric's, would touch her heart. Eden drew a nervous breath. Oh, for it to be over. Oh, for that final satisfaction. An end to a story long overwritten, to dark chapters that seemed to drag on and on. To kill for justice and not for vengeance. She had wanted it for so long and now the end was here.

Eden closed her eyes and let it come back to her. She would let the memory envelop her, as it had been pressing to do, just one last time.

The pop of the trunk latch above their heads, the sudden gush of air onto their faces. The right side of the tape over her eyes had come unpeeled in the sweat on her face. The child Eden looked up through the red light into the faces of the men who had taken her, panting and sobbing as they pulled her out of the car and threw her on the ground. "Jesus, Benny," someone stammered. "Jesus. What have you done?"

"Fuck off, mate, you were firing too. That bloke was gonna go at me and you knew it as much as I did."

"Shut up, the both of you. We need to talk about what the fuck we're going to do now."

They forced her to kneel. Eric was kneeling beside her. Though she couldn't see him, Eden could feel the warmth of his body, hear the whimpers coming from his throat. The stones under her knees were sharp. She could feel them cutting into her feet. Screams rose up in her throat, meeting her shut lips and turning into growls. She couldn't stop the noises. They seemed to come with every breath.

"Shut up, you little bitch."

Someone shoved her into the gravel. Blood filled her mouth.

"This is not a complete loss," one of the men said. Eden watched him pacing, a faceless shadow in the dark beside the road. "We can still ransom them. They've got to have aunties, uncles."

"We've been through this. You fucking idiot, you just shot up the only family they got."

"We'll sell them," a cold, calm voice said, one of the men standing by the back of the van, smoking a cigarette. "You can get ten grand for a kid in the city. The girl's pretty. Nice long hair. A desperate pedophile might pay fifteen or more."

"No pedophile's going to buy two kids of a dead millionaire. No one in the world's that fucking dumb."

There was silence. Eden tried to snuggle into the safety of Eric's body but her bound wrists and ankles wouldn't allow the movement. Her dress was soaked, she didn't know what from. The silence pressed on and on as the two children knelt in the dark.

"Who's going to do it?"

"Oh come on, man!"

"Listen, you try to drop these brats off on a street corner and someone will see you. Someone's probably seen us already. This whole thing is a huge fucking mess and we need to clean it up now, man. Kids die every day. Don't be such a fucking baby."

"I don't want any part in this."

"I know a place we can get rid of them."

A pause. Panting breaths, curling mist in the dark.

"My mate told me about this guy who runs a dump down at Utulla. Twenty grand, he'll take them and we can forget this ever happened. We need to move fast, cover our tracks. We're looking at life here, fellas, and I don't know about you but I'm not going back to the fucking Bay."

More silence. Eric was crying. The sound of his crying brought on the hacking sobs the child Eden had only just managed to control.

"Will this guy . . . will he do it all?"

"Nuh, he only takes stiffs. We gotta do it."

"Well, I'm not fucking doing it."

"I'll do it," someone said.

"You can't shoot them."

"Why the fuck not?"

"You want to do it?"

"Don't shoot them. It won't take much. They're little. You shoot them and you'll get them everywhere. I don't want any part of them in the car."

With her untaped eye, Eden saw one man walk into the line of trees, grabbing at a thick branch hanging low to the ground. From nowhere, a hand tossed two folded blue sheets and a roll of duct tape onto the gravel in front of her.

Now, in the bathroom of her apartment, Eden looked in the mirror, stared into her own eyes as the intercom in her living room announced the presence of her brother on the street.

The last man. She would finally be free.

27

One of my ex-wives, I can't remember which, used to tell me that if I was going to bring her something it should be something she could eat or wear or she didn't want it. So when I arrived at Martina's that night I was carrying a plastic bag with two containers of Harthi's best Indian and a couple of big naan breads. Women love food. You can't go wrong. You can buy them the wrong ring or a tacky necklace or last season's handbag but when you bring a woman food and she's hungry, well, you might as well be Prince Charming.

Martina unlocked the door. She looked at me, then at the bag hanging off my index finger.

"You got a thing about chunky women or something?"

"No," I said. "But you've got free rein up to five hundred kilos. Then I might need to reconsider things."

She took the bag from me and kissed my lips. She was wearing studded earrings in the shape of red ladybirds that were anatomically correct, as though two of the insects had decided to curl up there for the night. I smiled and felt one of them with my fingers. She held my hand as we went to the table. It had been years since a woman wanted to hold my hand.

All her cutlery and plates and cups were mismatched, as if she'd just bought singular pieces she liked the look of in second-hand shops. Each was beautiful in its own way. I went through her cupboards and gathered everything. She stood by the balcony doors, lost to me, her fingers wandering in the lace hanging beside her. I stopped and watched her, knew she was watching the two patrol officers in the squad car on the street. I remembered my second wife telling me that there were times that I would come home and I would be away at the same time, a shell of myself, inaccessible to her. How unfair it was, she would tell me, how teasing to have my body and not my mind. I knew what that loneliness felt like then. Martina was a ghost. The loss of her stung.

I went to the window and put my hand on her arm, and some warm and bright flicker of herself returned. We wouldn't eat. We put the food in the fridge, stripped off and climbed into her bed together, and she fit the curves of her body to mine, her hands folded under my chin. We were still strangers and I was glad for it. There was so much to learn. The scent of her hair under my nose was new and welcoming.

"When I was little," she whispered, "I'd fight with my brothers. Play fights. There was never any competition in it but they enjoyed how worked up I could get. I used to like it until that moment came when I would be pinned and I would test each limb, each muscle, to try to find an escape. When there was none, there was always fear. I knew we were playing. I knew they loved me, sort of. I'd come to realize though, at that time, that my power meant nothing. All my power meant nothing. It was a game but . . . it wasn't a game. That's what it was like in those days in the cage. That's what it's like now. I'm pinned, Frank. I'm pinned just by knowing he's alive."

It was utterly dark and her voice sounded small, like it didn't matter if I heard her words or not. She was asleep almost instantly, as though she had been waiting years for a safe time.

The night has many shades. For Eden they came on like a blessed heat—the warmth of a job begun, the intense blaze of time as it ticked away. She was sweating as she pinned the black plastic sheet over the large wooden table, folding the edges into perfect forty-five-degree angles to form hospital corners, which she taped tightly. Eric stood by the door to the fish-gutting room, staring out at the stillness of the marina.

All about them the stink of fish was thick, a sour and salty smell, and the only sound was the familiar roar of the duct tape and the sloshing of water against the pillars beneath the boathouse. The licking of the waves sounded, to her, like the clunking of approaching boots. Eden trembled. She fancied she could hear, with her heightened senses, the sucking and gaping of barnacles and other sea creatures when the water receded. She laid out the cable ties, one at each corner, for Benjamin Annous's wrists and ankles. From a black leather pouch Eden extracted three long, spotless blades: a serrated hunting knife, a narrow filleting knife, a pointed chef's knife.

At the screech of the blades against their sheaths Eric walked back into the room and closed the door quietly. Along the wall hung less precise instruments, the weapons of the fishermen—hooks and picks and cleavers and scrapers. In the corner was a large and menacing machine, its munching teeth ajar and welcoming, rows of unlabelled cans lined along its shelves. This was Benjamin's workplace. He spent his days and nights here, snuffing out small, dumb lives hour upon hour, pulling innards from pulsing bellies, stripping vitality from wet flesh.

Benjamin Annous. The one who had begun the shooting.

Eden stood at the table, her gloved palms spread on its surface before her, leaning on their weight. Eric came up beside her and picked up the nearest blade. He smiled. He was remembering now, part of his ritual. Eden reached up and pressed his hand down, sinking the blade back onto the table.

"No," she said. "This time it's my turn."

28

The night has many shades. I felt them coming on like acts in a play as Martina lay beside me, moving restlessly through layers of dream. A cop's favorite hours are those first ones, when no one is drunk yet, fathers home late from work are falling asleep in front of television sets, children are whispering and giggling in the dark. At midnight, bars thrive and waitresses sigh at their watches, night cleaners vacuum vast meadows of empty carpet and the elderly, unable to sleep, read newspapers by lamplight. The witching hours come, cold and still. Drunks abuse taxi drivers. Bottles shatter in the street and bins are tipped over. Renegade teens stamp out fires on the black beaches and wander home, tight-lipped. My phone sprayed blue light against the ceiling. I thought it was lightning at first. Slipping my arm out from under Martina, I took the call at the balcony doors. I looked out and noticed that the patrol car was still there.

"You said it was urgent," Anthony said.

"It is."

"Yeah, well, I got everything you asked for. The house in Mortdale belongs to a BT Annous. The same Annous shared a cell with a Stanley J. Harwich and a Michael A. Nattier in Silverwater back in '91. Harwich and Nattier are missing."

I exhaled sharply, staring around me in the dark. Martina's cat came and rubbed its thin body against my leg. I nudged it away.

"A lot of people have received late-night phone calls to chase this stuff down. You might want to come round the station with a slab sometime soon."

"Thanks," I said. "I will."

I hung up and the phone slipped out of my fingers, hitting the floor with a dull thud. Six names. Five of them missing, extracted from the living world cleanly like cancers cut from flesh. Why were they doing this? What were they doing to these men? Immediately, a flood of poisonous thoughts entered my brain in retaliation to the wild fear that was infecting my body. *You can't prove anything. No bodies, no crime. They're cops, Frank. There's a proper explanation. There's an innocent story behind all of this.*

Pushing aside the thin lace over her windows, I saw the plainclothes cops sitting in a car across the street, one texting on his mobile phone, the other staring idly through the windscreen. I went to the bedroom door and looked back at Martina. Her hair had fanned out on the pillow in one short peak like a parrot's crest at the back of her head, jagged and feathery at its ends. Her hand was curled in the place where I had lain. The cat sauntered past me into the room and curled in the crook of her left knee, its upper body resting on her thigh.

I left.

*   *   *

Annous's house was dark. I approached from a street away, jogging on my toes along a curving concrete path, ducking under wet frangipani trees that hung over back fences. The scent of flowers followed me into the street where I crouched, looking for a car I recognized. There wasn't one. The truck that Annous owned was still in his driveway, the back shutter rolled down revealing a cartoon of a large sapphire blue fish. I waited ten minutes, then dashed across the street to the uncertain yips of a small dog wandering one of the yards.

I couldn't remember the nights being as cold as this on my police beat. My eyes stung as a gentle rain fell, beading in the hair on my forearms. The night felt trapped in the kind of stillness that made me wonder if I was alone on the earth, the only creature left in existence to move and creep and wander. End of the world. No crickets chirped in the grass. No bats flew overhead. No moon. I crept down the side of the Annous house and tried to stave off a slowly intensifying fear, the kind I had not experienced since I was a child, the kind that twisted shadows into figures and gave weight to empty air. I stood at the corner of the house and listened. Nothing. Benjamin Annous's back door was unlocked and slightly ajar. I eased it open and stepped inside.

When I was a little kid, maybe five or six, my grandmother used to come to our house regularly and sleep in a renovated garage at the back of our property that usually served as a kind of rumpus room. My father, a short-tempered workaholic, had forbidden me to sleep in bed with my parents no matter the terror that infected me at night, so my grandmother's visits were an opportunity to seek adult protection from my fear of the dark. The trek through the house, across the yard and into the garage, however, was horrific, laden with long stretches of impenetrable blackness. One night, trembling and sobbing, I made the journey through the house, out the back door, across the yard and into the depths of the long, cluttered garage, whispering Nanna's name with relief when I finally made it to safety. I found an empty bed, neatly made under my hands. She had left that evening on the late-night bus, long after I was put to bed. So there I was, in the dark, miles it seemed from my bed, having expected the company and security of another only to find that I was alone.

I remembered that night as I walked through the Annous house and found it empty. Strangely, I had expected someone, even if it were Eden and Eric, even if that would mean I had been right about them all along, that I was in danger. To find no one there was even more chilling. I stood in the kitchen and struggled to breathe, paralyzed by the emptiness around me. I looked down at the gold and orange tiles and noticed a drop of blood, the size of a coin and perfectly round, ink black in the minimal light.

The new morning was aglow. Jason stood in the garden with his face uplifted, watching the heat of his breath billow towards an untouchable sky. His skin was shivering cold, yet a fire roared against the curved and rolling insides of his flesh, a power that defied muscle, bone, veins. He felt it glowing behind his eyes and sizzling in his fingertips. The wet garden alone contained him, ropes of hanging flowers and mesh of leaves, a fragrant cage in which to settle, collect himself, before moving on.

He set down his bag and turned on the rusty iron tap on the side of the building, using the water to rinse his arms and hands. As he was running it over the toes of his shoes he noticed the orange light blinking against the bricks where he leaned. He turned.

A man stood there in a high-resolution vest, a hand on the first of the garbage bins lined up at the edge of the street. The young man looked at Jason's hands, the pink film of rinsed blood dripping from his fingers. Jason reached up and straightened his hair.

"Morning," he said, a statement of fact. The garbageman backed towards his truck.

I couldn't control myself. When Eden and Eric arrived outside her apartment building at half past four, a twitching, shivering rage whipped through me. I was covered in sweat. When they exited the car, neither of them spoke. It seemed strange, their silence. Eric's eyes moved to me a little lazily as I approached, as though he had always expected me to be there, and his hands remained by his sides as I took hold of his jacket and slammed him into the car.

"What did you do?" I snarled, feeling my knuckles crack under my grip. "What the fuck did you do?"

"Frank—" Eden gripped my shoulder. I shoved her off.

"My, my. It's way past your bedtime, Frank." Eric grinned. "Come on upstairs and you can sleep off the morning in the guest room. I'll even make you a nice tuna sandwich."

Eden covered her mouth with her hand.

"I know about Annous," I panted. "I know about all of them. I saw the list in Eden's wallet. I know they're all missing."

The air in Eden's lungs seemed to leave her at once. She crumpled in the middle like a paper bag. Eric, however, remained unchanged. He stared down at me with a kind of pity in his eyes, as though I were mad. It was the kind of look I had expected from him.

"Whatever you think you know, Frank, it's wrong," Eden murmured. "You need to back right off this, right now."

"Just like Doyle, huh?" Eric asked her, his eyes still fixed on mine. "I told you from the moment he laid eyes on you that he was going to be a problem. It's you, Eden. You're the problem. They just can't get enough."

His hand seemed to close on all of the front of my shirt at once. He used the fabric like a handle to just about lift me off my feet, the way a man might pick up a doll. His strength was unnatural, impossible given his size. My weight, the bulk of my shoulders and chest and belly, meant nothing. He spun me and shoved me into the car.

"Didn't I tell you, Eden? I'm always right, aren't I?"

"Put him down."

"What did they do to you?" I asked. "What did they do to you?"

Eric's phone began ringing. I used the distraction to scrape my shoe down his shin. His hands loosened. I punched him in the stomach and pushed him away, giving it all my strength, everything I had. He barely moved. His hand forced my jaw up, the night sky collecting in my vision as he punched me in the sternum, a body-bending blow.

I sunk to the ground, my breath gone and my lungs unable to draw more. His boot slammed into my stomach, cracking ribs. I couldn't make a sound. The pain was something in the very air. I was drowning in it. I was drowning in a hot, red sea.

My phone began ringing. Followed by Eden's phone. A calling of all agents. Nothing less could have stopped Eric's hands as they grabbed hold of my arms and hurled me into the road.

"Jason Beck, confirmed in Randwick. We got to go, Eric. We got to go!"

Eden was almost screaming. I used the hood of my car to drag my body upright. Sickness pulsed through me but I refused to succumb to it. I staggered to the door and fell into my car as Eden and Eric screeched away from the curb.

Randwick. Martina lived in Randwick.

As soon as I started to drive, everything I knew about Eden and Eric, everything I suspected they had done, was washed away by my desire to get to Randwick by any means possible. I gunned the car through stop signs, intersections, over roundabouts and through oncoming traffic lanes. The road was wet, the rain steadily increasing, driven sideways into the car by a growing wind. All across the city people were waking to an ominous day, a storm of brooding tension, the clouds low and purple. There was no sun. I swallowed my heart over and over, feeling the power of the vehicle surge through the steering wheel in my hands. My shoulders began to ache. Hills of uniform darkened apartment blocks rose and fell beneath me.

I left her. I left her. I gave him what he wanted. He was waiting for me to leave.

Eden and Eric careered into my path from a side street. They were upright, rigid in their seats like an elderly couple on a morning drive. I followed. On Avoca Street, I began to notice people running—not from the rain, there was more of an urgency in their stride. Umbrellas abandoned, pulling children by the wrist, teenagers fighting in the opposite direction, coming up against the spread palms of nervous cops. Blue and red lights flashed and sparkled in the rain. I shoved the car into an awkward park on the footpath outside a wedding photography shop, almost taking the painted front window with me.

There were cops everywhere. Civilians battered my shoulders as they passed, looked, bewildered, into my eyes. I glanced around at the sheets of rain splashing on the windscreens of dozens of patrol cars crisscrossing the intersection like discarded toys. The clouds above the Sacred Heart Church were black, as though burned.

I took a vest from the nearest cop. He seemed to know who I was and was holding it out for me as I jogged towards him. Eden and Eric were loading their weapons by a car at the front of the gathering.

"What's happening?"

"A garbageman called in a sighting of Beck about an hour ago on the opposite side of the shopping district. Said the guy was rinsing bloody hands in a garden tap, if you can fucking believe it. We went, looked, didn't take it seriously until we got another sighting up near the park—said he was trying to play with a stray cat. We chased him back here. He's just gone in and fired a couple shots to clear out the morning mass. Our chief's ordered us to pull back and block the street off."

"Anyone hurt?" I asked.

"Can't tell."

There were still people leaving the church through the side and front doors, those who had fallen and been trampled in the rush. The Sacred Heart 5AM mass was one of the biggest in the eastern suburbs. I knew the mass well. My grandmother had forced me to it every Saturday morning throughout my childhood, and if I mucked up, we'd go back for the Sunday repeat. Thunder split the air, a ripping sound like the tearing of fabric. We stood back and watched the church tower, which seemed to lean against the moving sky. A white marble Mary presided over the double front entrance above pointed arches inlaid with stained glass. Howling saints. A blood-spattered Christ. I buckled the vest and ran forward, splashing rain up my ankles and into my boots.

I jogged to the front doors, catching sight of Eden and Eric, their guns low, creeping along the side of the building. The windows in the foyer were shattered, glass on dusty tables laden with idols, cards, brochures. I crouched beneath a sandstone pillar and listened. Wind howled through the broken windows, tossing papers and clearing shelves in the small shop. A *Catholic News* crumpled under my boot.

My training told me that now was the time to talk to Beck, to open up a line of communication and try to turn it over to reasoning. But I didn't want to talk to him. I had nothing to say. I didn't want to reason with him. I didn't want to coax him out of the church with kindness, with lies, with platitudes. I wanted to catch him and pull him down. I wanted to get my fingernails into him. My teeth ached. It was an animal thing, the rage and the sickness in me. I was hungry for him.

It was the ceiling that first drew the eye, enormous and gaping, ribbed with polished mahogany buttresses. Pointed arches lined each side of the roof, allowing what little light the storm would allow to filter in and strike the rows of pews. My jeans were dripping rain onto a royal blue and gold rug that ran a hundred meters forward to the altar. There were bags and coats and umbrellas in the pews, scattered prayer cards on the hardwood floors. Everything pink, aquamarine, gold. Faces littered the alcoves, statues and carvings, infant angels, a bemused Mary, a moaning Jesus.

"Beck?"

My voice billowed outwards and upwards, causing pigeons to flutter in the roof near the north and south transepts. The thunder gave an answer. I crawled to the right, wedging my body under a full-sized reproduction of Michelangelo's *Pietà* in fiberglass. Paint had rubbed off the Lord's knees and Mary's palms from the touch of thousands. Christ's face, peaceful, emotionless. I thought of Martina's sleeping eyes.

A figure dashed across the front of the altar. I heard gunshots, noticed a flash from the rows of pews. Beck's jacket caught a stand of lighted candles. It crashed, echoing, to the carpet.

"Eden!" I called. More shots. I moved forward, fixing my eyes on where I had last seen Beck. Ahead, smoke curled between the pews. I rose up on my feet and ran forward in a crouch.

It was no more than a sharp tug, the bullet catching my arm and spinning me backwards into the space before the doors to the confessional booths. My gun slid away from me on dusty marble. The sound came after the pain, a clap that rattled off the high walls. A figure rose from where it crouched. The image of it was surrounded by green light. I shifted back against the door beside me and realized it was sprayed with my blood.

Eric had clipped me right on the edge of the vest, in the meaty place between my shoulder and arm. He walked towards me between the pews, grinning, his cover forgotten.

He sighed, shaking his head. "You know, we were actually willing to forgive Doyle his unique tastes because he was too close to us, because he might bring us unwanted heat. We let him play the monster. He was a curious dog, wanted to dig, just like you. He dug and dug until he uncovered something he wished he hadn't. You can't say you weren't warned, Frank."

His gun rose to my face. I turned away and felt the heat of the fire before the altar on my cheeks and brow. I thought of nothing but her eyes. Faced with Eric's gun, Martina was there, as though the memory had been waiting for my attention.

I don't know what I expected from the gunshot. The fear swelled and seemed to cripple me, cut off all sensation, stifled my breath. Then the noise. My body jolted, wood-stiff. I opened my eyes and exhaled sharply, terrified of the pain.

Eric slumped onto my legs. His blood was on my palms, which had been turned out in surrender. It was on my face. Eden's body was turned towards the fire, her silhouette outlined against a broken window like a cat against the moon. She was trembling. Her whole body seemed to constrict inwards as though she were sickened. I saw the moment when what she had just done hit her after the seconds of silence between the blast and her brother falling and her finger coming off the trigger. Done, finished, the decision made. Her face crumpled, she drew back her lips and a small, pained growl came out of her. It wasn't simply the sound of hurt. It was the sound of hurt trying to be acknowledged, trying to come out, and her furious determination to keep it in. She straightened and wiped the sweat from her brow with the back of her gun hand.

Her eyes were black as they lifted from Eric's body to mine. They took in nothing of the lightning when it pulsed red and green against the stained-glass windows. She seemed to eat the light.

"He was also warned," she said.

I shoved Eric off me. By the time I got to my knees she was gone. My limbs felt dead. I picked up my gun and crawled towards the north transept. A painted figure of Mary stood on a huge globe, a serpent writhing under her bare toes. I caught my breath, my eyes dazzled by the fire that had begun to climb the velvet curtains by the altar, a yellow-backed beast.

"Eden!"

A door slammed. I ran. There were wooden stairs, warped and unpolished. Gunshots split the stale air. I ran up the stairs, feeling the heat from the floor below throbbing in the walls around me.

My body seemed to bounce off the corners of the high, wide tower, leaving handprints everywhere. Plastic roses in terra-cotta pots adorned the landing under a window depicting a frowning St. Anthony.

Eric. She shot Eric.

Sweat poured down my chest. Eric's blood was all over me. I remembered the photos of Eden covered in Doyle's blood.

I kicked in the door to the tower room. My aim flew to the only standing figure. It was Eden. Beck's hands were splayed on the floor, his palms flat on the polished wood. Windows were breaking on the bottom floor. I heard glass tinkling onto the stones of the altar and shouting voices rippling off the walls. Eden looked at me. Her boot was clamped on the back of the killer's neck. Her thumb flicked off the safety, swift. A guilty child.

"Put your gun down," I said gently, "and cuff him."

Eden's hair was tight around her skull. I could see her brother in her then, the sharp edges of her face and jaw, the malice. She looked wild. Blood was running down my belly. I flicked the safety off on my own weapon.

"He's not being cuffed," she said.

I shook my head. Found myself laughing.

"You don't have the right."

The heat from the floor burned in my feet. Eden smiled, as though listening to the ramblings of a madman.

"You don't have the right," I snarled. "You're denying closure to hundreds of people. They're going to want to see this out in full. He's not yours."

"If they knew what's in store for him, they'd *give* me that right." She was suddenly almost crying, trembling with rage. "Jesus, Frank, how can you not understand? You know what Maximum is like.

The comfort. The security. The counselling. The fucking vocational classes and guitar lessons and fan letters and the magazine interviews. No one will know that I've done this. No one knows what I've done before. There's a line, Frank, that has to be crossed sometimes. He can't be allowed to live. He forfeited that right."

"Put your gun down, Eden."

"No."

"Put your gun down!"

I was far enough away to see Beck move, but Eden missed it. His hand swung around and grabbed her ankle, pulling her leg out from under her. I threw myself at Beck just as he rolled up into a crouch. I had my weight alone to fight with. My arm was useless, my head swimming. He shoved me down and rose onto his knees. His wet teeth grazed my cheek.

"There's no gratitude. There's no loyalty."

Eden hollered and beat him back onto his stomach, the butt of the gun cracking against his temple.

I lay on the floor and looked at the earrings lying beside my hand, simply looked at them, aware without having seen it that they fell from Beck's shirt pocket. Two ladybirds, perfectly fashioned, glossy in the sparkle of lightning around the tower. I scooped them into my bloody palm and sat up. The air shuddered in and out of me as though whistling through barbed wire.

All of my pain was gone. It was replaced by a cold, shrill emptiness. A door had been closed on all that led to this moment, sitting on the floor in the tower, with her earrings in my hand. Everything behind the door was cut off, inaccessible, gone. Eden stood above me, watching me, Beck lying on his side under her gun. She was calling me but I couldn't hear her. He was laughing, I think. Or barking. I can't remember. I stood, shaking, my eyes locked on my palm. I might have been speaking. I don't know. Both of them were looking at me. Smoke was curling past the windows, flames beginning to throb in the wall behind Eden.

There was no thought. I had none of the rationality that Eden had used, the cold calculation of who deserves what and who has the right to take life. All I could think of was Martina in the bed where I had left her, the cat curled against her leg, her hand on the sheet where I had been. All I could think of was her mismatched china and the posters on her walls and her fat landlady and the stairs to her apartment, red-carpeted and empty, always dark. I don't remember deciding to shoot Beck. I didn't feel anything when I did. My hand simply moved, lifting my pistol. I watched his head buck as the bullets entered it and thought of an animal.

The gun was empty and clicking. Eden pushed my hand down. The room was on fire, making my eyes water and my scalp tic with the furious beat of my heart.

Ash was falling from the ceiling in a light black snow. It sucked towards Eden's lips as she panted. We looked at each other. Time was nothing.

EPILOGUE

I figured myself pretty lucky that no one stopped me as I signed out of the Prince of Wales just four hours after surgery on my shoulder. The press mobbed me in the parking lot, their voices echoing off the bulbous glass awnings that crested over the patient intake center. They were there again on the steps of headquarters, milling around a coffee vendor, raining cigarettes around him as I stepped from the cab. No one touched me. I was poison. The owls scattered when I entered the bull pen, unable to meet my eyes. Two street cops had been waiting for me there, helplessly pacing around my desk, chewing on my pens. The two who had been assigned to watch Martina's apartment, to protect her after I'd left. They rushed forward, unable to look at my face. I already knew what they had to say. They had received a call in from a public phone that another patrolman was taking a beating from a gang of youths in an alleyway a few streets over. They had gone, instantly. It was an old trick. Beck had known they would protect one of their own over a stranger. He knew they were loyal dogs. I walked past these men without allowing them their explanation.

The only person who looked straight at me that evening was Eden, when I opened the door to the interrogation room.

She lifted her eyes and locked them to mine with an expression I had seen many times—a cold exterior hiding weighty thoughts the way the black ocean surface will hide a shark. She had been sitting with her hands beneath the table, staring at an empty pale yellow notepad, the pen aligned beside it like a scalpel.

I went to the chair across from her and sat down, adjusting my sling carefully. There was silence, ringing, the world enclosed in concrete walls. A camera hung over us, the light slowly blinking.

This is my life now, I thought. Each moment, each sensation, could be afforded directly to the hands of the woman sitting across from me. The seconds and minutes and hours that had ticked by since she had killed her brother to save my life were hers and hers alone. I knew, looking at her now, what he had been to her. Partner and savior, tormentor and protector. She looked smaller without him in the world. More frail, yet something new, something wavering in unknown sunlight, daring to grow. I knew, looking at her eyes, that some part of her had hated him. But she didn't know how to live without him either. Eden owned me because she had chosen me to take his place and, rightfully, she was beginning to hate me for it and would hate me for some time. She owned the agony that I had still refused to address, the aching details that would come with the processing of Martina's body, with the collecting and distributing of her things. Eden had given me this. Eden owned my every breath. I felt hatred swell, hot and tickling, through my chest and down my arms.

She owned me, and yet some part of her was now mine, the

way I had unconsciously desired it from the moment we met. I was stained now with her life, with the understanding of what she was, the dark hollows of her being. Intimate. *This is my life now.* I think I had known somehow from the moment we met that she was a wild thing, that she was different from any woman I've ever known before. In the beginning it had drawn me in, lured me, a calling that made me curious, a danger that I wanted to test and feel. I hadn't known then that I was dealing with a monster. Now I knew and there would be no way I could get away from her. To run would be to awaken that predatory instinct in her, to invite her to cut me down. I would have to remain her partner, her secret keeper, her watchful slave. I had promised her a secret once. Now she had it.

Her eyes wandered over my face, silently, like a creature of another species analyzing the danger, assessing the movements of a foreign thing. Calculating.

I lifted my own yellow notepad onto the table. She looked at the paper, then at my eyes. I set my pen on the first line of the page and she reached forward and did the same.

"You start," I said. "I'll follow your lead."

She nodded and started to write her statement. When she was well ahead, I began my own.

ACKNOWLEDGMENTS

I've always been a storyteller but I could never have had the success my writing has brought me without the influence of many passionate and talented writing teachers. James Forsyth, formerly of the University of the Sunshine Coast, my first "fan," spent a year teaching me how to rein in my young writer's excitement and how to embrace my darkness. Ross Watkins and Gary Crew taught me the mechanics, and Kim Wilkins of the University of Queensland taught me the business. Ros Petelin and Caroline McKinnon taught me how to love my language, cut the chaff and never settle for close enough.

I'd like to thank Camilla Nelson of the University of Notre Dame in Sydney for listening to my story, and my tough-talking agent Gaby Naher for going into the ring for me. I owe a great deal to my lovely publisher Beverley Cousins, for her faith, excitement and hard work.

To my family—thank you for biting your nails while I waited for answers, cheering when it looked like I'd won and crying with me when I failed. Thank you, Mum, for reading every word I've ever written, listening to my drunk phone calls when I was rejected and introducing me to strangers in the street as your daughter, the writer.

Candice Fox is the middle child of a large, eccentric family from Sydney's western suburbs composed of half-, adopted and pseudo-siblings. The daughter of a parole officer and an enthusiastic foster-carer, Candice spent her childhood listening around corners to tales of violence, madness and evil as her father relayed his work stories to her mother and older brothers.

As a cynical, troublemaking teenager, her crime and gothic fiction writing was an escape from the calamity of her home life. She was constantly in trouble for reading Anne Rice in church and scaring her friends with tales from Australia's wealth of true crime writers.

Bankstown born and bred, she failed to conform to military life in a brief stint as an officer in the Royal Australian Navy at age eighteen. At twenty, she turned her hand to academia and taught high school through two undergraduate and two postgraduate degrees. Candice lectures in writing at the University of Notre Dame, Sydney, while undertaking a PhD in literary censorship and terrorism.

Hades is her first novel, and she is currently working on its sequel, *Eden*.

Don't miss Candice Fox's next searing thriller

EDEN

Coming from Kensington in 2016.